TH
CHI
BEFORE

BOOKS BY MICHAEL SCANLON

Where She Lies

MICHAEL SCANLON

THE CHILD BEFORE

bookouture

Published by Bookouture in 2019

An imprint of StoryFire Ltd.

Carmelite House
50 Victoria Embankment
London EC4Y 0DZ

www.bookouture.com

ISBN: 978-1-78681-939-0
eBook ISBN: 978-1-78681-938-3

This book is dedicated to my late grandfather, fondly known as Jock, survivor of the Great War, storyteller, and a bit of a lad.

PROLOGUE

Winter is slow to loosen its grip here. Here in this place where tectonic plates once ground and crashed, forcing up sandstone and granite rock from the deep, wild Atlantic. Here, where nature has shaped the landscape, forcing trees into bent and crooked posture, tearing the coastline into a jagged wound. And it is here that the town of Cross Beg awaits the first sweet, warm breath of summer that surely, eventually, must come.

But this year it is different. Summer does not come slowly, or tentatively; does not, as in other years, creep in. No. It arrives suddenly, overnight, and although it is still mid-May, people wake one morning to find their cold, damp rock basking in sunshine beneath a clear blue sky, while the carcass of winter still lies fresh and unburied on the ground.

CHAPTER ONE

October 1954

The only light in the small, decrepit cottage came from a single candle burning on a saucer and secured in place by the falling wax that cooled about it. Its flickering flame threw shadows onto the wall like petals around the pistil of a flower. In the stone hearth, the fire that usually never went out was now nothing but a pile of grey ash. Outside, the night was cold, the sky a black canopy pinpricked by a thousand stars. There was no moon and the place they called Kelly's Forge was washed in a grey darkness. Here was nothing more than a collection of thatch cottages, a Clachán, *the inhabitants farming the commonage and scrubland thereabouts, seeking in each other a common strength for a common purpose: survival.*

A cold wind rustled the branches of the trees. Frost had begun to form, and even in the grey light, it radiated a dull glow on the narrow gravel track that ran through the centre of this place.

The girl stood in the doorway. There was not enough light to lend her a silhouette. Instead, she appeared as part of the darkness itself. For her nightdress, once white, was now of such a deep crimson that, in the dim light, it appeared black. But the reason for this was simple. It was soaked in blood.

She began to sing, the girl. Her voice was soft, so soft it was almost of the wind. It was a lullaby. She cradled her arms, rocking them gently back and forth. Back and forth. Back and forth. As if she was holding a baby. But she was not. Her arms were empty.

CHAPTER TWO

Beck had tossed and turned for much of the night, unable to sleep. The words of a radio talk show host from somewhere in the distant past played over in his mind: *'Folks, did you ever wake in the middle of the night and all that is wrong with your life, all that you worry about, all that makes you anxious, all that troubles you, everything, all of it, together, suddenly hits you in the face? Did that ever happen to you folks? Bang! Right in the face. There it is. Well, that happened to me last night.'*

Beck had never forgotten those words, because it meant that other people felt the same way he sometimes did too. But now, his tossing and turning was not to do with something wrong in his life, although he had much of that already. No, this was about something that had been so right in his life. Something, however, he just didn't have any more. But even when he did have it…

He imagined her face. Natalia smiling, her particular smile that came only at particular times. A smile of cunning and lust. The smile of a woman cuckolding her husband, her husband who just happened to be Beck's old boss. It was a relationship ultimately toxic, morally corrupt, yet irresistible in that it had that which most people seek: excitement. And without which relationships can flounder, disappearing beneath the waters in a sea of apathy.

Stop it, Beck.

This was useless. He gave in, abandoning any attempt at sleep, and decided to get up and face the day, even if it was still the middle of the night. But then, as he lay there, he felt his eyes starting to grow heavy. Sleep, now that he was no longer grappling with it, turned to him, luring him in. It would not be ignored. Finally, he drifted off through an open, waiting door.

He slept for an hour or more without interruption, not deep enough for his dreams to come up from below, but just enough for them to stir. Before they could fully come alive he was jarred back to consciousness, and in that moment before his eyes snapped open, he thought he heard something, a scream maybe, and a sound like that of a baby crying. But it was something else that had awoken him. He heard it again. Like drumming.

Someone was banging on his front door.

He immediately moved from the bed and crossed the room to the window, parted the curtains and peered out.

Maurice Crabby, big fish in a small pond, owner of the town's main supermarket, was standing on the street below, in his ridiculous lycras, the bicycle that cost him a fortune discarded on the ground behind him. Crabby was agitated, hopping from one foot to the other, unable to stand still. He banged on the door again.

'Hold onto your hat, calm down, I'm coming,' Beck said to himself as he looked around for his trousers. He couldn't see them.

He went down the stairs and opened the door.

'There's a body,' Crabby blurted.

'A body?'

Crabby was shaking.

'Are you deaf? I said a body!' Crabby repeated.

The man was normally so polite.

'Where?'

'A body. Murdered. There's blood everywhere. Oh Jesus.'

'Where?'

'I left my phone at home, went off on my bike you see, so I couldn't ring…'

'Can you calm down?' Beck said, stepping onto the street now. He realised he was wearing nothing but his boxer shorts. He took

Crabby by the shoulders and shook him. 'Where? Where's this body you're on about?'

'My wife doesn't like me taking off like that. So I didn't tell her. I did leave a note though.' Crabby garbled on.

Beck shook him again.

'One more time now, Mr Crabby. Where is this fucking body?'

CHAPTER THREE

The village that literally died. A photograph hangs in the library, of the last inhabitant of Kelly's Forge, standing by the stone bridge over the River Óg, a tributary of the Brown Water River. May flowers and gorse are teeming over the ditches all about, wild flowers sprouting from between the rocks of the bridge itself. He stands there. A tall, proud, white-haired man. If you looked closely enough you could see he was hiding a cigarette in the cup of his hand. The brass plaque beneath reveals the year, 1957, and an inscription: *Michéal Peoples, Village Elder, who assumed a role akin to an old Gaelic Chieftain. It was he who established the Clachán on the site of a medieval forge. Its people were his tribe. The inhabitants of the place known as Kelly's Forge were rehoused in Galway in 1956, the year the village was finally abandoned.* The man stares from the faded photograph. He looks lost, bewildered even.

Now, standing by this very same place, Kelly's Forge, Beck thought of this photograph. He'd seen it on a visit to the library once, hanging prominently in the foyer for all the world to see.

But the existence of that place was an aberrant, a freak, an oversight, something that had fallen between the cracks of a stagnant society, a society that did not want to be reminded of the ways of the past, of how it had once lived. And so they did what people in such situations do, they ignored it, maligned it, and ultimately, feared it too. And because of this, Kelly's Forge did not abide by the rules of the established order. Rather, they ignored them, created and abided by their own.

Leaving Crabby in the squad car, Beck walked with Garda Fergal Dempsey towards the gap in the hedge at the narrow road's dead-end. The sky was a clear blue and the heat of the sun like an unexpected kiss. Dempsey was wearing shiny shoes, something he always did on the 7 a.m. early shift, the time to catch up on admin work, the registering of fines and transferring of outstanding incidents to Pulse and such like. And, on a Tuesday, to attend at the district court for the prosecution of cases. Dempsey had told Beck once that the 7 a.m. shift was what returned him to a state of being a normal person, of having lunch at a proper hour, of being home in time for the early evening news on TV. It was a shift where only occasionally someone might shout in his face or need to be arrested. Usually for shoplifting, or being drunk and disorderly, usually because they hadn't sobered up from the night before. Generally, you could wear shiny shoes on the day shift and get away with it. Now, Dempsey was clearly trying to keep his shiny shoes clean as he followed Beck in through the gap in the hedge.

As they passed through, Beck spotted the back end of the car as described by Crabby on the drive over, registering that it was a Citroen Picasso, two years old. He paused, preparing himself for what was to come. People don't act the way Crabby had without good reason. Beck walked over to the car and slowly stepped out from behind the rear.

It doesn't matter how many times a person witnesses the aftermath of a violent death, it leaves its mark. That is, if the person witnessing it possesses the normal faculties of emotion and empathy. And Beck, despite his flaws, did.

He observed the head, shoulders and arms of the female victim protruding through the open front passenger door, noted she was lying on her back, her head at an odd angle, hanging so far back it appeared to be on a hinge. He observed all this and wondered: Why?

Beck took a couple of steps forward and stopped. There was a long, wide, gaping wound to the neck, stretching from beneath the earlobe on one side of the head to beneath the earlobe on the other. Blood smeared the bottom half of the windscreen by the passenger door, tapering towards the door. Considering the severity of the wound, there wasn't as much as would be expected. Then, he noticed the large patch of crimson on the ground. Had the victim been trying to escape the car when the wound was inflicted? He turned again to the victim. Her eyes were wide and stared ahead, frozen. A mass of light brown hair tumbled to the ground, some wisps stuck to the grey flesh of her forehead. Dempsey started to speak, but Beck raised his hand.

'Get tape from the car, Dempsey. Bring it here to me. And check the reg plate. I want to know who this person is. And I want you to go round to the registered address the first chance you get. Take somebody with you. Got that?'

Dempsey nodded, but didn't move.

'Now! Dempsey. Get on it now.'

Whatever Dempsey had wanted to say, he didn't say it. Instead he turned and headed quickly back towards the squad car, showing no regard now for his shiny shoes. Alone, Beck approached the car, stepping carefully through the grass. The passenger seat was semi-reclined. He noted the victim's feet were in the footwell on the driver's side, cork-heeled sandals discarded next to them on the mat. Half of each foot disappeared under the seat. Beck imagined she had used her feet as an anchor, wedging them in under the seat in an effort to stop herself from being dragged from the car. She was slim, her arms stretched out behind on either side of her head, frozen in rigor mortis. The body itself was remarkably blood-free. It appeared to have just that one, single, fatal wound. The floral-patterned blouse she wore had been ripped open. Beck could see buttons scattered on the floor of the car, and two others on the grass outside. Her bra had been partially pulled up, exposing one breast. She was wearing a short skirt, pulled half way down over her hips where it appeared to have become stuck, the centre crumpled and pulled up over her crotch, revealing purple underwear, the elastic broken, the material puckered and frayed. Someone had tried with great determination to pull those off. The glove compartment was open and the contents had spilled out. Beck took in the rest of the interior. Beside him, directly behind the passenger seat – the door pillars had obscured it until now – was a baby seat.

He stepped right up to the rear passenger door and pressed his face close to the window, peering in. The baby seat rested on the grey, suede-like fabric of the seat. At the other end, a loaf of sliced bread and a two-litre container of milk. The writing on the bread wrapping, 'Crabby's Shop Rite Wholemeal Bread'. In the footwell below lay a half-empty baby bottle of milk.

Beck attempted to reassure himself, thinking that just because there was a baby seat in the car, it didn't mean there had been a baby. He thought of Garda Jane Ryan, who parked her car at the station for the duration of her ten hour shifts and it always had a couple of baby seats in the back. He told himself he didn't constantly have to expect the worst.

But deep down, he knew he was kidding himself. Because he did.

Returning to the back of the car again, he pulled his shirt out from his trousers, wrapping the fabric around his index and middle finger. Fumbling for the boot lever, he found it and pressed it open. Inside were two long-life shopping bags, a pair of sneakers, and a set of jump leads wrapped in an elastic band.

And something else.

Pushed towards the back was a folded pushchair, and just in front of it, a baby bag. The baby bag was open, revealing a couple of striped nappies and a bag of baby wipes, sealed shut.

Only then did he realise that he had been holding his breath. He exhaled now with a loud whoosh.

Beck felt a coldness. It crept through him, like an icy stream.

He felt sure now: A baby. Yes. There had been one.

CHAPTER FOUR

October 1954

The boy lay huddled beneath the blankets and old coats in the hag, the hollow in the wall by the fire, the warmest part of the house, alongside his grandmother. He had lain there, still and silent, since they had left and gone into the forest, listening only to the sounds of his grandmother's breathing. He had lain there when they had come back again, shouting and agitated, his mother screaming, her nightclothes drenched in blood. He had lain there too, when the policemen had arrived, among them the big hulking detective shouting, demanding his mother tell him where the child was.

The child.

His sister.

Bernadette.

CHAPTER FIVE

'Mr Crabby,' Beck said. 'When you found the car, was there a baby in it? Can you tell me that? Did you hear or see a baby?'

He was sitting alongside Crabby in the back of the squad car. Crabby appeared to have calmed down, staring straight ahead, completely still. Which wasn't good either. He turned his head slightly, his eyes swivelling to the corners of their sockets. It gave him a shifty look.

'Mr Crabby,' Beck said. 'When you found the car, was there a baby in it? Can you tell me that? Did you hear or see a baby?'

'A baby?'

'Yes. A baby.' Beck was struggling to keep his voice calm.

'I can't be certain. I didn't see a baby... I don't think. I can't be certain'

'Okay. And you were out for an early morning cycle, is that right?'

'Yes.'

'What brought you here, to this spot?'

Crabby shrugged his shoulders. 'It's, I don't know, pretty, isn't it? The bridge. I've always liked it. There used to be a tiny village you know, Kelly's Forge. All ruins now. It's very peaceful. I like peace...'

'Did you recognise the deceased?' Beck asked.

'You mean the person in the car?'

What?

'Yes. The person in the car,' Beck said.

Crabby bowed his head and folded his arms tightly across his chest. 'Her throat was cut. I could see it.'

'Did she look familiar?'

'I don't know?'

'What do you mean you don't know?'

'I don't think I even looked at her face, you see.' He paused, before adding. 'All I can remember is her throat. I couldn't take my eyes off her throat.'

'I see,' Beck said. 'By the way, how did you know my address?'

Crabby unfolded his arms and they fell by his sides. He looked down, then up again at Beck. 'You don't remember?'

'Remember. Remember what?'

'The bottle of tequila. You came into my shop. I had actually closed, was locking the door. I didn't want to sell it to you, you understand, but you were very, very, persistent. I knew you were a policeman, so I offered to drive you home. You were, you know...'

'Oh,' Beck said, his mind whirring quickly. 'I'd like to thank you for that. And apologise at the same time. It was a reaction to antibiotics. I had a virus at the time.'

Crabby was silent.

Beck wondered if he believed his lie.

The truth was he had absolutely no recollection of the event. He didn't even like tequila. But it did explain one mystery. During a particularly bad bender not so long ago, he had woken to find a half empty litre bottle of tequila on his bedside locker. He'd called it a gift from the Mexican tooth fairy.

'I'll have someone drive you home,' Beck said. 'But we'll need to talk to you again. You're not planning on going anywhere are you? Certainly not in the near future?'

'No. I'm not. When do I get my bike back?'

'We'll have to hold onto that. It shouldn't be for long. I'll get word to you. You can come and collect it from the station, or we can drop it back. Whichever you'd prefer.'

'Why?' For the first time a change in the pitch of the voice. 'Why do you want to hold onto it?'

'Because we'll need to forensically examine it, that's why.'

Crabby thought about that. 'And why? Surely… Surely you don't think I had anything to do with this?'

'I don't know,' Beck said. 'I don't know anything. Not at this moment. You can understand.'

Crabby stared at Beck. 'Listen,' he said abruptly. 'Actually, I don't understand. This is my reputation you're talking about. I'm not involved in this dreadful business. Do you understand?'

'Understand? I understand there's a killer out there who needs to be found. And there's probably a baby missing too. That's what I understand. Anything else, such as your reputation, well, it pales into insignificance, doesn't it?'

Crabby pursed his lips and looked out the window, away from Beck. He muttered something under his breath. Beck couldn't quite catch what it was, but it sounded like 'I gave you a bloody bottle of tequila.'

CHAPTER SIX

October 1954

They were outcasts. The people of this place. This Clachán, *this hamlet known as Kelly's Forge. The boy knew it. Knew it in the way the people of the town avoided them. Knew it in the way they looked at them. In the way they spoke to them. In the way they ridiculed them. They did not belong. Their world was the world of the forest, where the monsters dwelled, the banshees, the faeries. That was their world.*

He did not like looking at his grandmother's face, so he avoided it, turning away from her now. Because it held a tortured grimace, as if she was suffering the most indomitable, insufferable pain, as if her skin was being burned alive, dripping from her body. He knew the cause, one word: stroke.

The boy watched as the people congregated around the door of the cottage, the light from their burning rushes a glowing pit in the darkness. They stood there, stooped figures for the most part, one or two women with babies beneath their shawls, the men in ill-fitting jackets, their faces gaunt and shadowed in the flickering light that reflected on the uniform buttons of the two guards who stood inside.

He watched as the big hulking detective pushed the rickety door closed, the light from the burning rushes disappearing, appearing to squeeze through the small narrow windows, where faces were pressed against the dirty panes of glass.

The boy would later learn the big detective's name: Inspector Padráic Flaherty, of Mill Street station in Galway.

He watched his mother. She was sitting on a wooden stool by the table. In that night dress. That was drenched in blood. He saw that she was shivering, and wanted to go to her. Wanted to protect her. Because that's what men did. But he was not a man. Not yet. He was still a boy. And so he could do nothing. The boy turned his head on the hard pillow. And was startled to see his grandmother staring at him. In the black pits of her eyes he could see his face. But he did not recoil. Instead he reached out for the old woman, held her close. And he could feel her hand on his back, gently pressing into him.

CHAPTER SEVEN

'Do we know who she is?' Superintendent Wilde asked.

The commanding officer of Cross Beg Garda station looked at Beck, biting his lower lip.

'No,' Beck said. 'Dempsey's just gone to the address of the registered owner of the car. We should know something soon.'

They were at the end of the cul-de-sac. The narrow roadway behind was clogged by marked and unmarked cars parked one behind the other. When the Technical Bureau van arrived, whenever that might be, it would be a slow reverse procession back onto the main road.

Inspector O'Reilly was standing a short distance away. He looked to Wilde, then to Beck, his eyes lingering on Beck a fraction longer than was necessary. O'Reilly forced a smile, which Beck thought strange. Because O'Reilly rarely smiled, and at a time like this, a smile was out of place. It just didn't belong. Since Beck's banishment to Cross Beg, in punishment for an unstated misdemeanour, O'Reilly had harangued and roared. But now, cleared by an investigative committee whose finding would remain secret, Beck had been restored to his rank of Inspector. Although he had seniority by virtue of length of service, O'Reilly could no longer behave as before.

'The new CRI, Gerry?' Wilde called. 'You up to speed on that?'

O'Reilly stepped across and nodded.

'In relation to missing children,' he said, like answering a question in a pub quiz. 'Goes out on radio, television, the internet and Facebook, oh, and motorway roadside electronic signage too. That the one you mean?'

'Yes. That's the one. Set it up so we just have to press the switch? Have it ready to go. Let's hope the child is with her partner. Ring that patrol, Beck, for Christ's sake, and see if there's any word.'

CHAPTER EIGHT

October 1954

The boy could hear them talking, the big detective's voice like a shovel running through pebbles.

'Kathleen, a grá', he said, pulling a stool across the rough stone floor and sitting down.

The boy could see the big detective glance toward the windows, to the faces pressed there against them. He shouted to the other guards, 'Run them, for God's sake. One of you. Run them.'

The sergeant's heavy boots pounded to the door and he shouted out into the night. The glowing light at the windows dwindled and was gone, taking with it the ghost-like faces. The inside of the cottage was almost in darkness now.

'You'll tell me now what happened,' the detective said, all softness gone from his voice. 'This minute. Or I'll have to take you with me to the barracks in Galway. Where you'll be locked up in a cold, lonely cell. You don't want that now, do you?'

The boy saw that his mother was shivering continuously now.

'Have you not got something to put over yourself?' the big detective asked, his voice gentle again.

'It came and took my bábóg,' she mumbled, as if to herself. 'We heard the banshee. And the door opened. And the creature came in. And then it grabbed my bábóg. Oh, my bábóg...'

The boy wondered. And was confused.

Why had his mother just lied?

CHAPTER NINE

Claire Somers didn't do tears. Or so she thought. Anyway, it had been a long time since she had.

She wiped her eyes with the tissue again and looked at herself in the rear-view mirror. She sighed. A long sigh. A sigh of hopelessness. Also of confusion. But above all, of loss.

Was it the same for straight couples?

She was immediately angry she had even asked herself this question. It was the sort of question sure to get up her own goat if she'd heard someone else ask it. It was a question up there with, *well, how do you actually, you know, do it?*

Whatever, this had been the longest week of her life. It was now eight weeks since they'd got the news. The IVF cycle was now complete. Over. Finished. The result delivered. The preamble, the jargon, it went on and on, but she had known right away. Because they don't do preamble and jargon unless they want to hide the bad news at the end. And the bad news at the end was more or less the same as the bad news on the previous two occasions. Eggs had been harvested, but only one fertilized, and this had rejected the donor's sperm. The clinic had wanted to try again. They said to keep positive. Easy for them to say, so long as they were getting paid. But Lucy and Claire decided that enough was enough. For now. Maybe in the future they would try again, maybe with Claire's eggs next time. But for now, it was too difficult to continue, each failure was too much of a numbing loss in itself, and it was taking too much of a toll on their relationship.

The clinic would not use the word failure when this was really what they meant. Why couldn't they say it like it was? Why did they feel the need to colour the result with the same enthusiasm they had coloured their promises at the start of the process in their bloody colour brochures. It would have been easier if they'd just said it like it was.

The process.

Jesus.

And she didn't do make-up either. Or so she thought. Anyway, it had been a long time since she had. But she needed colour to her pale, gaunt face. Because Beck had already rung twice. And she couldn't keep putting him off. She had to face people. She had to present a normal image to the world.

Her phone rang again.

She picked up, 'I was just th…'

'Where the hell are you?'

'Keep your shirt on, Beck, I'm on my way.'

CHAPTER TEN

October 1954

The big policeman was angry. The boy knew it. He could see it in the way he clenched his fists and in the way his arms hung down by his sides, his mouth set like a cross dog.

'Stop your nonsense!' the policeman shouted at his mother, kicking back the stool and standing. 'Enough of it!'

The boy shuddered.

'It's the truth,' his mother shouted back. 'I swear it to you I do. It's the truth.' She began to wail. 'Oh, my bábóg.'

But just as suddenly, she fell quiet, staring at the table. The weak light from the candle glinted on the nail heads in the rough-hewn wood.

'Have you a husband?' the big detective asked.

The boy stiffened at the mention of his father. But it was not his mother who answered. It was the sergeant.

'Her husband is in England. He left to find work.'

'Did he?' his mother said. 'That's more than I know. He told me he was leaving. For good. Said he'd had enough. Have I not had enough as well, I ask? But where can I run off to? I can't, can I? No. I can't. Are marriage vows worth nothing any more? The curse of God on him.'

'Have you got a torch?' the inspector asked the sergeant.

The boy saw the sergeant fumble under his coat. A moment later a powerful beam of light lit up the small hovel.

'What in the name God is…?'

The detective pointed to the open hearth. Lying on the stone floor in front of it was a calf.

'What in the name of God is that doing here?' he demanded. 'I thought such days were over.'

The boy's mother did not answer.

'So, tell me, why didn't it take that then? This animal here. The creature that took your* bábóg. *Why didn't it? Explain that to me.'

His mother gave the detective an odd look.

'Because nothing will take a sick animal. What? And for it to get sick itself? No. No. No. It took my* bábóg. *Look at here…'*

She stood suddenly and crossed to the wicker basket near the door. She picked it up and brought it to him. She held it out.

'Look at here.'

The big detective peered at the basket. There was a soft green blanket in it, splattered with blood.

'Will you get out of that nightdress and put on something decent?' he shouted. 'You are covered in blood and half naked… God, this cursed place.'

His mother dropped the basket, stood with her hands open, then collapsed to her knees, wailing.

'My* bábóg. *My* bábóg. *Will you not get me my* bábóg?'

CHAPTER ELEVEN

The windows were open, but the breeze did not offer much respite from the sun beaming into the car. Beck liked heat, for a time that is. Winter Costa del Sol heat. The thought of a cold beer slipped into his mind. What could be wrong with a cold beer? Nothing, he lied to himself. And then he could see black clouds gathering, the flash of lightning, could hear the rumble of thunder in the distance, the barking of a dog, straining at the end of its leash.

'The victim's name is Samantha Power,' he said as they drove. 'The missing baby, her daughter, is called Róisín.'

'And the partner is Roche?'

'Correct. Edward.' Beck tapped the folded search warrant against his knee. 'He's refused members entry. That's why we're going there.' He held up the warrant. 'And why I have this.'

Claire slowed as they reached the turn off for Ravenscourt Drive. She drove into the small estate of semi-detached red brick houses, arranged in a semi-circle around a central green area.

She was wearing make-up, Beck noted. He had never seen her wear make-up before. He didn't think it suited her either. She wasn't the type. They could see the marked patrol car ahead against the kerb.

'Right there,' Beck said, pointing.

'I can see it. I'm not blind.'

As Beck walked up the garden path he looked at the small, wide-set man standing in the open doorway, dressed in Snickers cargo work trousers and a black polo shirt, arms a colour palate of tattoos, his face sporting a heavy moustache and stubble. He also noted the logo on his polo shirt, *Elegant Print and Design Company*. This was Mr Edward Roche. A couple of feet in front of him was Dempsey, facing the door, his back to Beck. Beside him was another officer, the pale blue epaulettes of a probationer on her shoulders, her back against the wall. She straightened up when she saw Beck walking towards them.

'Who're you?' Beck asked as he approached.

'Probationer Smyth. Helen. On secondment from the Training College.'

'Right,' Beck said, nodding towards Roche. 'Keep an eye on him?' Then, to Dempsey, 'You come with Detective Garda Somers and me.'

Roche folded his arms, standing in the doorway, refusing to let Beck pass.

Beck forced the lid down on his voice as he spoke. 'It's likely… no, no, let me start that again.'

'Easy, Beck,' it was Claire, from behind.

'… It's certain,' Beck continued, ignoring her, 'I think it's certain, the body of your partner is lying back there in a car registered to your name. On the back seat of which is a baby seat. But there is no baby.' Beck held the paper in the air. 'This is a search warrant. Now let us in to the property.'

Roche raised his arms, fisting his hands, placing them in front of his face in the defensive boxer's position. His eyes narrowed. Beck wondered if it was within operational guidelines for him to head-butt the man, aim for the nose. The blow to the soft cartilage would cause an instant overpowering pain and a flood of water to the eyes. Deciding it probably wasn't, he stiffened his left leg in preparation for bringing his right up and kneeing him in the balls instead. He'd have a better chance of explaining that, if he absolutely had to.

But Roche moved first. And not in a way Beck could have imagined. He began pummelling… himself. And as he did so, his face took on a tormented grimace, his mouth opened in an imitation of Edvard Munch's 'The Scream'. From his throat came a long grinding sound, like a low gear of a motorbike engine. And then he collapsed on his knees to the floor.

Beck stared. Should he clap or commiserate?

'Look after him, Smyth. Dempsey, come on.'

The probationer gave Beck a nervous glance, nodded her head. But Beck didn't have time for this. Roche's reaction concerned him. Was there a body in here too – that of baby Róisín?

They went through all the rooms. Looked under beds. Opened wardrobes. Went to the attic. Emptied boxes; old clothing, and stuff. Into the kitchen. Checked the cooker, the fridge/freezer, the refuse bins, even looked in the microwave. Went to the rear garden, a tiny green area, grass faded and uncut, some attempts at flower beds along the edges, but mostly bordered by weeds. They went back into the kitchen and through a door here into the garage. Beck was giving up hope now of finding any baby, and felt relief and disappointment, both at the same time. He detected a smell, like cinnamon, as he pressed a switch on the garage wall. A florescent light flickered and buzzed to life, revealing bare concrete walls, and a single window covered by wallpaper and a metal bar across the back of a door opposite.

There was a work bench just inside the door, running the length of the wall and in the centre a black machine, without definition, like a lump of metal offal, just sitting there. But the plate with black lettering on a red background bolted to the front gave it away. It said, 'Original Heidelberg'.

It was a printing press.

Beck walked over and looked at it. He touched it with a finger. It was cold and clean. He knew now the smell was not of cinnamon. It was ink. There were two rollers attached, like an old-fashioned clothes squeezer. Hanging from one end was a thin braided leather bracelet, loops of red thread woven through it, with a broken clasp. On the floor was a canvas cover with a corner rolled back, revealing tins of ink beneath.

Beck considered that. The man was a printer after all. On the work bench was a stack of booklets. He walked over, picked one up, turned it over. The title: *Living the Word. The Magazine of St. Joseph's Parish, Mylestown.*

CHAPTER TWELVE

October 1954

The boy could see a change come over his mother. She had grown very quiet, sitting with her arms folded, not speaking, her back against the wall in a corner of the room. Not once did she turn his way, to look at him. There was a look in her eye, like she could see things others could not. He didn't like that look. It told him that something was gone, a part of her was missing. Maybe the leprechauns had crept in while no one was watching?

There was a terrible stench in the place now. The boy thought the sick calf had died, because it lay so still on the floor. No one was paying any attention to it. He could hear people outside, voices, and a dog barking, an occasional wail of a woman.

He saw the big detective go to the door and stand before it.

'Sergeant,' he said. 'Come with me. Leave your other man here.'

He opened the door and stepped out into the night, the sergeant following. The boy could hear their footsteps crunching and fading as they walked away. A brief silence followed, and then the big detective's voice boomed:

'You will all make yourselves useful. Men, women and children. Everyone. You will do as we direct and leave no stone unturned. I want this place scoured. Scoured. Do you hear me!? Enough of your guff about banshees and monsters. I won't hear of it any more! If that baby isn't found by the middle of this night, Kathleen Waldron will

be returning to Galway with me. From there she will be taken to the asylum in County Clare. Now, get on with it.'

But no sound of movement followed. Only silence. Then the booming voice of the detective came once more:

'I said. Get on with it. Now!'

At that moment, a sound tore through the night from outside. It was a howl, swirling through the air, filling the entire world. The boy froze, staring into his grandmother's tortured face. A panic rose in him but he pushed against it. He was hot, and pulled the blanket down from about him, but instead of cold air he felt something warm on the back of his neck, like a moist breath. He snapped his head around, and looked into the face of a monster, nostrils wide, ears large and protruding, eyes circled by rings of brown.

It was the calf, standing by the hag, staring at him, its tongue protruding from a corner of its mouth. For the first time, the boy began to cry.

CHAPTER THIRTEEN

In the living room, there was a fireplace with a stone surround full of tissue paper, takeaway coffee cups and cigarette butts. This was not a tidy house. In a corner of the room was an empty playpen, brightly coloured plastic animals strung across the top. Roche was quiet now. He sat on a white settee beneath the window, a very low settee so that his knees were almost level with his face as he leaned forward, arms tightly held across his chest. He gently rocked his upper body back and forth.

Beck was staring at the playpen. It seemed to shout out to him, drowning out all other sounds by its very silence. He looked at the faces in the room. Was he the only one to hear it?

The uniforms sat on the settee along with Roche, one on either side of him.

Beck went and sat in a white leather armchair beside the fireplace. It was covered in black crease lines. Claire sat in the armchair opposite him, turned it so that she was facing Roche.

Silence.

For a long time Roche remained in the same posture, arms folded, staring at the floor.

Silence.

Slowly he raised his head and looked at Beck. His eyes had lost their defiance. He looked beaten. For the first time Beck felt some sympathy for the man.

'Why did you not report your partner and daughter missing? Can you explain that?' Beck asked.

'Because, like I already said we'd had a row. She stormed off. She's done it before. She always comes back though. When she cools down. But I didn't think she'd stay out all night. If I did, of course, then, it would have been different, I would have reported it. I really didn't think she'd stay out all night, okay. The row wasn't so bad. We've had worse. I can't even remember what it was about now.'

'You told us it was about you playing golf and not being home,' Garda Dempsey said. 'That's what you told us when we got here. Remember?'

Roche did not strike Beck as the golf-playing type.

'Oh, ya,' Roche said. 'Look, this is wrecking my head.'

'Where do you play golf?' Beck asked.

'What? Oh, Cross Beg golf club. On the driving range, nothing fancy.'

He's lying, Beck thought, but let it go for now.

'But they didn't come back,' it was Claire, 'that's the thing. They didn't come back. And you did nothing about it.'

'I thought she'd gone to her mother's, or one of her friends',' Roche said softly, hanging his head again. 'The baby's probably with one of them.'

The baby's probably with one of them.

And Roche's earlier meltdown seemed to have passed in double quick order. Specifically around the time he'd realised that they were coming in no matter what.

Beck noticed now the picture frames on the mantelpiece above the fireplace. And the large framed photograph high on the wall beside the settee. The photograph on the wall was of two people. There was Roche, in an open neck white shirt, the same stubble on his cheeks that gave him a permanently unwashed look. He was smiling. But it was a forced smile. Beck guessed that smiling did not come easily to the man. Next to him was the woman. The woman from the car. Samantha Power. In death there is no beauty, but in life she was surprisingly beautiful, Beck thought.

Even allowing for high-heels, she was taller than Roche. The dress she was wearing clung to every part of her slender body, merely emphasising the portliness of the man next to her, the physical differences between them.

He's not just punching above his weight, Beck thought, he's scaling a sheer rock face.

Beck looked at the frames on the mantelpiece now. There were three: Roche and two men in the nearest, wearing shirts and ties, a sombre occasion of some sort; the remaining two of Roche and different people – family occasions, he guessed.

'It may not be her,' Roche said. 'Will you take me there? So I can see. *Please.*'

Beck considered.

'I'm not so sure,' he mumbled, 'it's not procedure.' His voice rose an octave now, 'Mr Roche,' pausing again, knowing he had to build up trust, and continuing with his first name. 'Edward. Unfortunately, that's not going to change anything. I'm sorry to be blunt. Formal identification besides, we're pretty certain who the victim is. What you haven't told me about is your daughter. You don't seem very concerned, Edward. I'm beginning to get suspicious. I have to tell you that.'

'Concerned,' Roche shot back, his defiance returning now because it had never really gone away. 'Of course I'm bloody concerned. Look at me.'

'Edward,' Beck said, 'where are the photographs of your daughter?

Roche opened his mouth, was about to answer, but before he could there was a crashing noise and with it an explosion of glass. There were no curtains on the windows, and the fragments showered the settee. Instinctively, the people sitting there covered their heads with their arms. There was a dull thud as the rock bounced against the end wall, the one behind Beck's head. It landed on the floor at his feet.

Beck jumped up and crossed the room. He was just in time to see a group of children run along the street from the house.

'Feelings are beginning to get a little hot,' he said to no one in particular. He turned. 'Edward, why would that be? Why would children choose this house to put a rock through its window at a time like this?'

'Little shits. News travels fast around here. Very fast. They've heard something, haven't they? And having a cop car outside doesn't help. They don't like me, okay.'

'I see.'

'And I don't take crap from them either.'

Claire looked at Beck: *uh oh*.

'Have you been in trouble with the police before?' Claire asked.

Roche's head swivelled.

'What? What's that supposed to mean? Why do you ask? What's that got to do with anything?'

'It's a standard question.'

'That I'm not answering, because it has nothing to do with this. My partner, her child, are missing, and…'

'Her child,' Beck interrupted. 'Odd phrase. Isn't it your child too?'

Roche fell silent, slumping back into the settee, ignoring the broken glass. He sighed, closed his eyes, began massaging the corners with the index finger of each hand.

'She's not my child,' he said.

CHAPTER FOURTEEN

The house was big enough that most days they didn't get to see each other. It sat in a hollow on the side of the mountain two miles outside Cross Beg. It was not a big mountain, rising on one side of the Brown Water River basin, but big enough so that Crabby could see almost the whole way to the holy mountain, Croagh Patrick, way off in Co. Mayo on a clear day.

Since their two children – both boys – had grown and left home, their living arrangements had changed by mutual, silent, agreement; Julie lived in the top of the house, Crabby in the bottom. The kitchen and the outside deck were shared areas. Julie never went onto the deck anyway, even on the warmest of days, and with a little careful planning, they never were in the kitchen at the same time either. They existed in a state of marital purgatory, hating the sight of each other and yet at the same time neither willing to live without the other. Instead, she liked to silently torment him, just by her very existence. She liked to stand at an upper window when he was down below her on the deck, and watch him. Nothing more. Just watch him. He would feel her eyes upon his back after a time and could not help but to turn and look. And there she would be, looking down at him, with that strange smile on her face. A smile he was familiar with. Her father had it too. It only came out on special occasions. Christmas for example, when he cashed up at the end of the day. As the notes slid in and out between his fingers, it would be there. One corner of the mouth up, the other down, two front teeth poking out over the lower lip. It went against nature, a smile like that. It wasn't really a smile, but it wasn't a smirk either. There was no word for it, it was subconscious, it was an expression, of triumph. *I have won.*

The patrol car dropped him at the end of the driveway. Where it was difficult to see from the house, unless you were peering out from the very top of an upstairs window that is. Which she could well be, so he kept to the side of the driveway, against the bushes, hidden. At the top he crossed quickly and went around to the back of the house, then approached as if he were coming from the garage.

He entered through the kitchen door, but she was waiting for him, two fat feet poking out from beneath a long, white floral-patterned summer dress – a dress that only served to make her appear twice as fat as she already was. Her dyed auburn hair framed a still pretty face, despite the blubber on her neck and cheeks, the sharp green eyes still holding their sense of mystery. It was as if a new body had grown out of the old, all that remained was the kernel of who she once was.

She didn't speak, she didn't have to, because those eyes said it all.

He felt like he always felt around her, like a little boy, one who wanted to run away. But where to?

'I went for a cycle… ' he said, and a voice inside his head went, *you're pathetic!* 'Like I do… the weather… it was early… maybe a bit too early… I stopped at Kelly's Forge…'

The eyes: *Humph, Kelly's Forge.*

'I found… I found…'

As he fell silent.

The eyes stared, and she was silent. *You found what?*

He whispered: 'A body… there was a body… a body in a car… a d-de… a d-dead body… it was just… just *there.*'

A sound issued from his mouth that he had no control over, like a whine.

Her eyes now: *You're pathetic.*

He felt an overwhelming sense of sympathy, but for himself, and she could read it, she could read everything about him, this woman of tones, a different tone for every occasion. She was an apothecarist of tones, selecting from her vast collection, tipping in the appropriate essence. She selected one now, and it was contempt, dolloping it on.

'What were you doing there? Meeting one of your bitches I suppose?'

'Nooooo,' the whine never ending.

He cannot stop the whine.

He tells himself: *You are pathetic.*

'My father was right. The apple never falls far from the tree, after all. You did well out of us, my father and I, didn't you? And now your name is over the door. My father would turn in his grave. Is it one of the shop girls? I warned you about that.'

'I wasn't meeting anybody.'

'I hear the way you talk to them. There are laws about that now, you silly man. Don't you know that? Not to speak of the shame, for your two sons, for me, if... A body, you say. *You* found it. Whose body?'

'I don't know.'

'Humph. I'm thinking of the business. Not you. Of our sons' inheritance. If you destroy it, my reputation, their reputation. They have the bad luck to go through life now with your silly last name. My fault that, I admit. Yes, if you destroy it, you'll end up begging on the streets. You'll have nothing. I'll see to it. I promise you. I guarantee it, do you hear me?'

Crabby crossed the kitchen to the sink, leaned over it, placed both hands onto the window sill. He suddenly felt like he was about to throw up.

'Did you tell them, the guards?' she asked, selecting condescension now, pouring it on. 'I bet you didn't tell them *that.*'

The whine left Crabby's voice, replaced by surprise.

'Tell them what?'

He realised he and his wife were saying more to each other in that moment than in the entire previous year.

'Oh, don't act silly. Don't act silly, Maurice. You silly little man.'

Crabby straightened and turned from the sink. He looked at his wife now, directly into her eyes. It is she, Julie, who is taken by surprise on this occasion. But she doesn't look away, instead looks back at him. Silently they stare at one another.

'You were there, yesterday afternoon, weren't you? Kelly's Forge. Did you tell them that? Well, did you?'

Maurice said nothing.

'Well, did you tell them that, you silly little man?'

'No. I was not. I was not there.'

'You lie. You pathetic little man. And when you came home, there was blood on your clothes. Did you tell them that?'

Maurice covered his mouth with a hand and turned back to the sink, lowering his head, retching once, then twice, before finally vomiting up a stream of yellow viscous liquid.

CHAPTER FIFTEEN

October 1954

The boy knew it was very late when Mícheál Peoples had come to the cottage enquiring about them. He spoke with his mother briefly and when he had finished and was about to leave again, the big detective said, 'What is your name?'

'Mícheál Peoples. I came to see how they were.' He waved vaguely towards the boy and his grandmother. 'I am the village elder.'

'Are you now?' the big detective said. He glanced over without warning, and the boy ducked beneath the blankets before he could meet his eyes. He held his breath.

'Do you know who called us here?' the big detective asked. 'Word was delivered to Mill Street, but we don't know from whom.'

He could hear Mícheál Peoples tell him that he did not know.

The boy heard footsteps approaching, then the blanket was pulled down gently from his face. Up close, he thought the detective looked like a giant, with a head the texture and colour of stone.

'Young gossan,' he said. 'Did you see anything in here tonight? Did you?'

From the corner of his eye, the boy could see Mícheál Peoples watching him. He shook his head, his eyes so wide he felt as if they might pop out. The detective's rock-like face softened. He raised an arm and brought down the massive hand onto the boy's forehead, patted it twice. Then he turned and walked away.

The boy watched him go, and could see beyond, through the window, the first light of a new day beginning to scratch through the darkness. It was then he finally closed his eyes and went to sleep.

CHAPTER SIXTEEN

His lips barely moved as he spoke.

'*She's not my child.*'

Roche allowed the statement to hang in the air, then pursed his lips, sealing his mouth shut. Seconds passed, but no one was surprised when he did not speak again.

Claire said, 'That would be Billy Hamilton, wouldn't it?'

Roche's eyes widened as he looked at Claire.

'I checked Pulse,' Claire said. 'The assault, some months back, when you went round to his home and attacked him.'

'If you checked why did you ask if I was known to gardai? You already knew the answer to that.'

'Because I wanted you to tell me. You didn't. Maybe because when you went round to Billy Hamilton's place the tables were turned. Hamilton got the better of you. A fella like Hamilton always will. You also have some traffic offences, and a public order conviction from last year. There are also two domestic incidents, for this address.'

'You think I done it, don't ya? Killed Samantha.'

'There are aspects of this case which cause me concern,' Beck said. 'They would anyone. You would not allow entry to the uniformed gardai when they called just now. They were merely attempting to verify that there was not a baby on the property. Which is why I'm here, and I don't want to be, because there are other things I could be doing, believe me. And I'm being forced to come across a little heavy-handed, but you leave me no choice.

Now, can you run me through where you were from, say, lunch time yesterday until night time?'

'Are you looking for voluntary admissions? Isn't that what you call it?'

'You're watching too many crime programmes on TV, seems to me,' Beck said. 'I'm just asking a very obvious question. Could you just drop the attitude and cooperate.

Roche intertwined his hands, and Beck could see the colour of his flesh change, becoming whiter, as he squeezed and squeezed.

'I can save you a lot of time,' Roche said slowly. 'I didn't kill her. I… I love her. You're wasting your time. Don't waste your time. Find the real killer. When the gardai called, I was nervous, okay. I couldn't take everything in. I'm sorry.'

'Where were you then?' Beck said. 'Let's start again.'

As he began to speak, Beck watched Roche's body language, because he knew from experience, that people who lied often displayed specific body language indicators. This usually meant that their posture became closed, they crossed their arms, or their legs, maybe touched their face, especially by the mouth, or they over explained things, became conversational, tried to win over their interviewer's trust, their ultimate goal to take control. But a good interviewer would stimulate proceedings, would have already gained the suspect's trust, would have played along in a respect. And Beck knew he had not done a good job in gaining Roche's trust.

None of which Roche does now, because his hands still squeeze together, and he is sitting back into the settee, legs loose but not man spread.

'I was working yesterday. Until just after six o'clock. You can check.'

'Did I hear you correctly?' surprise in Beck's voice. 'Didn't you just say a moment ago you had a half day off and went playing golf?'

'No. I said I was *planning* on playing golf. But I *didn't* say I played golf. After the row, I changed my mind, I didn't bother. I worked and went home. I thought Samantha and the kid would be here.'

The kid.

'I waited in all evening, waiting for her.'

'You have no way of proving any of this, do you?' Claire asked.

Roche looked at his hands, parted them, then raised them to his face now and rubbed them briskly across it a couple of times.

'No… No, I don't,' with a sigh, holding the palms against his cheeks.

'You can see my predicament,' Beck said.

'Yes. I can see it. But you're barking up the wrong tree.'

A telephone rang, shrill and loud. Dempsey fumbled in his pocket and took out his mobile.

'Hello. Yes, sir, he's here. Yes, sir. Will do.'

He hung up, looked at Beck.

'Superintendent Wilde is waiting for you. He wants you back at the station right away for a briefing.'

'Okay,' Beck said.

'What about him?' Probationer Smyth gestured to Roche.

'What about him indeed,' Beck said. 'Edward, you want to make a complaint about your broken window?'

Roche shook his head.

'I'm not going to be here much longer,' he said. 'In this house. No. Forget the window. I want to see Sam.'

'Someone will be in contact with you about that. If you leave this property, and go stay somewhere else, which I think would be advisable, you must inform us immediately.' And, to Dempsey and Smyth. 'Stay with him you two. Take an official statement. Any more rocks through the window, deal with it. Prosecution can be secured under the public order act, you don't need a statement. I'll talk to you again, Edward. Goodbye. For now.'

CHAPTER SEVENTEEN

October 1954

It was mid-morning, but the daylight had never fully taken hold, shadows still crept about the room. The boy was awake. He had not slept for very long. He needed the toilet, his bladder pressed down inside him and his stomach was tender. But he would not move from his grandmother. He saw that the sick calf had been taken away. His mother had changed her clothing too. She was dressed in a frayed winter dress and cardigan, with a brightly coloured coat on top. He liked that coat. The colours. They gave her a radiance, one that was out of place in the dark gloom of this place. She wore a hat too, tilted to one side. He considered this strange, and wondered: Was she going somewhere? She was sat at the table with the big detective.

'Your bábóg. *Last chance. Tell me what you did with her?' The detective's voice was gritty and tired.*

'I told you,' her voice strangely content. 'The monster took my bábóg. *But I am happy now. I have prayed to God and I know my child is in heaven. She is with the angels and the saints. She is with my blood and kin who have passed before. She is safe. She is happy. Yes, I am happy now too. So I wore my hat. You can take me now. To that place you told me about. I am ready.'*

'Then say goodbye to your boy.'

'There is no need. I have already done so. Take me now.'

The big detective stood and walked to the door, opened it. The boy's mother stood and followed. As she stepped through the doorway the boy was about to call out to her. But he did not. She and the detective walked away and the door banged shut behind them.

His mother had not said goodbye to him. She said that she had, but she had not.

She had lied again.

In the silence of the room, the boy's life had changed forever. The events of this night would never leave him, they would be with him always, a torment, one he would constantly relive, silently, within himself, every day from this moment on.

CHAPTER EIGHTEEN

Colette Power's life was one of suffering. That was apparent immediately in her face; the flesh like crumpled parchment paper, and the eyes, peering out from their deep sockets. She looked to be in her mid-fifties, but it was hard to tell, life seemed to have slowly, inexorably, ground her down, pushed her towards the edge where she had precariously balanced for years. All it would take was a gentle nudge and she would topple over now.

And this was not a nudge. This was a sledgehammer blow, even if Garda Jane Ryan had decided to come here herself and deliver it as gently as she could. Colette Power had opened the door of 121 Chapel Park just enough to place her head through, peering out at her.

'Can I come in, Colette?'

'What's happened?'

'Can I come in, Colette?' Garda Ryan repeated.

The head remained, poking out from behind the door.

'Who's that at the door?' a voice from somewhere behind her, with a distinct antipodean accent. 'The guards d'ya say? Bloody Nora.'

'What's happened?' Colette asked, the door opening fully now.

From down the hall came a tall and gangly male, a mop of dirty blonde hair above a deeply tanned face, dressed in Bermuda shorts and a T-shirt with a cartoon of a kangaroo and the words 'Fair Dinkum' on it.

'It's your daughter, Mrs Power,' Garda Ryan said. 'We believe her body was found this morning.'

'Whoa, what the hell,' Crocodile Dundee said. 'Wha'ya just say?'

'What did she say?' Colette asked too. 'What did she say? Samantha. What about her? Did you say a body?'

'Can I come in, Mrs Power, *please*?' Garda Ryan tried one more time.

'What the hell,' Crocodile Dundee said again.

'Who are you?' Garda Ryan asked.

'Who am I? I'm Mikey. Sam's brother. That's who I am.'

'He's home on a holiday,' Colette said, turning and walking away. Garda Ryan followed her down a short hall and into a tiny living room. It seemed to be taken up completely by a large leather settee and two armchairs with lace antimacassars on the backrests. There was a cabinet along one wall filled with cut glass trinkets. The air was musty, the room spotless, seldom used.

'You sit there, Mum, eh?' Mikey said, guiding his mother to the settee. 'I'll deal with this.'

He stood with his hands on his waists, a gatekeeper.

Colette wrapped a wizened finger around wisps of long, dirty blonde hair, pushed the finger against the hollow of a cheek.

'Shut up, Mikey. Will you? For Christ's sake.' She looked at Garda Ryan. 'What? Please. Tell me.'

Garda Ryan's hi-vis jacket was too warm for this weather. But still she wore it. It made a loud squealing noise as she sat down into an armchair. 'Colette, I'm awfully sorry to have to tell you this. But a body was found this morning. It's Samantha.'

Colette Power stared at Garda Ryan. 'What? It can't be. I've already lost one. A son. Kevin. No. Not again. Please.'

'No way,' Mikey said, coming and sitting beside his mother now. 'You coppers are always getting your facts arse-ways. How d'ya know it's my sister, eh? Who the bloody hell ID'd the body, eh?'

'Samantha,' Colette said, ignoring her son, her voice calm, then, as understanding crept in. 'And Róisín? Where's my grand-daughter?'

'We thought she might be here,' Garda Ryan said.

'Here? No! Róisín is not here. She's with Samantha. And, what? Samantha's… dead? Is that what you're telling me?'

'Don't listen to them, Mum. You go and ring Samantha right now, you'll…'

'Shut up, Mikey! They wouldn't be here unless they were certain. Don't be an idiot.'

'Her body was found this morning, Colette,' Garda Ryan said, leaning forward in her chair.

The noise of that damned jacket.

'You're certain?' Colette Power said. 'That it's Samantha.'

'Colette, we're as certain as can be. I have to ask, do you know where the baby is? Have you any idea at all?'

'Róisín,' Mikey said, his voice gentle. 'Ah, Jesus.'

Colette Power was so still she seemed to have stopped breathing. Her eyes stared ahead and did not blink, the spiny finger had stopped turning the wisps of hair about it. It was as if her life force was leaving her. But then she blinked. She could not leave, not just yet.

'Her father?…'

'Eddie?' Garda Ryan asked, and realised immediately her mistake.

'He's not the child's father. Billy Hamilton is,' Colette's voice a monotone. 'He might be a lot of things, but he's a good father… after all, he's had a lot of practice.'

'That bastard,' Mikey said, his eyes blazing. 'And the other one, Roche. If either of them two…'

'Will you shut up,' Colette said. 'This is hard enough.'

'Ya,' Mikey said. 'Everyone knows Hamilton's going through the young women of south Galway like a rampaging bull.'

'But Róisín is his only girl,' Colette continued. 'That might have had something to do with it. All the goodness he had he gave to Róisín, and all the bad, the evil, to Samantha. How could he be so cruel to the mother of a baby he loved so much, or seemed to love so much anyway?'

'Cause he's a bastard,' Mikey said. 'That's why, eh.'

Garda Ryan considered the news that Billy Hamilton was a good father. The last time she'd seen him was a night recently when he'd been stopped walking through the town with a pit bull terrier on a lead in one hand and a samurai sword in the other. He was strung out and rambling to himself. But it was obvious he wasn't on his way to make a friendly house call.

She saw a picture on the mantlepiece of the fireplace, of Samantha and a baby.

'This Róisín?' she asked.

Colette nodded, closing her eyes, then opening them again slowly.

Garda Ryan noticed a slight blemish on the side of the child's forehead, a faint red blob. She felt certain it was a birthmark, a strawberry birthmark.

'Can I take this?' she asked. 'I'll get it back to you.'

Colette nodded.

'Drove Roche mad, so it did,' she added. 'He's a jealous bastard that Roche. Samantha had her trouble with him too, told me she was going to leave him. Said she just wanted to wait a little bit longer. He earns good money down at that printing shop. Samantha wanted to wait until she had something sorted out. Just a little bit longer she said, just a little bit longer… How did she die?'

'Colette,' Garda Ryan said, reaching out and holding her hand. It was cold and bony, brittle, like if she squeezed too tight it might turn to dust. 'It appears she was murdered.'

A shooshing noise then as Colette sucked in air. She stared ahead, silent.

Mikey got to his feet, his fists clenched. 'I'll get whoever did this. I…'

Colette slumped forward, her chin falling against her chest. Garda Ryan felt the weight of her body shift now too.

'Colette. Are you alright?'

'… Swear to God.' Mikey went on, 'if any—'

'She's unconscious,' Garda Ryan shouted. 'I need an ambulance here now!'

CHAPTER NINETEEN

The operations room at Cross Beg Garda Station was really just a fancy name for a large room with desks and chairs in it. Modern desks and modern swivel chairs granted, but still, nonetheless, mere desks and chairs. There was also a bank of small personal, personnel lockers at one end. Blue, chosen to match the blue chairs which had been chosen to match the blue tiled floor. The desks were of wood veneer with metal legs and contoured tops so that each officer could reside within, rather than outside, their work station. Functionality, it was called. The ceiling was acoustic with bright, even harsh, florescent lighting that remained on day and night.

But this was a façade. Beneath it all, the building was an antique over a hundred years old, built during the reign of Queen Victoria, when all of Ireland was within her realm. This room, where Royal Irish Constabulary officers were once billeted, where they ate and slept, where an open fire burned and the sun shone through the narrow windows and rooftop skylight. Where they shined their boots throughout the day lest the district inspector should call unannounced. If he did and their boots were scuffed, they would be docked a shilling from their wages. The building now was of historical significance and retained some original features, the heavy green wooden main door for instance, and the tiled reception area. The acoustic ceiling had been installed the year before in the interests of energy efficiency. It concealed the old skylight, eliminating much of the cold winter downdraughts. But last winter had seen more officers taking sick days for colds and flu than ever before. In the wall of the Ops Room the large old fireplace had long been filled in, but its outline was still visible, its green marble mantelpiece jutting out with its fancy corbels beneath, and the slate surround sharply defined against the pale cream of the brickwork. It seemed the building could not decide whether it was a museum piece, an heirloom, or a modern police facility.

Beck went and stood alongside Superintendent Wilde at the top of the room.

'Where's Inspector O'Reilly?' Wilde asked.

Beck shook his head. He didn't know, and that suited him just fine.

'Very well,' Wilde said, looking about the room. It was a mixture of Cross Beg and district gardai. 'Listen up people,' he said, 'thank you. The victim is Samantha Power, mid-twenties, exact age to be verified. From what we can tell, killed by a single deep laceration to the neck. Found this morning by a cyclist, Mr Maurice Crabby. Yes, of the supermarket. We believe she had her six-month-old baby daughter with her. Name, Róisín. The child appears to be missing. We are very concerned for her safety. A CRI alert has been issued within the past hour and a half.'

'What's a CRI alert, boss?' The uniformed officer who'd asked was heavy set, with bushy white hair and red cheeks. He held a stubby finger in the air, peering over his half glasses. He could sniff retirement on the air, Beck felt certain, so didn't care what people thought either of him or his questions.

You've heard of it, you just didn't listen.

Superintendent Wilde ran through it quickly, added, 'It's already been disseminated through the media, Garda Kennedy. Motorway electronic signage too. And all ports and airports have been notified. Clear, Frank?'

The older officer nodded once.

'A mobile phone,' Superintendent Wilde went on, 'was recovered from the car. Initial analysis shows nothing unusual. A request through local media channels has been made for search volunteers, and Civil Defence are sending a coordinating officer. A dog unit is on the way too, also a request has been made to the Aer Corp for a helicopter… Inspector Beck.'

Beck cleared his throat.

'First off,' Beck said. 'We are also looking for a murder weapon, a great big bloody knife, in all probability. The water unit is on notice to attend if we can't find it. A case number has been created on Pulse, and it's very important that people use it because this will provide us with some joined up, strategic information. The case number is simple: 1-2-3-4. Everyone think they can remember it?'

Beck fell silent. Heads nodded.

'Suspects,' Beck said. 'We spoke to Mr Edward Roche.'

A murmur went through the room.

'The victim's partner?' someone asked.

'That's right,' Beck said. 'The victim's partner.'

'That's where I'd be looking then,' the same voice. 'Definitely.'

'He does fit the frame,' Beck said. '*Definitely.* And we've taken a statement. Nothing more we can do with him for now, but we'll keep an eye. Hourly patrols of Ravencourt's estate, to be logged on Pulse under the case number, until we see how this pans out. We may need to request phone records too.' He looked about the room. 'Anyone know where Billy Hamilton is? We need to speak to him.'

'I heard he's in Glasgow,' Frank said solemnly. 'Supposedly. Don't know where I heard that, but I did.'

'Glasgow,' Beck responded, surprised. 'Like, as in permanently?'

'No. A football game.'

'Okay.' There was exasperation in Beck's tone. 'You know where he lives in Cross Beg?'

'Billy Hamilton?' Frank gave a rumbling laugh, and a look, *are you serious?* 'He sleeps in a different bed every night of the week, that man. He's a stud.'

'He's a slut,' a female voice offered. 'If it's good enough that a woman can be called that, then it's good enough for that lowlife.'

'That's enough,' Beck said. And to Frank. 'Round you go then, and check, good man, all known addresses for Billy Hamilton.'

Frank wasn't laughing any more.

'Moving on,' Beck said. 'What's important now is that we gather as much CCTV as possible. The victim had groceries in her car, purchased from Crabby's supermarket. That'll be our first port of call.'

'The man who found the body?' someone put it as a question.

'That's correct,' Beck replied. 'Maurice Crabby knocked on my door this morning. He knows where I live, obviously. He'd forgotten his phone. He thought it quicker to come to my house than the station.'

'Bit of a coincidence, don't you think?'

'Anything's possible,' Beck said. 'At this stage. But it is the biggest supermarket in the town so I'm inclined to disagree, I don't think it's much of a coincidence.'

Beck turned his attention to the small, stocky sergeant sitting near the top of the room.

'Sergeant Connor?'

Connor nodded. Beck knew he had only just returned to day shift following an extended period working nights. The collar of his shirt was tight around his bull neck, the veins inside prominent, and his chin extended from his face like an overhang. But he looked happy, like nothing could remove his sense of perpetual optimism now that he was working day shifts again.

'CCTV, sergeant. If you can take charge. Everything you can get your hands on.'

'Yes, boss.'

Beck looked about the room.

'Garda Jane Ryan?'

'That's me.'

Garda Ryan stood. She had the harried look of one juggling too many balls in the air, and all at the same time. She looked uncomfortable, her uniform seemed too tight, and Beck wondered why she was wearing a hi-vis jacket on such a hot day.

'When I had my third child,' she said, 'Samantha Power used to come and help me out with a few things.'

'What kind of things?' Beck asked.

'You know. Bit of tidying, cooking, that sort of thing...'

'You mean, like a housekeeper.'

Garda Ryan shook her head.

'I wouldn't say that. Not a housekeeper. She just helped out, that's all.'

'What was she like?' Wilde asked. 'Can you tell us that?'

'A grand girl. She was with us three months...' She looked at Wilde. 'Sir, do you mind if I sit down?'

Wilde nodded. 'Of course not.'

'That was a year and a half ago now,' Garda Ryan said, resuming her seat. 'I haven't seen her since.'

She fell silent, folded her arms.

'Where was she living back then, do you know?' Wilde asked.

'With her mother. I know because she didn't have a car at the time. I had to collect her, drive her back home when she'd finished... By the way...'

'Yes,' it was Wilde.

'Because I knew Samantha, I volunteered to go round to her mother's place this morning. To inform her, see too if she had the baby. She didn't of course. I had to call an ambulance because she fainted. Her brother was there, Mikey, lives in Australia. He's home on holiday, has an attitude by the way. Oh, and baby Róisín, looks like she has a little birth mark, on one side of her forehead, a small red blemish, a strawberry birthmark, looks like to me. I got a photograph.'

'Right, we need to get it to the press office ASAP. Anyone else? Father? Other siblings?'

'There was another brother,' Garda Ryan said. 'Kevin, but he was killed in a motorcycle accident years ago. No one knows where the father is, she once told me he left when she was only a kid.'

'Previous boyfriends,' Beck said. 'Would you know?'

'Billy Hamilton, he's the only one I know about, apart from Roche that is. But Hamilton was the one, definitely. I had to tell her to turn off her phone more than once because she was getting no work done, he was always ringing her. It caused a bit of a problem between us, so it did, she was besotted with him. Other than that she was a great girl, hard working. It was as if she was under his spell. He's a bad egg, a hash and a piss-head too, but he looks good, I'll grant you that. We all know him. And such a lovely girl…' She shook her head. 'I could never understand it. I mean, the way she was drawn to him, and the other eejit, Roche, like a moth to the flame.'

'When did Roche turn up?' Beck asked.

'He's been with her since before the baby was born. They'd just moved in together. Roche has a job, so he offered her some type of stability, I suppose.'

'You think Hamilton or Roche are capable of doing this?' he asked.

'Complete morons, the two of them,' Garda Ryan said.

The room laughed softly, a release of tension.

'But this. Are they capable of it? Of killing her?'

'I don't know,' she said. 'Killing her is one thing. But the baby. Neither of them would touch the baby. Not even Roche. He was jealous of the child if you ask me. And yet if the baby was in the car, I don't think either of them would have touched Samantha. But I don't know. Hamilton has a temper, so he has. Who knows what he's capable of. They both knocked her around. Ah, why did she put up with the likes of them? Bringing all that on herself.' Garda Ryan shook her head.

Damned if I know either, Beck thought. Damned if I know.

*

Superintendent Wilde took a deep breath. They were seated in his office that looked like a set from a period drama. Beck noticed a wad of fifty-dollar notes on the desk top, wrapped in an elastic band.

'They've just arrived,' Wilde said.

'What, those?' Beck said, pointing to the money.

'No. Forensics.' He picked up the wad of notes. 'Counterfeit fifty-dollar bills. They're everywhere at the moment. Easier to forge than sterling or euro. People love to get them. Shopkeepers and publicans and the like. They put it in their going-to-America-on-holiday stash. The least of our worries, I think you'll agree. Although finance up in HQ is like a dog with a bone about them. I've been getting some very sticky emails on the matter recently.'

Beck nodded.

'In this heat, there won't be much left to work on if they don't get started soon. Any word from Inspector O'Reilly, if I may ask?'

The old window behind Wilde's desk had been lowered and hung lopsided now. Beck could see the taut rope pulley to one side. The window was stuck.

'You certainly may ask. No, is the answer. I haven't heard from him. I've tried ringing, but there's no reply. I'm getting a little worried, to tell the truth.'

'Really?'

'Because it's not like him. Not at all. And his timing's terrible. But he is a grown man, and grown men can act, shall I say, strange at times. You would know about that, Beck, wouldn't you?'

'Yes, I would… but not him.'

'Granted, not him. I'll give it another hour or so, then send a car round to his house. In the meantime, I should go and talk to forensics.'

'Why?'

'What do you mean, why? Are you serious?'

'Is a hospital manager present during surgery?' Beck asked. 'No, is the answer. So, if you want to observe forensics at work, watch TV. You'll be getting in the way otherwise.'

Wilde narrowed his eyes.

'Remember who you're speaking to. You think I don't know what I'm doing, is that it?

Beck shook his head. 'No…' but he didn't sound too convinced.

'I can see why O'Reilly has a problem with you,' Wilde said. 'Let's not fall out, Beck, okay. Anyway, I didn't want you going to the scene, because I have something that requires urgent attention and I want you to look after it.'

'Yes,' Beck said, curious now.

Superintendent Wilde turned to his computer, tapped the keyboard, clicked on the mouse, tapped on the keyboard again.

'A recent arrival to Cross Beg,' he said. 'Residing at number four, Rafferty's Flats. He's on the sex offenders list, recently released on parole. He just passed his post-release supervision period and decided to move to the country, make a new start, where he doesn't know anybody. The pervert is living here, Beck, in Cross Beg, and after what's happened, we need to talk to him. Immediately. This man served fourteen years in Arbour Hill prison for the carnal knowledge of a minor. Abducted and raped an eleven-year-old girl in 2003, the dirty…' Superintendent paused. He peered at the computer. 'He reported his change of address within the mandatory seven days. Go and have a look. I think Samantha Power might be out of his age range. But the baby isn't.'

Beck leaned forward. There was something very familiar about what he had just heard.

'Name?' he asked.

Superintendent Wilde peered at the computer screen again.

'Jonathan Tiery…'

'I know the bastard. I was the one who arrested him.'

CHAPTER TWENTY

They pulled up outside Rafferty's Flats. The sun was beating down now. The roadway was narrow and there was no footpath. In the centre was a patch of tarmac darker than that surrounding it which had melted. Claire tucked the Focus as close as possible to the warped railing at the front of the property. They got out and walked through the railing – there was no gate – and across a rectangle of concrete that had once been a small garden. They went up steps to the front door, the stub of a missing railing along the edge of each step embedded in the concrete. Next to the steps were three overflowing wheelie bins. The door was a faded blue with scuff marks along the bottom. On the wall next to it was a panel of doorbells, each bell with a space beside it meant to display the name of the tenant. But all the spaces were blank. The front door was not flush with the frame, and so not properly closed. Beck wiped the sweat from his forehead and pushed – and it opened. He stepped into a hallway, and Claire followed. The hallway was dark, clammy and hot, with a musty smell. A wide wooden staircase ran along the right wall and twisted upwards. The banister and spindles were ornate – at one time these would have been impressive, but now were faded and dusty. A large window high up in the wall by the stairs threw down some light, but a set of dirty half-closed heavy curtains blocked most of it. Another set of stairs to the left at the back of the hall led down into the basement.

There was a white, heavy wood-panelled door to the left and another beside Beck on his right, but neither had a number. The doors were likely original Georgian, Beck thought. The whole place looked like it had come straight from the pages of a Charles Dickens novel.

Beck went to the door to his right, was about to knock when the door opposite creaked open, just enough for a woman to put her head through, pale skin, black short hair, small facial features, surprisingly young. Surprisingly, because Beck thought everything to do with this house should be old. She looked at them without saying a word, then sniffed a couple of times. Beck looked at Claire, and slid his eyes sideways.

Claire walked across to the door. 'Flat four. Can you tell us where it is?'

'You the cops?' The woman's voice was low, raspy.

Claire nodded.

'Number four. He lives right above me he does.' The girl jerked her head upward. 'You going to arrest him?'

'Why do you ask that?'

'No why,' the woman said. 'He's an oddball. A header. Don't like him. Makes me nervous every time I see him, he does.' She began to close the door.

'Is he home now?' Claire asked.

'He's always home, so he is. You can hear him walkin' around all hours.' And the door closed.

The stairs creaked like an old wooden ship. At the top, a hallway led to the left with three doors, identical to those downstairs, wood panelled, painted white. Beck knew the last door, at the front of the house, had to be number four.

They went down the hall, stopped in front of the door. Beck gave three hard, business knocks. He put his ear to it, listening. He could hear a shuffling sound from the other side, followed by what sounded like newspapers rustling. Then, silence, a static silence. He waited. Nothing, just that static silence, like white noise. He took his ear from the door and knocked again, three more taps, louder, more insistent. He placed his ear to the door again. A creaking sound, right next to him: someone was standing on the other side of the door.

Beck stepped back, mouthed to Claire, 'Someone's standing there,' and, joining his index and middle fingers, raised and lowered them against his thumb in a speaking motion, mouthing, 'Talk to him'.

Claire spoke, her tone friendly. 'Hello. Jonathan. This is the Gardai. Can we have a word?' No reply. 'Jonathan, we know you're in there. Can you open the door? Please?'

They waited. Then, the sound of a latch sliding back, and the door knob began to turn. Finally, the door opened and Jonathan Tiery was standing before them. He'd changed, was Beck's first thought. Gone was the mop of curly hair. Instead, his head was shaved, the shadow of a hairline visible along the sides way back on top. Beck thought: Why bother shaving your head if, according to what we've just been told, you don't even bother going out? He'd lost weight too, but not in a good way, his cheeks were hollow and the shoulders bony beneath the round-neck jumper he wore even in this weather. His glasses were plastic rimmed and far too big for what was now a small head, and he looked pale and sick. Beck didn't think he'd have the strength to cut a carrot.

'*You*,' he said, looking at Beck. Beck had forgotten how high-pitched his voice was, like a child's.

'Hello. Long time no see. Can we come in?' Beck asked.

Tiery grunted and turned, walked into the room. 'Do I have a choice?' he muttered.

Beck and Claire followed. The room smelt of stale cooking oil. A bed took up one corner, next to it a sink and above it, a small circular mirror was fixed to the wall, its edges blackened with age. Across from the bed was a cooker and fridge and beside these a narrow, open, window. On the other side of the window was an old portable TV on a small shelf. In the centre of the room there was a narrow table with a cheap plastic floral design tablecloth, a red plastic chair on either side of it. Everything in the room was within a forward lean and an arm's reach. Beck thought it could be a museum exhibit, titled 'Bedsitting Room, early twenty-first century'.

Tiery stood by the window, leaning against the wall. He looked at them, these people filling his tiny room. There was no expression on his face, nothing.

As Beck watched this cold face, he was sent back to all those years ago.

The girl ran along the crowded city street, screaming. No one came to help her, too shocked to know what to do. The girl was naked from the waist down, her blouse torn open, bright red blood splattered about the area between her legs. When the police were called, Beck was one of the two guards to respond, waiting for her at the top of the street. When she reached them he took off his jacket and wrapped it about her. She was only eleven. Eleven!

Beck pushed his rage down inside.

'So you're out,' he said. 'What a small world. We meet again.'

Tiery turned his head and looked out the window, folded his arm. 'Cut the shit. Why are you here?'

'We're investigating a very serious crime, that's why.'

'It's the murder, isn't it? I heard. Hard luck. It's not me.'

'Yes, Jonathan, you would say that, wouldn't you? You've been out now a couple of weeks, is that right?'

'So.'

'And you come to a kip like Cross Beg to hide away from the world. Where you thought no one would know you. Where you could live happily ever after. What were you thinking?'

'You can't believe how much easier it's made my life.'

'Oh I can imagine. It's made *your* life a whole lot easier. Good for you. By the way, you go out much?'

'Jesus, am I ever going to be left in peace?'

'Probably not. Maybe you should have stayed in Dublin.'

'Believe me, if I could…'

'… You would. So why didn't you?'

'I hate you people. So callous.'

'You dying, Jonathan, is that it? You look like crap.'

Tiery looked into Beck's eyes for the first time, his expression one of sadness, but defiance mixed in there too.

'You are, aren't you? You're dying?' Beck said.

'Happy now? Stage four bowel cancer, had all the treatment and its spread everywhere now. So yes, I am fucking dying.'

Beck thought: good, but we're wasting our time here.

Tiery suddenly jerked his head to one side. 'Hey, what the fuck are you doing?'

Beck walked to the bed and pulled back a corner of the flimsy duvet. Underneath was a laptop, an image frozen on its screen, of a woman, spread-eagled by her wrists and legs, tied to something out of camera shot, a plastic ball in her mouth, a man behind her, holding a long cylinder type object in one hand. Tiery moved from the window towards the computer. Beck blocked his way.

'Play it,' Beck told Claire. 'See what it's about. Anything illegal on there and we have him.'

'It's a DVD,' Tiery said. 'See for yourself. An over-eighteen. There's nothing illegal about it.'

'You got anything else in here?' Beck asked. Then, to Claire. 'Check out the DVD.'

Claire crossed the room and opened the computer drive and took out the disc, peered at it, then tossed it onto the bed. '"Exclusive Fetish Series Three. Carla Goes Extreme." Over-18s.'

'I have nothing else,' Tiery said, his tone sad, like someone who'd had his toy taken away.

'I don't believe you,' Beck replied. 'Mind if we have a look?'

Tiery's vocal pitch dipped. He said, 'Don't you need a warrant?'

'Correct,' Beck replied. 'I do. But not if you invite me in to have a look around. The only reason you wouldn't invite me in to have a look around is because you might have something to hide. And in that case, I'd have to apply for a warrant. At this hour…' He checked his watch, '… hhmm, it's getting late, at this hour, that'd take a little time. I'd have to leave someone here, to make sure you didn't destroy any possible evidence, you know, while I went for the warrant. And before you ask, *Jonathan*, yes, I can do that.'

Tiery shoulders slumped. He walked over to the bed and sat down, cradling his head in his hands. 'I've stage four cancer. It's spreading into my liver and spine. I just, look at those things sometimes, that's all.' He turned his eyes upward to Beck, demeanour now one of sadness and pleading. 'Couldn't you just leave me in peace? To die? That's all I ask.'

Beck, who had been trying to operate inside Garda Mission Statement guidelines, really trying to do the right thing, to show respect and tolerance and all that, tossed them to one side now.

'You mean like the little girl in the park, the one you took behind the bushes, you miserable bastard. Why couldn't you leave her in peace? You sick pervert. You sick pervert! I'd love to get a sharp blade, hang you upside down, peel your skin from your body and leave you in a sewer. And even that, even *that*, would be too fucking good for you.'

Beck was shaking. The images were still there. Of his own abuse. They would always be there. Even if he had made sure he would never be able to see them. Because he'd stored them in an iron vault deep within himself. A place where he did not go. Where he never would go. Where he never could go.

He wanted to kill Tiery. Knew he was capable of it, at this moment. And not only that, he would relish it.

He felt Claire's hand on his shoulder. She whispered, 'Steady Beck, don't let him get to you.'

Tiery spotted it, and it excited him. 'Why don't you listen to Miss Bulldyke there? What's your name by the way? We weren't introduced.'

Tiery grinned, exposing small, crooked, teeth. It was then Beck noticed his hands in his pockets, mooching around. He was feeling himself.

'Tell me Bulldyke, what's it like? Do you wear a strap-on?'

In one fluid motion, Beck took a stride and clamped one arm around Tiery's neck, hoisted him up and smashed him against the wall. The wall, just a partition, quivered, making a hollow sound. Claire made a move to follow him, but stopped. She was uncomfortable. This was an assault, the same as all those assaults she'd witnessed down through the years, whether in pubs, outside on the street, in the living rooms of family homes, big, small, rich or poor, it made no difference. Except now it was a guardian of the peace who was being the aggressor.

For now, she said nothing.

Beck squeezed, the sleeve of his jacket acting like a dampener, stopping Tiery's skin from bruising. Tiery's eyes went so wide they looked like they would explode. His breathing sounded like air through a straw in an empty glass. His hands came up and pawed at Beck. Beck relaxed his grip.

'Wha'ya got, Tiery? Wha'ya got?'

'Please... you'll kill me... please... I have cancer...'

'Good. I hope you die screaming, you deserve it, you prick.'

'Please... please... under the sink, in the press under the sink...'

Beck slowly relaxed his grip, finally took his arm away.

Smiling, he said, 'Why didn't you say so in the beginning?'

Claire watched Beck. What made it worse was that Beck seemed totally relaxed about it. He wasn't even breathing hard. He'd done this before. He looked almost... she searched for a word, *satisfied*.

'Have a look under there,' he said to her, nodding towards the sink.

Claire stepped over, got down onto both knees. She opened the press door and maneuvered a torch from her belt with her free hand. She fumbled about, lay down on her belly, and wiggled in under the sink up to her shoulders. Grunting noises, what sounded like skittles falling over, and she came wiggling back out. In her hand was a sheet of paper.

'There's about six of these in here, I just grabbed the first one I saw.' She stood. It was a glossy A4.

She looked at it, went 'Whoa,' and turned the sheet over for Beck to see. On it was printed images no normal person should ever want to see.

Claire took her handcuffs from her belt and said, 'Place your arms out straight in front of you and your wrists together. I'm arresting you, Jonathan Tiery, for the possession of child pornography...'

It took an hour to process Tiery back at the station. He did not dispute the charges. Beck warned him that if he did, he would crush his balls in a nut cracker. Tiery believed him. By lunch time, a car was taking him back to Arbour Hill prison in Dublin, the prison where the majority of sex offenders in the country were housed.

CHAPTER TWENTY-ONE

The news had travelled quickly. As bad news always does.

And those people who had grudges and resentments and normally stayed away from any community activity, set aside their grudges and resentments. And those who were busy, or feigned being busy, they made time. And those who were lazy, found the energy. Rich and poor. Small fish in a small pond. Big fish in a small pond. They all swam together now.

Because it didn't matter.

Not now.

Because there was a baby missing. That transcended everything. No one, not even the most cantankerous, bitter or introverted individual in Cross Beg or its hinterland could ignore that. And they didn't.

Over 200 people had assembled in the general area of Kelly's Forge, trailing back along the narrow roadway and gathering on the far sides of gates into fields. The local meals-on-wheels had already assembled a refreshment station: two trestle tables piled with sandwiches and urns of tea and coffee. It was a coming together, a common raw bond of the most basic form, a search for a child, one of their own, the baby named Róisín.

*

Crabby slowed as he passed the turn off for Kelly's Forge. On either side of the hard shoulder, along the main road, cars and pick-ups were parked bumper to bumper. People were heading down to the

Forge, some carrying long beating sticks, some in groups, some on their own. Subconsciously he took a hand from the steering wheel and ran it over the fabric of his Italian cotton shirt. The wound was sensitive to the touch, but already beginning to scab over. He took his hand away again, thinking. How did his wife know he'd been there? Yesterday. How did she know? The sat nav pinged once. Crabby glanced at it. And then it pinged again. He cursed, reached out and turned the tracker off. He had just found out.

CHAPTER TWENTY-TWO

Sergeant Connor had been waiting over half an hour already, sitting on a hard wooden chair in the hallway at the back of Crabby's supermarket. He drummed his fingers on his leg and glanced at his watch again. Opposite were three red painted wooden doors. On the first was stuck a piece of paper with a strip of Sellotape across each corner, the block handwriting on it: 'Toilets for customer use only. Please ask for key at front desk. Leave as you find. Thank you.'

In other words, go do it somewhere else.

Connor was sitting opposite the last door. There was a sign on that too, a thin metal stripe on a wooden block screwed into the door panel, the word 'Office' in black across it. He looked at the door, then got up and massaged his arse cheeks with the thumb of each hand, looked down the hallway and walked out into the main body of the supermarket. To his right were banks of freezers, to his left the butcher's counter. Other aisles stretched ahead. He detected a smell, a mixture of freshly baked bread and cooked meat, the result a chalky aroma that reminded him of wood shavings.

He saw Crabby ahead now, coming in through the main doors. Behind him his wife. The sergeant could not remember ever having seen them both together. Crabby was without his usual flourish, his shoulders were drooped, head hung down between his shoulders. Not as normal, like he was master of the universe, head held high, rotating slowly, almost in a full circle, an owl, taking everything in. His walk today was little more than a shuffle. His wife waddled behind him like a duck minder.

'Mr Crabby,' Connor said as he approached.

The man did not acknowledge him.

'Are you deaf,' his wife snapped. 'Someone's talking to you.'

'Mr Crabby,' the sergeant said, louder this time. 'CCTV. Someone spoke with you earlier in connection with it.'

Crabby stopped.

'Yes. What is it?' He seemed not to have heard a word the sergeant had said. He finally looked up and took in Connor. Immediately, his expression changed. He forced a smile, displaying those unnaturally white teeth of his, like he'd just had them spray-painted. His eyes, however, couldn't hide it. To the sergeant's practised gaze, the man looked petrified.

Connor introduced himself.

'I'd like to see your CCTV, Mr Crabby. Is that okay with you?'

There was a hesitation, fleeting. But a hesitation nonetheless.

'Of course that's okay,' Mrs Crabby said before he could answer. 'You don't have to ask him.'

'Um, of course,' Crabby said. 'In my office. Follow me.'

'His office! Ha!' his wife muttered.

He took a key from his pocket, unlocked the door marked 'Office' and pushed it open, turned on the lights. Connor saw now it was really a storeroom with a desk and a couple of chairs in it amidst stacks of kitchen and toilet paper, boxes of baked beans and dog food.

'Let me just set this up,' Crabby said, moving behind his desk and sitting down. He indicated a chair in front and the sergeant sat down.

'This place is a mess,' his wife said. 'I can see I need to start involving myself more in the running of my father's business. Yes indeed.'

Crabby began pressing keys, turning his back to his wife. He picked up the desk phone, pressed a button.

'Would you like a tea, coffee, sergeant?'

'Tea. Coffee. At a time like this,' his wife said, screwing her eyes, and looking heavenward.

The sergeant nodded though. 'A coffee wouldn't go amiss. Thank you. And if we could start with the exterior cameras first.'

Crabby nodded quickly. His wife came and stood by the desk, making no attempt to sit, the wonky smile back on her face, her eyes hooded, watching.

'Louise,' Crabby said into the phone. 'Bring in two coffees. And don't forget some biscuits.' He was about to hang up. 'Well,' he added, 'I don't know, I…'

'You don't know what?' his wife demanded. 'I have a mouth on me too you know. She's asking if I want something as well, isn't she? Tea, for God's sake.'

'Two coffees and one tea,' Crabby said and hung up the phone.

When the tea and coffee had been drunk, and a couple of biscuits eaten, still Crabby showed no sign of showing the CCTV to Sergeant Connor.

'I need to get started, Mr Crabby. If you don't mind.'

'You want me to help? I could help you look through it. Maybe spot something that you miss.'

'I'll do this on my own, thanks, I've worked CCTV systems before.'

Mrs Crabby folded her arms, her green eyes like a lizard's, watching. She said nothing.

Crabby pushed back his chair and stood.

'I'll leave you to it then. If you want to come around this side. I have it set up for you.'

Sergeant Connor pushed his notebook and pen to the other side of the desk and stood. He went around and sat in the chair vacated by Crabby.

'Thank you. I'll take it from here.'

'If you need me, I'll be somewhere about on the shop floor.'

'So important, aren't you?' his wife mumbled to him as he passed by.

He went to the door and opened it, hesitated, then walked out, the door swinging shut behind him. Still, Mrs Crabby stood there.

The sergeant glanced at her.

'Don't look at me,' she said. 'I'm going nowhere.'

'Then I'll download this footage and take it back with me to the station. Which will cause a delay. Because I'd prefer to watch it here. On my own. If that's okay by you, Mrs Crabby? I need to be sure there isn't the potential for a security breach by having a civilian third party viewing it at the same time, you see. Do you understand?'

'I'm not stopping you.'

'I don't need distractions.'

'I don't like your tone. This is my property. I pay quite substantial taxes. Taxes which help pay your wages. And commercial property rates too. I have every right to stay here if I want to.'

The sergeant pursed his lips. 'Fine,' placing his hands onto the desk, about to stand.

Mrs Crabby appeared uncertain by his muted response.

'Mm…' she said, but her voice trailed off.

He started to rise.

'Fine. Fine,' she said and crossed to the door, banging it shut behind her.

Sergeant Connor pulled his chair closer to the desk. He had memorised the registration number of the blue Citroen Picasso. Or, to be precise, the cobalt blue Citroen Picasso. There were three camera icons in the top right corner of the computer. He pressed on the middle one. The screen became a still shot of the supermarket car park. All he had to do was regulate the speed and press play. He set the footage to play from 14.00 hours the previous day, increasing the speed to one and a half times real time.

He pressed play.

CHAPTER TWENTY-THREE

The sliding window to the public office was open, a welcome breeze blowing in through the open front doors of the station and into the operation's room. Beck sat alongside Claire at her desk, which was directly next to a window. Already Claire had lowered the blind in an attempt to keep the glaring sunlight out. But the flimsy white material that looked like a piece of ship's rigging did little to block it. Indeed, it seemed to radiate the heat itself. Beck could see small beads of sweat forming along the hairline of her forehead. She had reapplied make-up, and badly.

He realised he was staring. She glanced at him, absentmindedly touched the old wrought iron radiator next to her. She pulled her hand back, shaking it.

'The bloody thing is boiling. Can you believe it? Central heating's on. On a day like this. What a waste of tax payers' money. Typical public service.'

'Samantha was never in trouble herself,' Beck said, not paying attention, nodding to the computer screen. 'Her brother, Mikey, he had a few run-ins alright. About ten years ago. A spate of five incidents to be precise, one after the other. Public order, drink-related stuff. It was enough to make him head for a new life in Australia, I suppose. You know, people were sent there for a lot less one time. Stealing a head of cabbage, for instance, during the famine, or Travelyan's corn. Think of it, generations of people are now Aussies because someone, way back, stole a head of cabbage… mum Colette, there's nothing on her either.'

Claire moved away from the radiator and leaned against the wall beside it. She appeared not to have even heard him.

'You were a little too heavy-handed back there, with Tiery,' she said. 'You pushed it too far.'

'What? What's that got to do with anything? Maybe I was. So what?'

'If you do something like that again while I'm around, I can't guarantee that I won't report you.'

Beck did not take his eyes from the computer screen.

'At least you're honest,' he said. 'You're right of course. I'm trying. I really am.'

'That's a start. I'm glad you see it like that.'

'I hear you, Claire. Now, let's move on. Billy Hamilton.'

He nodded at the computer screen again.

'Burglaries, shoplifting, possession for sale and supply. Wear out the cartridge on any printer if you tried to run that lot off. The poor girl could pick them, couldn't she?'

'What's that mean?'

'Why? Don't you agree?'

'Maybe she didn't know what they were like. Maybe they fooled her. Maybe she just didn't know what she was getting herself into.'

'Maybe,' Beck said. Was she speaking from experience, he wondered?

'Anyway, maybe we should go? Talk to forensics.'

'Forensics. Forensics. Forensics. People are obsessed with forensics. I know some people who could gawk at forensics all day and think they're getting something done. What's this endless fascination? It's not a CSI programme. Leave specialities to the specialists. We have to wait. Anyway, I have a better idea.'

'What?'

He looked at the Ops Room clock.

'I think the best possible course of action we can take right now is to go get something to eat. It's getting late.'

'You can't be serious?'

Beck got to his feet.

'We need to eat. Remember what people did for a head of cabbage. Van Diemen's Land. Botany Bay. What would those people make of it if you turned up your nose at the prospect of proper food?'

CHAPTER TWENTY-FOUR

The special at Frazzali's was fish and chips. Beck was pleased.

'Excellent,' he said, putting the menu aside.

The road outside was thrown half into shade by the buildings on the opposite side, the other basked in bright sunshine. An articulated truck rumbled by, and Beck could feel the vibration through the floor. Different accents and languages drifted through the busy restaurant. Summer in Cross Beg brought a transformation of the town from ugly duckling to swan, the town an eruption of colourful flower boxes underneath a clear blue sky.

While Claire was still looking at her menu Beck took the opportunity to observe her. Something was wrong. That much was obvious. To him at least. He watched as her eyes scanned the piece of laminated paper in her hands, her eye lashes flickering as she blinked excessively, her fingers constantly altering their grip. Beck said nothing, shifted his gaze from her.

'I'd feel better with a takeout,' she said finally, putting the menu aside. 'If we were actually doing something, you know.'

'Just because you're doing something,' Beck said, 'doesn't mean you're actually *doing* something.'

'What does that mean?'

The waitress came. They both ordered the special.

'It'll come to you, give it time,' Beck said.

'Bloody philosopher… But it's hard. Just sitting here. Knowing she's out there. Somewhere.'

'Unfortunately…' Beck said, 'A baby can't just disappear for Christ's sake? Not of its own accord. It's impossible. But…'

'But,' Claire interrupted, 'You and I have been around long enough to know anything's possible. She's been abducted most likely, or we're looking for a body.'

'Well yes, of course, but we'll continue searching. If someone has her, and they're very clever, we may never…'

'I know.' Claire said. 'I know.' She shifted her body, a shift of subject too, if only for a little while. 'You haven't changed your mind, by the way?'

'Changed my mind?'

'Dublin? Pearse Street?'

Beck smiled. 'Did you think I had?'

'You haven't mentioned it lately, that's all.'

'I haven't mentioned it because there's nothing to mention. I'm waiting on my transfer. Biding my time, as it were.'

'You make it sound like you're waiting on a bloody bus.'

'There are similarities,' Beck said. 'I don't have a lease, on my accommodation, it's week to week.'

He had turned a door handle, and now Claire pushed and came through.

'In your last place, what really happened? You don't talk about it. Can't have been easy, Beck.'

It was still fresh in his mind. The memory of finding the body of his old landlady, Mrs Claxton – murdered, and placed under his bed. Questions had been raised, and answered, thankfully. But Beck hadn't been back there since.

Anyway, he didn't want to be bloody reminded of any of this right now.

'Excuse me,' he said, getting to his feet, slamming the door shut again. 'I need the loo.'

*

When he'd finished and was making his way back to the table, two builder types came through the door. They entered in single file, flapping hi-vis vests and barrel bellies, their bulk making it impossible to see that someone much smaller had slipped in between them.

Beck sat back at the table opposite Claire again. When he looked up she was there, standing by the table: Claire's wife – Lucy Grimes. He was about to speak, give a false greeting. But something stopped him, her expression, and he said nothing.

'We need to talk,' Lucy said, ignoring him.

'There's nothing to talk about,' Claire said. 'And how'd you know I was here?'

'What does that matter? I saw you come in, okay?'

'There's nothing to talk about,' Claire repeated. 'Not now. And certainly not here.'

'What? You can't be serious. We have a lot to talk about.' She turned her head to Beck. 'Look at him. Could you go and leave us alone? This is a private matter.'

Lucy's voice was loud enough now for people to turn and look.

'No, Lucy,' Claire said. 'It's time for *you* to leave. Lucy. Go. I mean it.'

Lucy's eyes were still on Beck. 'You. You've been talking to her, haven't you?'

'Leave him out of it. I've told him nothing.'

'You've done alright out of me,' Beck said, unable to help himself.

Lucy leaned onto the table.

'What does that mean?'

'Your syndicated serial killer story. Nice little earner. Creative licence for sure. I have to say a great read, even if you made half of it up.'

'Get lost.'

The waitress appeared, clutching two plates of fish and chips. She sensed the mood, placed the plates on the table and walked quickly away. Beck busied himself with his food, grateful for the distraction.

'Lucy. Please go,' it was Claire. 'I mean it.'

Beck's phone rang on the table next to him. He could see the word 'Station' flash across the screen.

He nudged it with his elbow towards Claire, his mouth too full to speak.

Claire took it up, glanced at Lucy.

'Go.'

'Okay. For now. But we'll talk.' She pointed at Beck. 'When he's not around.'

Claire pressed the answer button but waited until Lucy had turned to leave before she spoke. Then: 'Claire Somers... Yes, Dempsey... Beck is busy, you can give it to me... Really... Okay... Of course... Goodbye.'

She put the phone back onto the table.

'Samantha Power's car has just appeared on the CCTV from Crabby's supermarket.'

Beck swallowed. Maybe they should have ordered a takeaway after all.

Sitting in the Focus outside, Beck draped an arm out the window, a cigarette held between two fingers, the smoke gently curling upward into the still air, while Claire fumbled with the keys.

'This is a work place, Beck. You're not supposed to smoke.'

She fanned the air in front of her face with a hand, looked at the cigarette, and then to Beck.

He took a long draw, placing his face out the window, and gave a theatrical wheeze as he exhaled, mock punching his chest a couple of times. Finally, he dropped the half-smoked cigarette to the ground and sat back, sighed.

'There. Happy?'

Claire turned the key and started the engine, pulled away from the kerb.

'That's criminal damage, by the way,' she added. 'Throwing a cigarette out the window like that. Comes under the littering act.'

'I'm quite the criminal then. What you going to do, arrest me?'

They drove in silence. But a moment later, Claire braked. Beck hadn't bothered to put his seat belt on, he'd merely pressed his thumb into the mechanism to stop the alarm from sounding. He grabbed the seat now with both hands to stop himself from tumbling forward.

He turned to Claire, who had her head bowed over the steering wheel. She was sobbing.

Beck stared, open mouthed. This was a woman he'd considered to be teak-tough. The woman who'd always stood her ground, held her place in a man's world, always gave as good as she got. This was that woman.

Beck felt helpless, his hands like dead weights too heavy to lift and reach out to comfort her.

She took her hands from the steering wheel and wiped her eyes, taking some of the make-up away, smearing her mascara so that it looked like black blood trickling down her face.

And as she did so, the dead weights became hands again. He reached out and rested one on her shoulder, the other just below the nape of her neck. He held her gently, reassuring her: I'm here, you are not alone. And that, more than anything, was what she needed right now.

'I've been doing this all day,' she said. 'Crying. I made sure no one was around to see me. I don't want anyone to see me like this.'

She took a deep breath.

'You want to talk about it?' Beck asked.

He thought it'd been a long time since he'd cried. Way back in what he called The Dark Ages, his school years. He'd had plenty to cry about back then.

'Thank you,' Claire said. 'I do want to talk about it, only just not right now. Lucy and I, we're going through something, okay? But we'll work it out. Sorry about what happened.' She took a tissue from her sleeve and carefully dabbed her eyes. 'Right now, we've got work to do.'

CHAPTER TWENTY-FIVE

The searchers realised it was not as easy as it had first appeared. The land was not a neat blanket that fell into place, tucking itself into the corners without sharp or rough edges. In some places the ditches along the borders of the fields hid steep inclines that disappeared into heavy undergrowth. The sun did not penetrate here, and the ground was boggy and waterlogged. It was only when the beaters had fought their way through the thorny bushes and placed their feet onto the ground at the bottom, that they noticed they were standing in a foot of thick sludge. And it was here, in these places, that they knew it was more likely than any other that a body could be concealed. A small body, a baby's body, one easy to miss. So they made sure they didn't miss anything, and took their time, beating back the bramble, sliding down the inclines, sloshing through the stagnant water and mud. The process was slow. Every hollow and cavity was searched, nothing left undisturbed, and only when they had done all this, when they were completely satisfied, only then did they move on. The sun had passed its highest point in the blue sky now, but still the heat was intense. The breeze had faded, and there was nothing to temper the harsh, uncustomary heat. A weather forecaster had already termed it a freak. Even as four o'clock approached, the heat did not diminish. Some beaters wore sunhats with handkerchiefs tied about the back of their necks, others T-shirts they had converted into bandanas. Everyone wore something. A helicopter had joined the search, a drab green military Agusta Westland AW139 that crisscrossed the sky, the chomping noise of its rotor blades dropping and rising as it went. The Civil Defence Second Officer, named Sharkey, looked at his map, at the rows of empty grid boxes and the wavy contour markers beneath that marked the terrain. He had crossed a mere handful of these off with his pen. If the baby was out there, he was losing hope with each passing minute, because, in this heat, he had to admit, she was probably already dead.

CHAPTER TWENTY-SIX

Sergeant Connor touched the screen with the tip of his pen.

Beck and Claire leaned in.

'It's right there. See.'

Beck already had. The cobalt blue Citroen. His heart began to canter inside his chest, the sound of his rushing blood filling his ears like a waterfall. He took a deep breath, held it, exhaled slowly.

'Play it,' he said.

ACTION: The world on the computer screen came alive. A car traversed across the foreground. There was the sound of wind, a hollow flapping noise, also voices, and engines, all rolled into one, becoming an indistinct low rumble. The camera was positioned high, the world through its wide-angle lens curved as if looking from the inside of a goldfish bowl, taking in the roadway and the car park beyond.

For a long time there was nothing, just that indistinct low rumbling noise. But then, the car driver's door opened and she got out. Beck stared. Samantha Power was taller than he had imagined. Looking at her now, at her tumbling hair, the clothes he had seen torn and partially pulled from her body, knowing that she wore purple underpants that someone would very soon try to pull from her, remembering her exposed breast, the underwire of her white bra biting into the flesh, knowing all this was like knowing an evil secret. If only he could shout and warn her, go back in time to stop her.

Jesus, run for your life girl.

If only he could stop it from happening.

But he could do none of these things. All he could do was watch.

Samantha stood by the door of the Picasso, and lingered, as if undecided about something. Leaning forward now, resting her knee onto the driver's seat, twisting her body and leaning over it into the back seat.

'Stop it right there,' Beck said.

The screen froze.

'Zoom in. I can't see the baby.'

The computer screen world fragmented, as if gravity had suddenly been sucked out, the pixels breaking free, suspended in air, tiny digital atoms. The wording on the sticker across the bottom became legible: 'Clementine's, Main Peugeot and Citroen Dealers – Athlone Road, Cross Beg'. The backseat headrests were visible too, something rising above the one on the passenger side.

Sergeant Connor tapped the screen. 'That's the baby seat. Right there. It's got a high back, so we can't see the child. But her little hands were flailing through the air earlier. See, Samantha's attention is on it?'

'Baby Róisín,' Beck said softly.

*

Samantha took a €10 note from her purse and some loose change from the central console of the car. She put the purse into the glove compartment, making sure it was closed tight, and looked in the rear-view mirror. Róisín was sleeping. She decided that she would not wake her daughter. She would leave her here. The child was exhausted, as was she. It was one row after another now, day in, day out. How much more of this could she take? Concentrate, she told herself. She only needed bread and milk, something for Naomi too. Her friend. Her saviour. Especially at a time like this, because without Naomi, it was either back to her mother's or sleeping in the car. If she had to, if she absolutely had to that is, and she wasn't sure which one of those two options she'd take.

Anyway, how long would her shopping take? A couple of minutes at most. In and out. No longer. Still, she paused, two fingers on the door handle, as she looked at her sleeping daughter in the rear-view mirror again, and felt it, as if her heart would burst with all the love it carried for her.

'I won't be long, my sweetheart,' she whispered, opening the door.

She got out, but paused again. Was it her imagination, or had Róisín's eyes just flickered? Carefully, she leaned into the car, resting one knee onto the driver's seat, peering into the back at Róisín. No, her daughter was sleeping soundly. The rear windows were slightly open, allowing a gentle breeze to waft in. Still, should she cover her with something? Róisín only had a nappy and a T-shirt on after all.

Samantha smiled and got back out of the car, telling herself she was fussing too much. She gently closed the door and pointed the keyfob, pressed the button, the squelching sound reassuring her the car was now locked. She would not be long. In and out.

She walked quickly. She did not want to meet or talk to anybody, did not want to be delayed in any way. Passing in through the supermarket doors, she headed straight for the bread section.

'Heeello.'

Samantha could not see anyone. She looked down. Mr Crabby was kneeling in front of the information booth, refilling crisp packets into the space beneath the counter. He smiled, his white teeth gleaming from his perma-tanned face.

'How are you today?' he asked.

Smarmy git.

'I'm fine thanks. And you?'

She cursed silently for not having merely walked on, a simple hello would have sufficed.

He squeezed in the last of the crisp bags.

'Swinging the devil by the tail,' he said. 'You know how it is. Yes indeed, swinging the devil by the tail. I must say, you're looking well today. Motherhood suits you.'

She smiled, a 'you can't be serious smile', and walked on. She doubted Mr Crabby even knew her name, it was all soft talk, from a salesman with a shop full of stuff to sell. She picked up a Crabby's Local Shop Rite Wholemeal Bread loaf and headed for the milk fridges on the other side of the supermarket. She grabbed a two-litre container of milk and a tub of low fat yogurt for Naomi and then it was straight to the checkout. In and out, just the way she'd planned.

Please, Róisín, don't wake up, I'm almost finished here.

At the checkout two people were ahead of her.

Come on!

The old dear in front was taking her time, counting out the coins from her purse, holding them up for inspection before placing each onto the counter. Eventually, it was her turn. The girl at the checkout smiled, said hello, ran her purchases through. Samantha watched the cash register tally, realised her loose change would cover it. Now it was her turn to count the coins, but she didn't care, because her €10 note had lived to fight another day.

She scooped up her items and headed for the main door. There was Mr Crabby again, standing by it, on his mobile phone, his back half turned to her, looking out the window. As she passed by, she could hear his voice: agitated. This surprised her, because the man suffered from chronic cheerfulness, even if, as Samantha had heard, his wife was a prime battle-axe.

She found herself turning as she passed, curious, and their eyes met. She felt uneasy, he was staring at her. His expression reminded her of Billy Hamilton's when he was brooding about something, which was often. Those were the times when it was best to make herself scarce. Because she knew what would happen if she didn't... Samantha walked on, feeling put out. She could see Crabby's reflection in the door watching her as she left.

*

Beck stared at the screen. Then he spoke: 'Return to normal resolution, and play on.'

Sergeant Connor zoomed out again, the pixels unifying, the screen becoming like a goldfish bowl once more.

'She's leaving the baby in the car,' Claire said, surprised, as they watched Samantha walk from her car and disappear through the shop doors.

Sergeant Connor clicked the mouse. The screen switched to show the interior of the shop, the camera mounted opposite the front door. The footage here was clear, the format standard, like watching a TV soap. Music played in the background, an insipid combination of horns, guitars, and drums. With it the rattle of shopping trolleys bunching together outside as the door opened and Samantha entered, her long thick hair bouncing with each stride she took.

They followed her through the shop like invisible ghosts. They watched as she passed Crabby, speaking with him briefly while he packed crisps underneath the information booth counter. They watched as she went to the bread aisle, picking up a Crabby's own-brand loaf of sliced bread, then on to the other side of the shop, picking up a two-litre container of milk and tub of yogurt, and finally to the checkout. They watched as she was leaving again, meeting Crabby a second time at the door. He was on his phone, partially turned from her, looking out the window. They watched as she turned to look at him as she passed, and then away again.

'Hold it right there,' Beck said. 'Can you replay that? That moment as she passes him.'

'What do you see?' Claire asked.

Beck didn't reply, waited while the segment was replayed.

'There,' he said, pressing a finger into the screen, causing a ripple on the liquid crystal display like a pebble into water. 'Look. As they both turn. She doesn't acknowledge him. No smile. Nothing. Not like before, when they seemed very friendly. Now she seems, I don't know, maybe scared is a little too strong a word. But something. Anyone else see it?'

'She doesn't look comfortable, definitely,' Claire agreed.

Sergeant Connor nodded, he could see it too.

Beck noted the time in the top corner of the screen: 16:43. He had no official time of death. Not yet. For this person, clutching a loaf of bread, two litres of milk, and a tub of yogurt, whose baby was sleeping in her car out front, and who would soon be dead, and whose baby would soon be missing.

Beck had never felt so helpless.

He wanted to jump through the screen.

Someone had to – and warn her.

The image of her body, throat slit, blouse torn open, skirt gathered about her waist.

Don't get in the car, please!

Samantha crossed the roadway outside the supermarket to the car. They could see her point the key fob. Then she opened the door, reached in, placed her items onto the passenger seat, and got in the driver's seat herself. The door closed, and a moment later the reversing lights glowed as she reversed. The car moved slowly along the roadway in front of the supermarket, following the curve as it completed the semi-circle between the entrance and exit points in the perimeter wall. They watched the brake lights glow as the car stopped briefly before turning left onto the main road. It drove on, out of sight.

CHAPTER TWENTY-SEVEN

What happened between the time Samantha Power drove from Crabby's supermarket car park and her arriving at Kelly's Forge? Ultimately, she had been killed, that was the short answer. But Beck didn't want the short answer. The explanation was in the long answer. Someone, somewhere, had gotten into that car, or, alternatively, she had travelled to Kelly's Forge and met somebody there? So the likelihood, Beck considered, was that it was somebody she knew, somebody she knew well enough to do either of those two things. There was no other explanation, not that he could see.

Beck was considering this as he walked to the hospital. He wanted to hear what Dr Derek Gumbell, the State Pathologist, had to say. He could have taken the shortcut, but he'd decided to take the scenic route, by Bridge Walk, to clear his head, to give himself time to think.

He went from Bridge Street across the stone bridge over the Brown Water River. It was 150 years old, with nothing added in that time but coatings of tarmac to its roadway. He passed along in front of the cathedral, its towering, brooding presence rising above the town. It was here that the majority of the town's inhabitants had had their heads sprinkled with holy water in baptism and would have their coffins sprinkled during the holy rites of burial. To the rear of the cathedral, hidden by a low hill, were the ruins of the presbytery. Beck thought of the night it had burned down, his fight for survival in the cold waters of the Brown Water. He glanced at the water now, calm and peaceful.

'Inspector Beck.'

Beck looked across the road to where the sound had come from. Father Ignatius Cruise was looking at him from behind the white-painted railings of the cathedral.

'One minute, Inspector,' he called, moving to the gates and crossing the road. 'We met before, briefly. Do you remember?'

Beck remembered. It was at the hospital. Beck was recovering from his injuries.

'Oh,' Beck said. 'I think an apology is in order.'

Beck had been sleeping, had woken to find a person in his room. He'd been dreaming of the man who had killed four people and who had almost killed him. Half asleep, he'd woken to find Father Cruise, whom he'd met before, in his room. Had shouted, threw a plastic jug filled with water at the man.

'It was understandable,' Father Cruise said.

He was a young man, mid-thirties perhaps. A little on the chubby side, with a fresh face and simple brown plastic-framed spectacles that sat at an odd angle on his face. He was dressed in black priest's garb, but his jacket appeared too small. Beck also noticed on his feet were a pair of frayed sneakers. He was not concerned with appearances, that was apparent.

'I just saw you passing by. I wanted to meet you.' He extended his hand and they shook. 'Have you fully recovered from your ordeal?'

Beck nodded.

'Yes. Some rest. That's all I needed. How is the presbytery rebuilding coming along?'

Father Cruise looked past Beck to the river.

'It's not.' He looked back again. 'The ruins will be pulled down. A presbytery is of another era. A simple memorial will take its place. We don't need presbyteries. That is my opinion. And the bishop agrees, thankfully. The church needs to be much simpler now. Inspector Beck...'

'Yes.'

'What do you think has become of the child? Róisín. Of course, nothing can be done for her mother. She is in heaven now I am certain. But the child. I helped in the search. Earlier.'

'Did you? That was good.'

'No, no. That is not why I mention it. Everybody was there. It was a refreshing display of community solidarity. If something is to come out of this, it would be that. But *where* is the child?'

Beck had no answer for that, so said nothing. In the silence, Father Cruise understood, and offered his hand again.

'If ever you need me, Inspector Beck, you know where to find me. I feel the church has wronged you too, in a sense.'

Beck continued on his way. He thought of what the priest had said, his feeling that the church had wronged him in some way. Father Cruise had no idea what an understatement that was.

CHAPTER TWENTY-EIGHT

The hallway leading to the mortuary was in darkness. There was still daylight outside, but inside it was permanently night. Ahead, Beck could see a rectangle of white suspended in the air. He walked towards it, pressed his face against the glass in the door. On the other side he could see Gumbell, dressed in blue medical scrubs, leaning over a stainless-steel table, white plastic chemical bottles by his elbow, writing on a notepad.

Beck tapped on the glass.

Gumbell turned. 'Who the hell is that?'

'Beck,' pushing the door open. 'May I come in?'

He immediately felt the welcome cool of the airconditioned room.

'Blast you, Beck, can't you see I'm busy.'

'I'll catch you lat—'

'No. No. Come in. Come in, man.'

Beck went and stood next to the State Pathologist, who ignored him, continuing to write on the notepad. Minutes passed.

'There,' he said, finally putting his pen down.

Beck looked at Gumbell's scrawled handwriting. It might as well have been Swahili. Or double Dutch. Whatever, it was all the same, completely illegible. However, the name across the top in block letters was decipherable: Senan Roy.

'Who's that,' Beck asked. 'I haven't come across anyone in this case by that name.'

'What name?' Gumbell said, untying the knot on his scrub at the back.

'Senan Roy. It's there, written on that notepad of yours.'

'Nothing to do with your case. That particular Senan Roy was found impaled on an iron railing on Monday in Kilkenny. He could have saved me a lot of bloody time and trouble if he'd just left a suicide note. I've only just worked it out now.'

'Oh,' Beck said.

'Oh, indeed. I'm a little behind, Beck. I'm an investigative medical officer as well as the State Pathologist it seems. Two for the price of one. Is this a social call?'

Beck looked at the bank of six freezer doors set into the wall, arranged three high in rows of two. His last case had almost filled them all. One door was open, the tray fully extended on its rollers.

'You sleeping in there tonight?'

This was a reference to Gumbell's endless griping about what he referred to as his miserable expenses account.

Gumbell grunted, trying to stop the corners of his mouth from doing what they were genetically predisposed never to do – to rise into a smile, which they did now, just about. But it was gone again as quickly as a fly before a swatting newspaper.

'Actually, I'm staying at the Brown Water Inn. I have hopes it will be a marked improvement on The Hibernian Hotel.'

The grass is always greener, Beck thought.

'Is your phone flat?' Beck asked.

'My phone?'

'I've been ringing you.'

'It's somewhere or other, damn nuisance of a thing. You know, before mobile phones were invented, we all got along perf—'

'I hate to interrupt…' Beck said.

'But you are anyway.'

'… I was hoping you might have something for me.'

Gumbell whipped off his medical scrub and carried it to the yellow plastic wheelie bin in a corner of the room. Stencilled across the front and sides, 'Non-Hazardous Surgical Only'.

'I thought you'd be back in the bosom of civilization by now,' Gumbell said, opening a press high on the wall next to him, rummaging through its contents. It seemed to consist of boxes of rubber gloves and bottles of hand sanitizer. 'In Dublin I mean. But you're still here in the swamps. Where is the damned thing?' His hand squirmed about amongst the sanitizer bottles. 'There. Have it.'

He withdrew a brown naggin bottle, held it out for Beck to see, snapped the seal, unscrewed the top, and raised the bottle to his lips.

'To your health, my man.'

Gumbell took a long swallow.

'My lord, it's good. Come on, before I finish it all.'

He walked over to Beck and held out the bottle.

'I'll pass,' Beck said.

'I should have known. It's your eyes, Beck. Too damn healthy. It's the best I've seen them in years. You on the wagon again?'

'Call it what you will,' Beck said.

'I've told you before, Beck. Ultimately, it's not in the best interests of your health. A body that's conditioned to poison builds up a defence mechanism against it. On the other hand, a temple to the gods of healthy living crumbles before the first onslaught. Trust me, I should know. I'm a doctor.'

Now it was Beck's turn to smile.

'You don't even know when you're being funny, do you? You've just turned the whole paradigm of medical science on its head.'

'If you're on the wagon, Beck, you're of no use to me. No offence old boy.'

'About the victim? What can you tell me? No offence taken, by the way.'

'That she's dead. That's a start. No mystery there. Nor the cause of death. A deep wound to the neck, severing both the trachea and carotid arteries. She would have been unconscious in seconds, dead within a minute. So, the first part of the puzzle has already been solved, unlike Mr What's-his-name.'

'The fact you can't remember that victim's name is an indication of the poison's positive effect on your brain cells,' Beck said. 'You've said the same about me often enough. I presume you mean Senan Roy.'

Gumbell took another mouthful of whiskey, held the bottle up to the light.

'These small bottles don't hold very much, do they? It's almost empty.'

He replaced the cap, and walked to the bank of fridges, pulled on the handle of the one to the middle right, and rolled out the tray. It was the hair. Beck knew immediately it was Samantha Power's body.

'Will the autopsy be tomorrow?' Beck asked.

Gumbell peered down.

'I don't think it'll be of much help. I mean, what am I looking for? Contents of her stomach? See if she ate her baby?'

Beck winced at Gumbell's gallows humour.

'If need be,' he went on, 'we can image the body. No longer is it necessary to fillet a corpse. Not in all cases. And I think this is one.'

He nudged the bottle in between the arm and ribcage of the cadaver.

'What?' he asked, catching Beck's look. 'She doesn't mind. Now, the deep laceration to the neck. Caused by a sharp, but blunt instrument, if that makes any sense. Not so much an oxymoron as you'd think. What I mean is the wound is not clean cut. It's serrated, depth varying from three to six centimetres. The flesh was pulled, or dragged, as opposed to cut smoothly. Hence, the item was sharp, but not *sharp* sharp.'

'A blunt knife?' Beck said.

'I would discount a knife,' Gumbell said. 'Something else. A shank maybe.'

Beck thought about that. He could smell the whiskey on Gumbell's breath, a contrast to the lingering odour of chemicals and decaying flesh, odours the extractor fans could never fully remove. These were part of the DNA of the building itself. But the corpse on the tray did not smell. Not yet. It was still within its sell-by date. Hence Gumbell's placing his bottle where he had.

'I've taken nail scrapings, but there is nothing to indicate anything other than subungual dirt,' Gumbell said. 'The body, other than that one devastating laceration, appears free of any other external injuries, apart from some bruising to the right knee and upper chest. See there...'

Beck looked along Gumbell's outstretched arm. High on the chest, beneath the shoulder blades, a flash of purple against the greenish and blue hue of the skin. Beck's eyes wandered to the wound itself, the dark crimson of congealed blood, torn muscles, the rubberised end of the severed trachea, and, to the rear, the exposed cervical vertebrae like a flash of sunlight.

What I mean is,' Gumbell added. 'There are no defensive wounds. There is just the one. The fatal, deep, oblique, incised injury to the neck. I would hazard part of the reason for this is that she did not try to save herself, rather she concentrated on saving her baby. The incision appears left to right, the killer is probably righthanded, and the wound was inflicted from the rear. The bruising to the knee, she hit it off something, probably the gear stick, the pattern is similar, consistent with its shape. He compressed her upper chest, maybe in a tight arm lock, maybe while pulling her back, inflicting the fatal cut.'

'He would be covered in blood then, wouldn't he? Even if he cut her from behind?'

'Well,' Gumbell said. 'The blood would have spurted outward. He certainly would have some blood on him, yes.'

'But there was relatively little blood inside the car.'

'Relative being the word,' Gumbell corrected him. 'Blood was in the car. But not much. Because I think the wound was inflicted while the victim was protruding from it, in the manner which she was found. Imagine this: the killer is in the passenger seat, he turns and grabs her while she is attempting to reach her baby in the back of the vehicle, he stretches forward, getting to his feet maybe, grabs her and pulls her back, they both fall backward, momentum carrying them partially out through the open door, at the same time, let's presume, he panics, slices the blade across her neck, inflicting the wound, and the sluice gates open, blood splashes onto the inside of the windscreen corner, some onto him too, but most onto the ground beneath her. This is how I imagine it. I may be wrong, of course, after all Beck, I wasn't there, but this description explains things the way I found them.'

'Time of death?'

'My best estimate is between 17.00 and 18.30 hours yesterday.'

'Was she sexually assaulted?'

'Depends what you mean by sexually assaulted. There was an attempt. Most certainly. That in itself is an assault. But she wasn't raped.'

Beck looked at his watch.

'Not keeping you from something, am I?' Gumbell asked.

'Actually, yes. I'm already running late.'

Beck considered that Gumbell looked disappointed at this. But he quickly recovered.

'Right then,' he said. 'You can get lost so.'

Outside, Beck gulped in the warm evening air, and, without realising it, rubbed his hands along his shirt, like a cat preening, trying to rid himself of all traces of death.

His phone rang, 'Private Number' flashing across the screen. He answered, but did not speak. No sound but the swirl of static. Beck knew who it was.

Natalia had said she would not ring him again. And it had stopped, for a while that is. But lately it had started again: The early morning, the middle of the night, anytime really, it didn't matter.

This was her now. He knew it. Even if Natalia almost never spoke.

But today she did.

'Finnegan. I miss you.'

And Beck felt it, like being back in secondary school, to the first time he had felt it, looking at Mandy North. A surge, barrelling through his entire body, a force capable almost of knocking him flat onto his back, of tying his tongue into knots, of making him act like an imbecile. Or of all three.

Mandy North had no interest in imbeciles, not that she even knew he existed. She didn't. Last he'd heard, she'd married a sheep farmer and was living in New Zealand.

Beck felt it all.

His thumb found the red icon on his phone screen.

He pressed it, and walked on.

CHAPTER TWENTY-NINE

Beck climbed the rickety stairs in Ozanam House and gently opened a door at the top. The room was full, and someone was speaking. He found a chair at the back, sat down, leaning forward, resting his elbows onto his knees, submerging himself beneath the heads around him. His entry had gone unnoticed. Or so he thought.

The room fell quiet. Someone coughed.

'Finnegan, glad you could make it.'

Shit.

Beck raised his head. The man at the top table had a smile like a fisherman who'd just gotten a bite, his eyes twinkly bright.

'Want to share?'

Shit again.

Beck sat up, pushing himself back into the chair until he could go no further. The eyes of the room were on him.

'My name is Finnegan,' he said. 'And I'm an alcoholic. This is my third meeting and I don't feel ready to share just yet. So I'll pass. Thank you.'

After the meeting, Beck picked up a mug of coffee from a steaming row by the sink in a corner of the room.

'Your sharing – or lack of it – does no one any favours you know. And you never help make the coffee. Think it just makes itself, do you? Think you're too good for it? How's your ego doing by the way?'

'What?'

The man wore a crisp blue suit, white shirt and bright red tie. His nose and cheeks had a red glow.

'I'm telling you like it is,' he said. 'Otherwise you're wasting everybody's time. My time. Your own time. Everybody's time. We want to hear real sharing. This is a life or death gig. We need people who are going to help us stay sober. We're selfish. We have to be. Sobriety comes first. It comes before everything and anything. Comes before any person. Comes before wife and kids. Comes before mothers and fathers. Comes before…'

Beck took a sip of coffee.

Then the man stopped talking, extended his hand.

'Jeff. I'm tough because I have to be, but that's what works. People were tough on me when I first came into the rooms. It's why I'm still here. AA doesn't need you, Finnegan, but you need AA. Keep coming back, it's that simple.'

Beck rinsed his cup at the sink when he'd finished, was about to place it onto the draining board when a woman standing next to him handed him a tea towel.

'It's called a tea towel. Works by revolving propulsion. Let me demonstrate.'

She picked up a mug, began drying it, turning it briskly in her hands.

Beck smiled.

She smiled back.

She had shoulder-length blonde hair, brown doe-like eyes, tight jeans hanging from wide hips.

'My name's Vicky. Jeff's right. Keep coming back, Finn. That's all you have to do. Fake it till you make it.'

Beck picked up another mug and started to dry it.

'Is everything in here a metaphor?'

'Don't knock it. It works. After we finish we're going to Frazzali's for coffee. Want to join us?'

'More coffee?'

'I bet you didn't say that when you were drinking? What, more alcohol? No, I don't think so. That attitude will help you pick up again. You know that? By the way, that mug is dry now.'

Beck put it down.

'Okay. Sorry. I'd like to. Thank you.'

She smiled.

'See. It's okay to drop the attitude. It's okay to be honest with yourself. Becaaaause, if you're like me, you'll have to learn everything all over again. From scratch. The right way this time.'

It still wouldn't change what Beck could see before his very eyes. This woman was a knockout. He was prepared to be honest with himself. She was the reason he was going for coffee.

Beck caught the look of the man who had come and was standing beside them now. He was on the small side, but wide and athletic. The type of body that comes from hours spent in the gym, the elasticated short sleeves of his shirt emphasised the results of his labours. He couldn't disguise the look. Not in his forced smile, not in his overly compensatory, too firm a handshake. The look of the Alpha male eyeing the approach of a rival.

'Joe. Finnegan here is joining us all for coffee at Frazzali's.'

'Great,' like he'd just been told of a death in the family.

At Frazzali's they pushed two tables together and eight recovering alcoholics, including Beck, took their seats. The meeting appeared to continue, each person regaling the group with tales from their drinking past, each story more fantastic than the one preceding, as if competing for a prize.

Eventually it was his turn.

'You're a policeman... I heard,' Joe said. He had made a point of sitting next to Beck, between himself and Vicky.

'That's right,' Beck said.

'Coming to accept one's past is an important step in recovery,' Joe went on. 'Step Four says we must make a searching and fearless moral inventory of ourselves. Some people are never ready to do that, they find it's too much. You need to prepare yourself for that step.'

At the end of the table Cathy shifted. She was a retired nurse. She hadn't touched alcohol in a quarter century, but suspiciously appeared to know the name of every psychoactive prescription drug on the market.

'It was all over the news,' she said now. 'The poor Frazzali girl, I mean. God rest her.'

And the others. Remember them too?'

The man who spoke reminded Beck of Humpty Dumpty. His expression was of someone who was about to burst into tears at any moment. Beck couldn't remember his name.

'Are there any developments with Samantha Power? The whole town is talking about it,' Humpty Dumpty asked.

Beck broke off a piece of apple tart with his fork, dipped it into the cream on the side of the plate, and held it in front of his mouth.

'No,' he said, opening and putting the apple tart in.

It was obvious he wasn't going to say anything further.

'And the child, the poor craytur,' Cathy said. 'Will they search through the night for her?'

Beck didn't answer. The search would be called off when darkness fell. But he didn't want to say that.

The group was silent. Beck swallowed, took a sip from his coffee.

'Was that a trace of anger?' Joe asked. He was smiling. 'It's understandable. I'm sure you can't discuss the case. But still...'

'It's a normal emotion,' Vicky interjected. 'If you feel it. Show it. That's what I say. Hiding has consequences. We all know that.'

She leaned forward, turning towards Beck. At the meeting she'd had on a light zip-up pink jacket. This was draped over the back of her seat now. Underneath she wore a low-cut top.

The broad back of Joe came between Beck and Vicky as he leaned onto the table, obscuring his view.

'I think we should be very careful what we say to Finnegan here. Remember, he doesn't have the time under his belt that we have.'

'How long are you sober?' Humpty Dumpty asked Beck.

'Come on,' Joe said. 'It's not about time. All any of us have is twenty-four hours. A day. A day at a time. That's it. We're all sober for today. One day at a time!'

'But you just said,' it was Cathy, 'that he didn't have the time. And now you say all we need is twenty-four hours. You said it, Joe.'

Joe took a deep breath.

'Promptly admit when we're wrong. Sorry. Okay. I did say it. I shouldn't have. Sorry. It's getting late. I think I'll go home. You ready, Vicky?'

Beck caught the switch. As the group lost interest in the discussion. Instead, they silently looked at Vicky, waiting...

The eyes of the old man at the end of the table, in a flat cap and Crombie coat, who had not spoken during the meeting or here at the restaurant, suddenly seemed to come alive. He stared at Vicky, his mouth open.

'That's alright, Joe,' she said after a long pause. 'It's a lovely night. I'll walk. You go ahead.'

Joe didn't move. He placed both hands onto the table. Slowly, he clinched them, tightly, and Beck could see the whites of the knuckles appear through the taut skin. The air became heavy, pushing down, like something was about to crack and splinter.

But then Joe smiled, and the air immediately lightened. And then he laughed, and it disappeared completely.

'Right then,' he said, getting to his feet, pumping false cheeriness into his tone. 'I'll be off. See you all on Saturday night I suppose.'

Voices called after him: 'Righteo, Joe, see you', 'Remember, all you have to do each day is... breathe', 'Keep coming back, Joe.'

Vicky watched him go.

Now it was her turn.

'Regards to your wife, Joe,' she called after him.

And for a brief moment, Joe paused. It seemed like he was about to turn around. The group watched him closely, like they were waiting for something. But then, Joe walked on.

'Hello, Vicky.' The man approached from a side table. He wore a dirty grey sweatshirt and jeans, baseball hat with the swoosh logo across the front.

Vicky turned her face up to look at him.

'Danny Black. You avoiding me?'

He grinned, his face slightly off kilter, nothing matching up. He wasn't avoiding Vicky. No man on earth would ever want to avoid Vicky. 'No. Course not. Next week. Maybe Monday. I've been in Galway for a few days, just got back, finished up a job there. You're next on my list, honestly.'

Vicky folded her arms, pushing out her breasts. 'You make sure I am, Danny. A girl can only wait for so long. It's leaking everywhere – the radiator I mean.' She laughed. 'Only teasing, honey. Can you make it this week, pretty please?'

'Okay, maybe tomorrow, or Friday. I'll do my best to be round one of those days.'

Vicky wagged a finger, her arms dropping by her sides. 'Okay. I'll be waiting in for you. It's summertime now, suppose I can do without central heating for a little while.'

The man smiled in that sweet innocent way of his, lingering, uncertain of what to do.

'I'll see you then,' she said, dismissing him, his purpose served.

'Okay,' he said, and started to walk away.

Vicky looked about the table, a ringleader in a circus arena of men.

The waitress reappeared, reaching in to the centre of the table where she had placed the bill earlier. She took it up and crumpled it in her hand.

'Tony says regards to the policeman. This is on him.'

Vicky brushed a hand through her hair and looked at Beck. He wasn't certain, but he thought he caught it. Something. He wasn't certain what.

Something.

CHAPTER THIRTY

In the last ten years of the total of fifteen he had spent in Dublin, Beck had lived in one property, the house he owned in the urban village of Ranelagh. Now, in the few short months he had been in Cross Beg, he was already on his second home. He had no choice, not really, because Beck had no wish to remain in a house where the body of a murder victim had been discovered. Nor, it seemed, did anyone else. That house had been vacant ever since.

Like his last, this too was a townhouse, but rented week to week from a management agency in Galway. Last time he had rented from the owner. She was the one found under his bed, his landlady, Mrs Sheila Claxton. But Beck didn't dwell on that, there was no point.

The current house he was staying in was one of a row of ten that stood, separated somewhat from Cross Beg, on the other side of what was called The Little Town Park. Which was, as opposed to The Big Town Park, an area once with high hopes of being turned into a spectacular public garden for the benefit all the citizens of the town. The Little Town Park was now an overgrown, Japanese Knot-infested example of what can happen when an undertaking is the ambition of just one person. Gertrude Wolfe, who had passed away two years before, would be horrified.

It was midnight. Beck was in his sitting room, a copy of a crime thriller on the armrest of his chair. He had given up on it. The author, an ex-Chicago police captain, had included plenty of technical details. Beck assumed these were correct. But as a policeman himself, even Beck wasn't sure. Nor were most policeman he knew, because specialities were best left to specialists. He also knew that when an expert writes a book, it becomes a manual. And so, he considered, had this book.

Although the search for baby Róisín had been called off for the night, volunteers were still searching. They did not want to give up. No one wanted to give up. So they continued, would search well into the darkness, using torches and spotlights in scouring an ever larger radius. Nothing had been found as yet. Nothing. Beck now could not rid his mind of images. Of baby Róisín, wondering if she was wrapped up warm and tight, sleeping? Or was she crying in some dank and dismal place? Or was she dead, lying in a ditch?

He took up the book again, he'd give it another go. He turned the page, forcing himself to concentrate, but after just two pages his eyes grew heavy and then closed, his head slumped against his chest and he began to gently snore. Natalia smiled at him, beckoning him to follow. The door was open, and she walked ahead into the bedroom, the moonlight through the windows silhouetting her body beneath the fabric of her nightdress. She lay on the bed, arranging her hair onto the pillow like a halo. He could see the veins on her long white neck quiver, pulsing against her flesh. She lay there and parted her legs, then raised them, the nightdress falling down her thighs as she folded her knees back. She reached out her arms, the palms of her hands flat, as they began dancing through the air.

She opened her mouth to speak. But the sound that came out was not what he had expected. It was of a baby. Crying. And then her neck, unaided, as if by black evil magic, opened up, and a geyser of blood erupted into the air. Yet still, her hands continued to move, dancing through the air, moving faster and faster.

Beck was rooted to the spot. He could not move. Natalia moved from the bed and walked towards him. That sound she had made of a baby crying had stopped. In its place came a hollow hissing noise as air escaped from her neck, like air escaping from a pipe, which essentially is what it was. She smiled at him. What's wrong? her eyes said. Still he could not move. She was almost upon him now, he could smell the sweet metallic aroma of fresh blood. But the face was no longer that of Natalia. It had changed. He was looking at Samantha Power. She tried to speak, but all that came from her was that hissing noise from the gaping wound under her chin. Still, he knew what she was trying to say, *'My baby is dead. My baby is dead. My baby is dead.'* Her blood no longer gushed, it had reduced now to a mere trickle. And her hands were almost upon him, almost touching his face.

Beck woke with a start.

He was slumped in his armchair. The book was on the ground. He shivered. It was cold now in the room. And with it came a feeling, solid and heavy, pressing down on him. Which was this. The baby was dead.

God, he thought. Please. God. Let me be wrong.

CHAPTER THIRTY-ONE

The new day was breaking through. Beck could not sleep and had come here. He stood to the side now, a silent observer, not wanting to get in the way. They were prepared. The garda search team had been waiting for the first lick of dawn to begin their work. Before the arrival of volunteers, before anyone. So they could have the area to themselves, and allow the search dogs to roam unhindered. Because if the dogs could not find the baby now, it meant the baby wasn't here.

There were three springer spaniels, the youngest, Casper, highly strung and with a question mark over his future in An Garda Síochána. Unlike the others, Casper now did not crouch low to the ground in the customary fashion of his breed. He did not sniff the ground either. Instead, he held his head high, and sniffed the air. His handler only saw him do this when hungry, usually at the end of shift, as he was being taken from the van.

The dog tugged on his lead now and whined. He didn't normally whine. And started to scrape the ground with his front paws. This was not what he had been trained to do. He had been trained to keep his nose low and move forward strictly on command. Any other time, while on operational duty, he was to remain calm and obedient.

Maybe he smells a bitch in heat. If that's the case, Casper my boy, it's the dog pound for you.

Casper turned his head and looked at the man. The dog's big, soft eyes had a quiet intelligence about them. Casper was very still, as if, the dog handler considered, his feelings had been hurt by what he'd just been thinking.

'Okay, Casper. Let's see what you can do.'

The dog pawed the ground again as the handler unclipped the lead. 'Off you go, boy.'

And Casper streaked away. It took him mere seconds to reach the far end of the field. He did not stop there, instead dove into the thicket of bushes and was gone.

The handler waited...

But Casper did not reappear.

... And waited, considering with a sinking heart that Casper's instincts indeed might have triumphed over his training.

And then he heard it.

Casper's excited barking.

He ran to the end of the field through which Casper had disappeared. There, he could see the dog peering up from the bottom of the ditch through a tangle of bramble, his brown and white coat camouflaging him perfectly into his surroundings.

Right next to his face was what appeared to be a rectangle of cloth. The dog was now doing exactly as he had been trained to do, which was to wait for the man.

'Fetch, Casper!'

Casper gripped the item gently in his jaw. He lowered his head and immediately began to make his way out again, his tail wagging in that frantic way of springer spaniels.

'Good boy, Casper, good boy.'

The handler brushed the dog's coat briskly and took Casper's reward from the side pocket of his cargo pants. He bounced the ball into the air and Casper jumped to catch it.

'Good boy, Casper, good boy.'

From his other pocket the handler took a pair of plastic gloves and a folded evidence bag. He pulled on the gloves and bent down, picked up the item carefully and placed it into the bag.

It was a bloodied baby's T-shirt.

CHAPTER THIRTY-TWO

The crows were shrieking in the trees as Beck walked through the field. The dog handler was waiting, the springer spaniel sitting at his feet. The animal looked at Beck, watching him with gentle, intelligent, eyes.

'His name's Casper. He found it. In there.' The handler pointed to behind him. 'I can show you exactly.'

They walked to the ditch and the handler indicated.

'Right down there. It was caught in the branches.'

Beck looked at the tangle of thick foliage.

'The dog pick up a scent anywhere else?'

'Casper got this on the wind. He didn't track it.'

'Really,' Beck said.

The handler looked genuinely proud. 'Not many canines could do that, springers anyway. There wasn't a track for him to follow. Not as such. Anything here is twenty-four hours old by the way. The T-shirt was dropped. That's the only explanation I can think of.'

Beck considered that.

'That you, Beck?' The voice came from the other side of the ditch, in the next field.

'Andy Mahony?'

'We're coming through from this side,' the SOC Inspector said. 'Clipping everything back, piece by piece, branch by branch.'

He grunted.

'Damn, I just tore my overalls again. Meet me at the van, Beck, I'll need a fresh set. Be there in a minute.'

The Technical Bureau Fiat Ducato was shoehorned onto the narrow roadway. Beck went along the side, the thorny bushes of the ditch pulling on his shirt sleeve. The back doors were closed. He saw Inspector Mahony crossing a gate and starting to walk towards him now, pulling at the shoulders of his one-piece forensic suit.

He nodded to Beck, opening the van door and pulling off the suit. He placed it into the bin just inside the door. The suit itself would be analysed later. Mahony was sweating. He ran a hand over his forehead, then reached into the van again, took a bottle of water, opened it and gulped down. He held out the bottle to Beck.

'No thanks.'

'The piece of clothing,' Mahony said, 'suspected to be baby Róisín's T-shirt, is on its way to the lab in the Phoenix Park on a Yamaha 1200 motorbike, running on lights and siren. It'll be matched with the victim's DNA sample that was sent yesterday. This time tomorrow we should have the result. That is, if the body doesn't turn up in the meantime. Either that or the child is long gone.'

'What about the car? Anything?'

'There were prints. On the roof by the passenger door, four finger marks excluding the thumb, and underneath the passenger door handle, index and middle finger. Both sets are a match. For the same person. Unfortunately, there's isn't a match on the system to identify who this person is. We took a mould of fresh tyre marks too. From the end of this road here, right by the gap in the hedge where the victim's car went through. Something big. Bigger than a car. Smaller than a truck. Tyre analysis should tell us the particular type, but not the actual vehicle model itself.'

'An SUV? Is that what you mean?'

'Yes. A large SUV. We've combed the area searching for the murder weapon. It's likely we'll have to dredge the river... Thought you'd have an easy life of it down here, didn't you, Beck?' Mahony adjusted the hood on his new overall. 'Or does death just follow you like a stalking cat?'

'If that's a joke, Mahony, I'd stick to the day job. Not that you're any bloody better at that.'

Inspector Mahony watched Beck walk away.

'I've heard you're on the wagon, Beck,' he called after him. 'It'd be a foolish man who'd place a bet on you staying there.'

CHAPTER THIRTY-THREE

Beck walked to the end of the road and paused, looking ahead over the low bank of moss and weeds that marked the entry to the lost village. On the other side, what had once been a gravel track was now high grass and scrub winding its way ahead of him, wild gorse and white hawthorns pushing in from either side where once the stone thatch cottages of Kelly's Forge had stood. Beck clambered over the low embankment and made his way along the covered trail.

It wasn't far to the end. This was marked by a ditch, on the other side of which a cow stared back at him, its lower jaw moving in a sideways motion as it chewed with a soft munching sound. Behind it the boggy ground stretched for a short distance before it was lost to the curve of a hill. Next to it a shimmer of green. Beck stared. He discerned ivy, stretching off in the other direction. Was that a wall there?

Beck looked either side of him and, crouching low and holding back the sharp hawthorn branches with a sleeved arm, pushed in through the bushes on his right. The thorns pierced his clothes and scratched his flesh, and just as he wondered if it wasn't too difficult to continue, the bushes gave way and he was standing on a carpet of pine needles. A bird flapped its wings somewhere above him and flew away, leaving the world completely still. Ahead were trees of Scots pine, widely spaced, indicating it had been thinned here in the past. The sun glinted on the pine-needled floor, leaving streaks of light and shadows through the trees.

Beck doubled back through the trees a short distance in the direction he had come. He stopped and looked about. He could see that they were part of the forest now, almost indecipherable, wilds roots having taken hold, tumbling down walls, covering the fallen stone in vines and moss. But there they stood, jagged mounds rising from the earth, the last vestiges of the buildings that had once stood here. Where the trees grew now, the villagers cattle had probably wandered, half-starved in winter with nothing to eat but the long acre, the grass along the sides of the public roads. And where once voices echoed, nothing now but stillness. All else was dead. Forgotten.

Beck felt a hard, ribbed, roughness beneath his feet. He used his shoe to brush back the thin layer of vegetation that appeared like a mat, revealing an old cart wheel beneath. It was moulded into the ground, blackened and rotting, its central metal hub reduced to mere twisted shards of rust.

Beck turned away and walked away from it, deeper in amongst the trees. He stopped after a couple of minutes and turned back again. This distance provided him now with the perspective he needed to see the pattern. Still, it was difficult to pick them out, but gradually he could discern the remains of the stone cottages at regular intervals interspersed through the trees. These reminded Beck of the headstones on forgotten graves, where no one any longer came to place flowers or pick tender weed roots before these could take hold. Now, the weeds had slowly devoured the graves, as they had devoured this place. Soon nothing would be left, all traces would be gone, everything having returned to the earth.

Or would it?

Beck closed his eyes, and a sudden rustle through the trees like the whispering of ghosts gave him the uncanny feeling that he was being watched. So powerful was it that he opened his eyes and looked about, trying to find the prying eyes. But he could see none. The trees rustled again, but louder this time, as if angered by his presence.

And then, on the breeze, he could smell it. Unmistakeable. It was the stench of rotting flesh. Of death. Beck walked ahead, in deeper amongst the trees. The branches weaved and sighed before him. The ground became rougher, stumps of long fallen trees hidden underfoot. Beck moved carefully, the ground beneath him soft and porous. He came to a stream at the bottom of an incline. It was very low, almost dry, the water hardly moving, the rocks on its bed jutting up, edged in lichen. If this weather continued, soon no water would remain. He jumped to the other side. The stench was much stronger here. A little further on the ground sloped away to an area of clear, rough ground. The stench was overpowering now. He held his nose, and looked down.

Hard, bare branches extended from the ground at the bottom. They were oddly shaped, and rigid, like spirals, a labyrinth of wood. He stood looking down, following the trail of spirals, trying to make sense of them, to what looked like a… He saw then what it was. A buck deer's head, and the spirals of wood were its antlers. He looked along, to the bloated body, could see towards the back, over the distinctive short white tail, skin had broken, a mass of pulsated larvae exposed, expanding and contracting like a grotesque beating heart. He felt his foot begin to lose grip and so he raised it and moved it back, attempting to anchor it more securely. But where he placed it was hollow beneath, and Beck stumbled and fell forward, grabbing branches as he went, successfully stopping himself from completely falling over but ending up stumbling onto one knee at the bottom of the slope. The movement had thrown the flies, big fat bluebottles, into the air, swarming around him now, the angry buzzing of their wings like an audio rash.

And in front, its yellow teeth bared in a death grimace, clamped around a long floppy black tongue, nostrils flared, inside of which, towards the back, Beck could see a sliver of that same undulating pulsating larvae.

But it was the eyes. They were immense. While the body had rotted, they seemed almost alive. The buck deer stared back at Beck, as if to say: *Well, what the hell?*

CHAPTER THIRTY-FOUR

Beck stood at the top of the Ops Room and informed the assembled detectives and uniformed members of the discovery of a baby's bloodied T-shirt in a ditch not too far from Kelly's Forge.

Silence followed.

It was the first and only find in the search.

'We'll know tomorrow if it's baby Róisín's.'

He paused, tempted to add that it probably was baby Róisín's. But he knew they were already thinking that. So why add to expectation? There was always the chance it might not be. Because coincidences, Beck knew, created unnecessary turns within an investigation already a maze.

He moved on.

'We haven't located Billy Hamilton. As you all know, Róisín's biological father lives with his mother and two older brothers. She says he hasn't been home in a couple of days.' Beck paused. 'And Edward Roche, Samantha's partner. His statement needs to be corroborated. That he was indeed at the Elegant Print and Design on the day Samantha Power died. Even if he was, he still had a narrow window in which he could have done it. He finishes at five. Theoretically, he still had time. Just about.'

'He's hitting the sauce I hear, Hamilton,' a uniform informed the room.

'He'll have heard by now, of course,' Superintendent Wilde said.

'He was in The Noose last night,' the uniform added. 'We parked outside at closing time. But we missed him.'

'Why didn't you go in?' it was Beck.

The uniform looked surprised.

'Billy Hamilton. The Noose. At closing time. You'd need the public order unit. Do I have to explain?'

'There's more ways to skin a cat,' Beck said, but not loud enough for anyone to hear.

Beck lowered his head, raising his eyebrows secretly. An image of a room of policemen filing into a maze and taking a wrong turn filled his mind.

'It would be hard to take the child out of the country,' Superintendent Wilde told the room. 'The CRI was activated within hours. But it's possible. She could be in a different jurisdiction by now. And consider we believe the motive behind the attack on Samantha Power was sexual. Taking that into account, it's possible therefore, I consider, the baby may have been abducted for the same reasons.'

For a moment there was complete silence.

'She's a baby for Christ's sake,' it was a perplexed Garda Ryan, mother of four children herself. 'Six months old. Sir, with respect, come on…'

The room broke out into chatter. Wilde raised his voice a couple of octaves.

'It may be part of a long term, planned scenario.'

'Sir,' Beck said. 'But we believe this was not a planned crime. All indications are that it was spontaneous.'

Superintendent Wilde frowned, took a step back, leaving the atmosphere in the room much heavier that it had been when the briefing had first started. There was a white-board next to Beck. Superintendent Wilde had wheeled it in earlier. Beck wrote bullet points in black marker on it out of respect for the traditions of the station. In reality, it was a complete waste of time. Everything had already been inputted onto Pulse. Lastly, in large heavy lettering, he wrote 'CCTV', underlined it twice.

'Sergeant Connor?' Beck called.

From the back of the room a hand rose. Beck was glad to see that Sergeant Connor's pallor had grown into a healthy pink glow now that he was back on day shift.

'Progress on CCTV,' Connor said. 'Because we now know the direction of travel of the victim's car after it left Crabby's supermarket, I requested footage from a filling station and a lumberyard along the Mylestown Road. It's a relatively short distance along here to the turn off for Kelly's Forge. I obtained one download already, from the filling station. But I won't have the other until later this afternoon. Once past the lumberyard, there are no more cameras until Mylestown, six miles further along. I also made a request through local radio for any dash cam footage that might be out there. Nothing has come back on that so far, unfortunately.'

'You look at the download you do have yet, from the filling station?' Beck asked.

'Of course. Everything appears normal. Samantha Power drives past. On her own. Nothing outwardly unusual.'

Sergeant Connor fell silent.

Beck turned his attention to Garda Ryan.

'Did she have any enemies, Samantha Power, that you know of, Garda Ryan?'

Garda Ryan began tapping her fingers on her hi-vis jacket folded across her lap.

Beck considered the jacket had a significance beyond the practical function of a mere item of clothing. He considered it the equivalent of an adult comfort blanket.

'If she had I would have told you,' she said. 'Of course, she had people who didn't like her. Don't we all? But you'd really need to hate someone awfully bad to do what was done to that poor girl, and I can't think of anybody like that. Not even Hamilton or Roche, to be fair. I met Naomi Scully, the girl she'd been staying with by the way. She came up to me on the street. Wants to know if anyone will be round, to search through her stuff. Not that there's much of it.'

'Look after that, will you?' Beck said. He held out little hope of anything coming out of it.

She pulled the hi-vis jacket closer to her, looking down at it, running a finger along one of the silver reflective stripes across the front.

'The prints on Maurice Crabby's bike are all his own,' Beck said. 'Anyone have any dealings with him in the recent past, by the way?'

Garda Ryan shifted in her seat. 'He's smarmy, that fella. Everything he says is loaded with sexual innuendo. 'Crime fighting keeping you out of your warm bed at night, guard?' That sort of thing? Gives me the creeps.'

Superintendent Wilde looked at her. 'If we can stay focused on the fundamentals of the matter, please.'

Garda Ryan looked like she was about to say something, but didn't, instead folded her arms and remained silent.

'The murder weapon has not been located,' Superintendent Wilde said. 'We're looking for something sharp, but blunt. That's an oxymoron by the way.' He noted the confused expressions. 'An oxymoron is…'

'With all due respect, sir. We know what an oxymoron is.'

'Not a knife,' Superintendent Wilde said, tetchy. 'At least not a sharp knife. And the State Pathologist believes it's not a knife. But what it is, we don't know yet.'

But Beck wanted to get back to the baby.

'I do think there is also the possibility,' he said, 'that the killer also killed the baby. Dumped her body. Somewhere.'

Superintendent Wilde placed his hands on his hips in that way of his and looked at Beck.

'Do you now?' Beck heard him mutter.

*

'Was it really called for?' Wilde asked when the briefing was over. 'To directly contradict what I had said in front of my officers?'

'I didn't directly contradict you. I thought I was being quite subtle. I do believe the baby is probably dead.'

'But you don't know. That's the thing. And speculation is dangerous. We must be openminded. To all possibilities. If you have opinions of that nature in future, tell me in private. Understand?'

Beck nodded. 'I understand. Anyway, where the hell is Inspector O'Reilly? I haven't seen him since yesterday morning, and he needs to be here, doesn't he? Has anyone heard from him? If not, isn't it time someone went round to his house?'

Wilde's brow furrowed. 'Someone has been round to his house. Apparently he's not there. I spoke to his ex-wife. She usually hears from him every couple of days or so. Because they still have a boy in college. But she hasn't heard from him in a while. That's how she put it. We spoke yesterday evening. She said he hasn't been himself for the last few weeks. Make of that what you will. Something wasn't right with him, she said. I really don't know what to make of any of it. Do you have an opinion on this?'

'Where does he live?' Beck asked.

'Just outside town. On the Loughrea Road. I don't know much about the man any more, to be honest. Not since he separated. Everything changed. Up to then we'd see each other socially from time to time, our circles would cross… you've heard the rumours of course, the sex party scandal from some years back, the swingers thing. He'd never get another promotion because of it. He was stuck, and he knew it. You've seen him. His resentment. You've had personal experience of it, haven't you?'

'For a time,' Beck said.

Over Wilde's shoulder, he could see Claire Somers enter the Ops Room. She crossed and sat at her desk.

'When you say you know he wasn't there, at home,' Beck asked. 'How do you know?'

Wilde raised an eyebrow.

'There was no reply, of course, when the patrol called earlier. No one answered the door. That's how I know.'

'Boss,' Beck said. 'I think you need to send someone round again and kick the door in.'

CHAPTER THIRTY-FIVE

Maurice Crabby sat on an upturned box at the back of the super-market storeroom. He liked everything about this storeroom. He liked the smell of it – like dried figs – he liked the grey-painted bare block walls, he liked the high-vaulted roof with its lattice of exposed metal girders. But most of all, he liked the fact that he could hide in here, amongst the shelves and row upon row of stacked goods, in this warren of cardboard walkways. Here he felt safe.

Today he had retreated further to the rear than he had ever done before, pushing beyond the staples, past the savouries, past the tinned soups, into the realm of the mango chutney and organic coconut milk, the almond butter spreads. Rarely did anyone come here. After all, a box of mango chutney could be expected to last a year. He settled himself into an alcove hollowed from the boxes around him, and sat with his head held on fisted hands, staring ahead. Opposite was a shelf containing an assortment of jars and bottles. These were plainly out of date, the tins specked with rust and the bottle labels mottled and peeling. A stash of back rowers that had never been rotated properly according to the policy Maurice himself had pinned to all the walls about the place. Left by a lazy teenager long since moved on to some university course or other.

He didn't care about any of it now. Because it was only a matter of time before they came looking for him. And he knew what would happen then. Because he had been there before. He had seen the windows that looked out onto the pretty gardens. But all was not as it seemed. The windows that looked out onto the pretty gardens had iron bars across them. And he had heard those pitiful screams that echoed along those gleaming corridors where shrouded ghostly figures glided with no sound but the flapping of their capes. Some nuns had great bunches of keys that hung from their waists. They were the nuns that the orderlies accompanied. The orderlies, big, barrel-chested simpletons selected from the orphanages and reared there for this very purpose. Bred more like, Maurice considered, like the Nazis bred Doberman pinchers. To keep order, in the Loony Bin. That's where they'd put him too. So Maurice kept his mouth shut.

He cradled his arms across his chest now and began to rock back and forth slowly.

He thought of the missing baby, imagining the screams of it so loudly he clamped his hands across his ears to drown it out.

But he could not.

He could still hear it. Louder than ever.

The baby. Crying. Screaming.

He pressed his hands tighter onto his ears and closed his eyes. Yet still he heard it.

Go away. Go away. Go away.

It did not. He heard it louder than ever.

'Gooo awaaaay,' a whimper.

It was no use of course. The sound remained.

She stood a little distance from him, watching, one end of her mouth up, the other down, two teeth poking over her lower lip. She heard him whimper, 'Gooo awaaaay,' and began to laugh. Crabby's eyes snapped open. He glared at her.

'You pathetic little man,' she said. 'Did you kill that woman? Well, did you?'

Crabby stood slowly, awkwardly. He raised his upper lip, pushing his two front teeth over the bottom one, made a clicking sound.

'You look like a rat,' he said. 'Do you know that?'

She blinked.

'Yes, maybe I did kill her. So what?'

That look on his face.

She took a step back.

Crabby took a step forward.

Again she blinked, took another step back, bumping into a bank of cardboard boxes. They quivered dangerously, before settling again.

'But maybe *you* finished her off,' he said.

'What?'

'Because you were there too. Weren't you? In the Range Rover. I didn't think of it at the time. When I was passing. But the sat nav pinged. It pinged twice. That new sat nav. Can do anything but boil a kettle. You forgot to clear it, didn't you? It pinged. Twice. I was only there once. You were there. In the Range Rover. Weren't you?'

Her mouth realigned, was no longer lopsided. Then it opened again, wide. She brought a hand up and covered it. He didn't think he had ever seen his wife look so helpless before.

CHAPTER THIRTY-SIX

Inspector O'Reilly sat reclined in the red velvet armchair with gold braid tassels hanging from the ends of the armrests. The curtains were drawn and the gaudy chandelier threw down shafts of weak light. A panelled mirror in the shape of a half moon fixed to the wall by the door reflected the light back in dimples. The curtains were parted just enough to reveal the marked patrol car pulling up outside, its two occupants opening the doors and getting out. But O'Reilly did not move, instead he stared ahead through the gap, waiting for the officers to walk up the garden path and knock on his front door.

Garda Dempsey lifted the heavy brass knocker and brought it down onto the brass plate three times, careful not to push too hard. This was the home of an inspector after all. When he received no response, Probationer Smyth tapped on the glass with the ring of a finger, *tack, tack, tack.*

'I think that's enough,' he said, when it appeared she was about to repeat the procedure.

She looked at him, holding her folded ring finger next to the glass.

'Really,' he said. 'I think that's enough.'

She ignored him. *Tack, tack, tack*, again, louder this time. Dempsey took a breath and counted to ten. It always worked.

There was no letterbox to look through. An American style postbox was fixed by the garden gate instead.

Still, Inspector O'Reilly did not react. The sounds of the knocking had reverberated throughout the property. A face blinkered by the palms of two hands appeared at the window soon after, two eyes swinging back and forth as they peered into the house. The inspector stared back, but the searching eyes did not see him.

'That window is slightly open,' Smyth said, pointing.

It was, very slightly, the window to the right of the door. They walked to it and looked through. A corner settee inside, a patterned rug in the centre of the floor, a coffee table, a large flat screen TV against the wall on the opposite side of the room.

'Wonder why the curtains are pulled in the other room and not here?' she asked, nodding her head in the direction of the other window.

She looked at Dempsey again. *Do something*, it said.

'What are you looking at me for?' he snapped now. This girl was irritating him. 'Try the bloody window yourself. See if you can open it?'

CHAPTER THIRTY-SEVEN

Beck stood next to Claire Somers, who was seated at her desk, head bowed. She did not look up at him. He waited for her to speak but she did not. She reached for some papers, began shuffling them.

'Fine,' he said, starting to turn away.

'Don't.'

He noticed the top sheet – it had the logo of an insurance company on it – appear before her a second time. She was shuffling for the sake of it. She stopped, put the papers down.

'I've left Lucy,' still not looking up at him. 'Temporarily. We need a break. That's all.'

Beck said nothing.

'I need a place to stay.'

Beck hesitated.

'You want to stay with me?'

'Christ,' looking up now. 'Do I have to spell it out?'

Again, Beck hesitated, before answering.

'That's not a problem. I have a spare key.'

'Are you sure? I feel like I've just asked you for one of your kidneys.'

Beck fished out a keyring from his pocket. 'I'm surprised,' he said, beginning to prise a key from it. 'That you'd want to stay with me, that's all.'

'But not that I've left Lucy?'

'Hmm, that too. You've only just gotten married, after all.'

He held out the key.

She took it.

'You think I don't know that. It's temporary, like I said. Anyway, I also said I *needed* a place to stay. Not that I *wanted* to stay. With you that is.' She smiled. 'Only joking. Thanks, Beck.'

'You know where the house is, right?'

'I know where the house is.'

'There's only one rule.'

'What's that?'

'I don't treat you as a visitor. That's too much like hard work. You make yourself at home. Do your own thing. Okay?'

'That's two rules.'

'The second is a clarification of the first.'

She smiled again.

'Understood.'

CHAPTER THIRTY-EIGHT

It was an old type, wooden-framed window. It was open just enough for Probationer Smyth to slide the hard cover of her notebook in and lift the latch from its holder and knock it to the side.

'You first,' she said.

If she went first, he'd have nothing to stare at but her arse. She didn't want that.

Dempsey latticed the fingers of both hands together and bent down.

'Here,' he said. 'I'll give you a leg up. Makes sense. You're lighter.'

Not by much.

'Come on. We need to get in. Quick. Do it.'

She didn't think about it, placed her right boot into the stirrup of his hands and started to lift herself up. She leaned forward through the window, saw a radiator directly beneath, and clamped a hand onto each corner. She understood at that moment the advantage of the baggy and formless uniform trousers she and the girls had been moaning about in training college. She twisted and slithered through the window until she could place both her feet onto the floor and finally, stand up.

She looked about the room. It was chilly in here. She noted the coating of dust on the mantelpiece above the fireplace.

'Get on with it,' Dempsey said. 'Open the front door and let me in.'

When she did, he crossed to the bottom of the stairs and called up, 'Anybody home? Inspector O'Reilly. Hello. This is the guards, sir.'

Smyth placed her hand onto the door knob of the room that had the curtains pulled. She turned it and pushed the door open. A light was on. A chandelier no less.

She saw a red velvet armchair some feet in front of her, tassels hanging from the ends of the armrests. On the wall was a large picture, of a naked woman, lying on a floor, her tongue curling from between closed lips, her legs crossed, one leg folded over the other, playfully concealing her crotch, an arm draped across her breasts. The room was what she considered a cheap whorehouse might look like.

She saw now that someone was sitting in the armchair. She could see grey hair circling a bald patch rising over the back of it. She knew that head. It was Inspector O'Reilly's, and he was sitting very still. She wondered if he was sleeping, and considered retreating back into the hall. At that moment, Dempsey came into the room.

'It doesn't seem anybody's home,' he said.

His voice was loud, which startled her. She jumped, quickly pointing to the armchair, mouthing the word: 'There'.

He followed her finger, and nodded. He approached the chair.

'Inspector O'Reilly,' he said. 'Is everything alright, sir?'

The probationer watched, holding back. She expected Inspector O'Reilly to wake about now and bark like an angry dog. The less he saw of her the better.

Dempsey moved to the front of the chair. Here it comes, she thought.

But Inspector O'Reilly did not speak. Dempsey did. Two words. *'Holy God!'*

CHAPTER THIRTY-NINE

'All airports and sea ports have been notified. We must continue to believe she is alive until we have verifiable proof to the contrary.'

Superintendent Wilde sat back in his seat, observing Beck. Who considered his boss was waiting to be challenged. Which Beck had no intention of doing, because Wilde was right, Beck did not know. The baby may not be dead, and watching the airports and sea ports was a good call to make.

But despite this rationale, Beck still felt it. And knew he was only trying to fool himself that he did not feel it. Because the feeling had not gone away. The intangible but as real as something he could reach out and touch feeling was only stronger now.

That child is dead.

'The press has finally drawn the distinction,' Superintendent Wilde said. 'Between the murder of Samantha Power and her missing baby. They have at last begun to treat the baby as a separate story. Which is good news. Means we might get a tip off. Jeez, we need it. One tip off could end this immediately, it usually does. Someone out there knows something...'

There was a loud knock on the office door, but before Superintendent Wilde could say anything, it opened. A young uniform was standing there.

'The patrol has reported back from Inspector O'Reilly's house, sir.'

Superintendent Wilde looked at the uniform, annoyed at his uninvited entry.

'What...'

'They found him.'

'About time. Is he coming in?'

The uniform looked surprised.

'No, sir. He's not. He's dead. His throat's been slit.'

*

For the second time in just two days, Beck found himself reeling out crime scene tape. He tied one end around a pillar in the garden wall and extended it to the last pillar on the other side of the gate. The house was a narrow three storey building with a grey peeling façade. The garden was overgrown but with splashes of colour from shrubs set in the gravel along the edges.

When Beck went in, SOCO Mahony was standing inside the door of the room where Inspector O'Reilly's body lay sprawled on the armchair, the smell pungent but not overpowering. Two dead bodies, their throats slit, in less than forty-eight hours. Coincidences didn't stretch that far, Beck knew. One person, he thought, a crazy person perhaps, was responsible, who was out there now, walking around, taking the air maybe, nodding his head in greeting as he passed people on the street.

The room was surprisingly chilly. And there were no flies. Beck thought about that. He'd come across bodies in the past in rooms where the doors and windows were tightly shut. Usually old men the world had forgotten about. Some had been dead for months. In such cases the skin tissue slowly and indecipherably turned into a slimy, stinking gel, before coalescing and over time becoming the texture of a wrinkled prune that disintegrated to the touch. There was no sign of forced entry, that Beck could see.

Mahony bent down and looked closely at the door panels while another technician moved along the wall, scrutinising it from top to bottom. Their first job was to look and appraise. The third technician recorded everything on a handheld camcorder. They were oblivious to the body. For now. Beck edged along the wall. He hadn't asked anyone if he should be here, because he knew what the answer would be. Next to him on a shelf was a marble clock, beside it a brown and white porcelain jug surrounded by brown and white porcelain cups, a collection of books at the end. He moved again, edging along until he came to a point where he was in front of the chair and had a view of O'Reilly's body. By its nature, death by murder comes swiftly, without warning, is always violent, sometimes brutal, and usually, but not always, a surprise. In Celtic mythology, it is believed it sometimes traps the spirit. Hence ghost stories rarely have their origins in deaths that are peaceful and natural.

Murder changed everything. Victims did not repose, because usually coffins were sealed. Where they were not, it was impossible not to look at the body in its velvet trimmed box and think, first and foremost: someone has taken this person's life from them. The natural symmetry between a life lived and of its passing was lost. Like now. This would be a closed coffin. O'Reilly's face was a blackened, swollen caricature, the mouth open, the underside of a purple, bloated, tongue curling up, filling the mouth, the veins limp and black, drained of their blood, the head lurched at an angle: hanging. But still, Beck was struck by the expression on the late Inspector's face. Despite everything, that look could be summed up in one word: relief.

The late Inspector's right hand was extended, the palm facing upward, the fingers slightly curled, as if he had been holding something before he died.

Beck turned and noted the books on the shelf. The title of the one facing him, *Bangkok Guide: Night Time Delights*. On the cover a picture of a female in a tight micro-dress, standing in front of a bar, a galaxy of neon lights behind her. Beck was wearing gloves. He reached out and separated the book from the others, straining to see its title.

'Beck!'

Inspector Mahony was glaring when he turned to look.

He pointed to the door. 'That way. Now piss off.'

CHAPTER FORTY

Beck snapped the visor down as he sat in the unmarked police car, leaning his head back against the headrest. He watched the half dozen or so crime scene-suited figures file through the front door into the house. Among the collection of marked and unmarked vehicles parked on the road was a purple four-wheel drive. A GSOC vehicle, the organisation responsible for garda internal affairs. The death of a serving garda under suspicious circumstances would automatically demand their attendance.

'The room. It was, like, almost kinky,' Beck said.

But he couldn't take his eyes off the purple four-wheel drive. This was a distraction no one needed.

'They interview you yet?' Claire asked, following his gaze.

Before he could answer the radio crackled.

'The Noose pub. Report Billy Hamilton's gone berserk. Anyone available?'

Beck reached for the handset, brought it to his lips, clicked the talk button.

'He still on the premises?'

'Don't know. That you? Inspector Beck?'

'Yes. It's Beck.'

'Can you take it, boss?'

Beck glanced at the purple four-wheel drive again.

'I can take it. Delta Five Two on the way. Out.'

Claire started the engine and spun the front wheels as she pulled away, turning on the blues and siren.

They were the first to arrive. A group of men were on the pavement outside, talking loudly and gesturing with their hands, smoking cigarettes. Sitting on the window ledge was a walrus of a man Beck knew to be the proprietor. He only knew him by his first name, Christy.

Beck got out of the car and stood observing the scene for a moment.

'Look-e there. If it isn't Dick Tracy himself.'

The man who had spoken was small, early sixties, and despite the weather, wore a heavy dark overcoat. A roll-up hung seemingly without any effort on his part from a corner of his mouth as he spoke.

'Jimmy Brennan,' Claire said. 'Haven't seen you in a while.'

'I gave up the drink for a while so I did, guard. Was going to them meetings up in Ozanam House. Look-e there, isn't that right, Dick Tracy?'

Beck looked at the man, who seemed familiar. The man smiled at him as Beck crossed to Christy on the window ledge.

'I think you'll need an ambulance.'

'Uh uh. No ambulance,' Christy said, holding a wad of tissues to his nose. 'It's worse than it looks. I've got to clean up me pub. Did you see what the headcase done?'

'I'm looking at it,' Beck said.

'No. To my pub I mean. Come on, I'll show ya.'

Beck followed him in through the doorway of the pub. There was scarcely enough room for the walrus to pass through. They stood inside, and Christy crossed to the counter, gripped it with both hands, and wheezed loudly.

'This is doing nothing for my heart y'know. I've a dickey ticker. I'll get him sorted so I will for this. I swear to God.'

'I'll pretend I didn't hear that,' Beck said. 'Tell me what happened?'

Christy squeezed the tissues against his nose and when he spoke it sounded like it was from inside a cardboard box. 'He came in, and I knew as soon as I looked at him something wasn't right. But it's Hamilton, ya, and we all know something's not right with him anyway. He ordered a pint and started talking weird…'

'A buck fifty, did you say?' Beck said. 'What's that?'

Christy took the tissue from his nose, which appeared now to have stopped bleeding. He touched it with a finger and winced. Most of the tissue paper was a deep red colour.

'I asked him that too. It's slang, that's what he said, from the 'hood, that's what he said too, for a hundred and fifty stitches. I'm tellin' you, he's a head case Hamilton, so he is. Anyway, he was annoying me so he was, going on and on like he was some kind of tough guy.' Christy's eyes widened. 'He's no tough guy, he's a big mammy's boy, that's what he is, but just 'cause he looks like Brad Pitt… Wait'll I get him, I'm tellin' you. Okay, okay, you don't want to hear about that.' Christy took a slow deep breath, continued. 'I lost my temper, told him to feck off and go and join those good people looking for his daughter. His daughter, I told him: His daughter! Anyway, he started talking real soft and apologetic, told me I was right, that's what he should be doing. "Come here," he says then, "I have something to tell you, privately like." And so I leaned in and that's when he done this. Headbutted me in the face he did, the absolute bastard, that's what he is. You'd need to get him quick, before I do, 'cause he's liable to kill someone the ways he's going on, so he is.'

'Any idea where he might have gone?' Beck asked.

Beck noted the floor was littered with glass, the linoleum strip separating the tacky carpet from the counter awash in spilt beer, broken bottle necks like buoys in a shallow sea.

'I'm not finished,' Christy said. 'What I want to tell you is he then went berserk. Went behind the counter and started knocking stuff over. Everything. Bottles. Glasses. Even the kettle, look at it there. He was pure mad so he was. Thank God he didn't cop the spirit bottles at the end. I can't claim on insurance for this y'know, put my premium through the roof, it's comin' out of me own pocket it is. And the bastard passed me a dud fifty-dollar bill so he did. I took it 'cause I'm going on a holiday to New York. The bastard!'

'Did he now?' Beck said. 'Hang onto that. We'll deal with that later, okay?'

'Oh, I'll hang onto that alright, what else can I do with it?'

'Any idea where he might have gone?' Beck asked again.

'I don't know. And I don't give a damn either.'

A patrol car had arrived when Beck got back outside.

'This town is gone to the dogs,' the female guard said to her colleague as they approached the pub. 'Hi, Claire.'

Claire smiled. 'Hi, Alice.'

Alice was medium built with short dark hair. Her smile disappeared when she looked at Beck.

'Can you take over?' Beck asked her.

'We were sent over because you're stretched. We were close by. Call this a favour. I can't investigate it. This isn't my area.'

Beck lit a cigarette and pulled on it so deeply the glow almost became a flame.

'There's nothing to investigate,' he said, exhaling a thick stream of smoke. 'There'll be no statement. We have to get this nutter before he does something even more stupid.'

Beck began walking towards the Focus without waiting for a reply.

The Ballinasloe mules didn't object. Without a statement forthcoming they had nothing to do but look official. That wasn't so bad.

Beck stood next to the car, smoking his cigarette down to the tip. He dropped it into the gutter.

'Let's go,' he said. 'I'll tell you as we're driving.'

*

They drove to 4 Ravenscourt Drive, banged on the door, but there was no reply. Beck peered in the windows, but the curtains were pulled. The window that had been broken was panelled over in ply board. Beck thought about forcing it.

'Has he left town?' Claire asked. 'He's not supposed to.'

Beck pondered that question, cursing under his breath. He thought of something.

'Just on the off chance. Come on.'

The Elegant Print and Design Company was really a newsagents shop at the front, a printing business at the back, and a kiosk with a yellow-and-red neon sign that said 'Keys Cut Here' to the side, tucked into a corner. It reminded Beck of an old seaside Punch and Judy booth. Inside it were rows of blank keys along the back wall, dusty, like they'd been hanging there a long time. A couple of aisles in the centre of the shop were devoted to books, separated into sections by genre, but too small to offer any worthwhile variety: Irish Literature, Popular Fiction, Biography, Non-Fiction, each with maybe three feet of shelf space. Other shelves along a side wall were sectioned into magazines and offices supplies – packs of printing paper, ink cartridges, pens, etc – the other side wall stuffed with cuddly and cheap toys. Beneath the counter, under the chocolate bar display, the daily newspapers were laid out. Beck ignored those.

A girl, seventeen or thereabouts Beck guessed, was behind the counter, in a white T-shirt, plucked eyebrows and a nose piercing. She turned to them, chewing gum.

'Can I help?' the voice unexpectedly friendly, smiling. Somehow, Beck hadn't expected that.

'I'm looking for Edward Roche,' Beck said, too late to take the cut from his tone.

Her eyes flicked from Beck to Claire as the smile disappeared.

'I'd better get Benny, the boss.'

She opened a door behind her and went into the back of the shop. There was a glass panel in the wall and Beck could see a man stacking sheets of paper at a table. The girl spoke to him and Beck watched as the man looked up, turning towards the window. The man nodded and wiped his hands on his apron, began walking towards the door, his head and shoulders stooped, like a defeated boxer. There was the loud clanking noise of machinery and the whirl of electric motors as he slowly opened the door and with it the smell of hot ink and paper. The door closed again and the man crossed to the counter.

His forehead was furrowed like a ploughed field, his expression like he had lost his life savings on a horse in the 4:45 at Chepstow. He stood before them, his shoulders narrow and slumped from carrying the weight of the world.

He spoke, a slow and throaty mutter, 'I don't have a lot of time.'

Beck could almost hear the black dogs straining at the end of their leashes as they dragged old Benny here along behind them. He looked into the man's wide, vacant, eyes.

'It's quite simple,' Beck said. 'We'd like to speak to Edward Roche?'

'Really? So why've you come here?'

'He works here, doesn't he?' it was Claire.

Benny's mouth opened, but no words came out. His face softened.

'This a joke, is it? I haven't heard a joke that could make me smile in ages.'

'No,' Beck said. 'Why would you say that? We haven't time for jokes right now.'

And the expression returned, as if he was walking away from the bookies with nothing left in the whole world but some jangly loose change.

'Roche,' he said. 'I fired him months ago. He doesn't work here.'

CHAPTER FORTY-ONE

Inside the front door of 4 Ravenscourt Drive, three bulging suitcases sat on the floor, pressed tight to the back so they couldn't be seen if someone looked in from outside. Even if the curtains were pulled.

The printing press in the garage made a munching noise as it spewed out each sheet of paper, like the sound of someone biting on a big apple. The noise was from a broken bearing in a roller. The machine was almost a hundred years old after all, and parts were hard to come by. But it did the job better than anything else for the money he had paid for it.

Edward Roche went into the living room, nudged aside the curtain with his little finger. If the cops were to come back, he'd have to be quick in shutting it down. Anyway, he was almost finished now. Just a little longer, then it would be over. He took his finger from the curtain and it fell back into place. He turned to go into the garage. And froze.

Shit!

Nobody else should be in the house. It was locked. Secured. He'd checked.

So why was somebody standing in the doorway?

CHAPTER FORTY-TWO

'G'day, mate. The girl who's been killed. Samantha Power. I want to speak to someone about it. The Superintendent, eh. The gaffer.'

The white-haired guard behind the public counter looked at the man standing before him, sun-bleached hair, deeply tanned skin, the corners of his green eyes concertinaed with laughter lines. But he wasn't laughing now. Garda Frank Kennedy stretched himself to full height, which wasn't much, and puffed out his chest. This was important business.

'Have you information, sir, about that?'

'Who's the boomer in charge, mate? That's what I want to know.'

'The boomer, what do you mean, sir?'

'Aye, the head chef. I don't care what you call him. You just go get him, mate?'

Garda Kennedy felt it important the public show due respect in dealing with the institutions of the State, especially the gardai, and he did not take kindly to at any attempt at undermining this authority. He was old school, and he didn't like the way Crocodile Dundee here was speaking to him. He reached under the counter for a notebook and pen and held the pen poised above the page.

'Your name there good man, and contact details, and the *specific* nature of your business, please.'

'Some things never change around here, mate, do they, aye? Once a bogan, always a bogan, aye?'

Garda Kennedy felt himself getting a little exasperated. 'I'm sorry there now, but I haven't a clue what you're talking about.'

'No, ya don't mate, do ya? Mikey Power is my name. Brother of Samantha Power, the girl who's been killed.'

Kennedy put his pen down.

'Why didn't you say. Take a seat please. I'll get somebody.'

'No worries, mate. You do that.'

CHAPTER FORTY-THREE

Roche didn't move. In the twilight of the curtained room he could see an outline standing in the doorway. He knew who it was. The arm of the outline reached out and flicked the light switch.

Hamilton's mouth was twisted. His eyes wild. A word came to Roche's mind: Deranged.

'How'd you get in?' no anger in Roche's voice, just mere enquiring, humouring him.

'How'd I get fuckin' in? I'm a burglar, bro, how do you think I got in?'

Roche felt his breathing quicken, each intake barely moving down his throat before it was coming back out again and he was gulping for more air. His body tensed, solid and brittle, both at the same time. It was a feeling that came with fear. No, more than fear, beyond that. He was petrified. Hamilton was a head case, everyone knew that. But even so, he would never admit how scared he was of him, not to anyone. This was the reason he had gone round that night, to prove to Samantha that a girl like her could be with a man like him, that he could handle the Hamiltons of this world. But of course he couldn't. Hamilton didn't even break a sweat, two punches and he'd be a heap on the floor. He'd never get the better of someone like Hamilton, he knew that now. But Samantha secretly liked that he had tried, as he'd known she would.

So, how was he going to get out of this?

'What is it, Billy? Why are you here?'

'Billy is it? Don't call me Billy. Who said you could call me Billy?'

It was then Roche saw the box cutter in Billy's hand, the blade twinkling like a shiny trinket in the light. He felt a looseness in his lower belly, a heat sensation emanating from his anus. He knew he was on the verge of shitting himself. The ultimate humiliation.

'Where's my child?' Hamilton asked calmly, taking a step forward. 'And before you answer, just so's you know, you're goin' to die either way. But if you tell me where my child is, I'll do it quick.' He laughed, a high-pitched sound of someone out of their mind. 'I'd do a nickel for slicing you, bro. I'll give you a buck fifty, man, across your motherfuckin face.'

And Roche felt a pressure building, and suddenly giving way, and a release, with it a noise, a crackling sound, and with it a smell like charcoal and fish as he stood there, as it ran down his legs, as he shite himself, and he began to sob.

Hamilton flicked the knife back and forth in his hand. 'You tell me where she is. You tell me Roche.' Another step forward.

'I didn't touch her. I didn't touch anybody. I swear it. I swear it, Billy. I had nothing to do with it. I had nothing to do with it. You've got to believe me. *Pleeeease.*'

'Where is?' Another step. 'My?' And another. 'Child?' And one final step. Right in front of Roche now. 'You stink, bro. Don't you have any self respect? How did Samantha ever fuck something like you? How?'

And from somewhere within Roche, it came. A defiance. A final last grasp at something resembling self respect before the inevitable. One last chance to roll back, just a little, on his utter humiliation. To at least *try.*

'Ya,' he said, surprising himself. 'She told me your dick was like a cocktail sausage, she had to finger herself to get off because you were crap at it.'

But not even that had any effect, except to make Hamilton laugh.

'What? Is that it? Is that all you can do? Man, you're pa-thet-ic. I'm hung like a donkey and every bitch in this town, no, in this county, knows it. You didn't make her pregnant, did you, bitch? It was me. You're not capable of it.'

He threw his head back and laughed.

And Roche took his chance. His only chance. His last chance. He ran for the door. But Hamilton, in a flash, brought up the knife and with one short, sharp movement, stepping to the side, out of the way, brought it down onto his face as he passed, slicing the cheek open with the ease of gutting a fish. Roche stumbled into the hallway, screaming in pain, fell against the staircase.

'Told you,' Hamilton said following, 'I'm goin' to slice you a buck fifty. Didn't I tell you that, homie? Here, *número dos*, bitch.'

Hamilton was bent over, holding one hand to the side of his face, whimpering.

'*Pleeease, pleeease. No Billy. Ah, Billy. Pleeease...*'

'You grovel like a bitch,' Hamilton said, running the blade down into his arm now, where there was a tattoo, of a mermaid, with long flaming red hair, voluptuous upper body, delicate green scales at the end of her tail. The knife ran through it, like ripping the canvas of a painting, but in this painting real blood poured, the mermaid's stomach torn apart.

Roche slumped to the ground.

This was it.

There was no use.

A buck fifty. His epitaph. The sum total of his life. *A buck fucking fifty.*

'Oh please God, make it quick,' nothing but a mutter now.

Hamilton laughed, and raised the knife again. And as he brought it down, a recklessness to the movement, because a person's back offered greater scope, greater freedom after all, angling the blade as a vague notion entered his head, to write his initials onto that wide sheet of flesh. But before the point of impact, just as the blade was about to puncture and slice through the skin, a sudden jolt, and the movement came to an abrupt, involuntary, halt. He saw that a hand had wrapped itself around his arm, just above his wrist. It was a hairy arm; further along he could see the folded back sleeve of a brown shirt.

He looked back over his shoulder, behind him. He recognised that face. The tall policeman. The one they called Beck.

'Drop the knife, Billy, there's a good man,' Beck said calmly.

Billy pulled on his arm, one powerful sudden jerk, designed to surprise, certain he could free it, but the grip became only stronger. He spun round now, lowering his head. He had a reputation for using that head. It was infamous as his close combat weapon of choice, when he had nothing else. He shifted on his feet, attempting to manoeuvre into a position to use it as a battering ram. But then he felt his knees suddenly give way as he was kicked from behind. He fell onto those knees to the floor, wincing with the pain. Claire Somers was behind him. She snapped the first ring of the handcuff onto one wrist, and Beck placed the other wrist into the second she held out for him. Claire snapped it shut. Hamilton stopped resisting. He lay still, his breathing heavy. He'd given up.

Beck stepped back and reached for his phone to ring it in, and as he did so he heard a sound from the direction of the garage, *crunch, crunch, crunch...* He glanced at Roche, who was writhing about on the floor, a widening pool of blood on the tiles beneath him. Claire went into a room looking for something to stem the flow of blood.

Crunch, crunch, crunch.

Beck looked in the direction of that sound. The kitchen, and beyond this to the garage. He'd felt sure when he first came here that Roche was hiding something. Now, he considered, he was about to find out exactly what.

CHAPTER FORTY-FOUR

The ambulance carrying Edward Roche sped off for the University Hospital in Galway. He had lost a lot of blood, and was stretchered to the ambulance unconscious by the paramedics. Beck had no doubt Hamilton had wanted to kill him. Once the ambulance left, the patrol car with Hamilton handcuffed in the back pulled away from the roadside, but in the opposite direction, heading for Cross Beg Garda Station.

Beck finally had an opportunity. He walked down the hallway into the kitchen. The door to the garage was closed. He crossed the kitchen and turned the handle, pushed. The door opened. *Crunch, crunch, crunch,* drowning out every other sound.

'Let's see what we've got in here,' to Claire standing behind him, but his words were lost, *crunch, crunch, crunch*.

He stepped into the garage. The air was stifling hot, heavy with the smell of fresh ink. The noise was so loud he stuffed a finger into each ear. The old black Heidelberg, clean and cold to the touch on the day he had visited, clanking away now. At one end, a slim metal plate slid out, *crunch,* while above a metal grill swung on an arm and down onto it, depositing a sheet of paper, *crunch*. The metal grill then rose again and the metal plate withdrew into the machine, *crunch*. A moment later, at the other end, a similar metal plate emerged, *crunch,* dropping a sheet of paper onto the ground where already there was a haphazard pile. But everything happened so quickly the noise was like a staccato, *crunch crunch crunch*. Beck noticed a junction box on the wall.

He walked over and pressed its big red switch. The Heidelberg was immediately silenced.

'Beck.'

Claire was standing in a corner of the garage, next to a heavy-duty trolley that had thick black wheels, something in her hand, a package.

'I believe the term is a bric,' she said.

She came over to Beck and handed it to him. The item was wrapped in clear plastic. He could see a face through it. Bearded. He knew that face. Ulysses S. Grant, the eighteenth president of the United Stated. In each corner two numbers, five and zero.

'Fifty-dollar notes,' Claire said.

'No,' Beck said. 'To be specific. These are not fifty-dollar notes. These are *counterfeit* fifty-dollar notes. Worthless, in the truest sense. Unless you can convince someone to believe that they are real. Trust it's called. The basis of the entire paper monetary system anyway. In that scenario, they are worth a lot of money. Real money.'

'And they're good, they're very good. You have to admit.'

Beck had to admit, they were.

*

Superintendent Wilde rang on the way back to the station and told Beck a wood chisel with an inch-wide blade had been found in a dredge of the River Óg. In good condition. Not there very long.

'Boss.'

'Yes.'

'Anything on Inspector O'Reilly?'

'Jesus no. Too early to tell. The GSCO guy is crawling all over the place. I don't need any of this right now. Two victims. Throats slit. Is there a knife-wielding slasher convention in town that I don't know about? Christ. Oh, and the search for the baby's body has been called off.'

The line went dead. Superintendent Wilde had hung up.

Beck looked at the phone in his hands.

'The search is called off,' he told Claire.

She said nothing, and they remained silent for the rest of the journey.

CHAPTER FORTY-FIVE

'That's not him, mate? I already met him. I want the head chef.'

Beck stopped midway across the foyer. Mikey Power was pointing at him. The young guard behind the public counter shrugged.

'What's up?' Beck asked no one in particular.

Mikey Power stood up. 'I haven't got all bloody day, mate. You'll do. Got a minute?'

Beck nodded, then to Claire, 'Go through, I'll catch you in a minute.'

They sat on the bench running along the wall beneath the window opposite the public counter.

'You any closer to catching the bastard did this to my sister?'

Beck wondered how long Mikey Power had spent in Australia, because he spoke like a native.

'What, mate, why you looking at me like that?'

'The investigation is progressing,' Beck said, ignoring the question.

Mikey angled his head and peered at Beck.

'Aye, mate, that the best you can do? You got to do better than that, eh?'

Beck folded his arms.

'Mr Power. I understand. This is a very difficult time. What else can I say? The investigation is progressing.'

'The blonde dude. Was taken in just before you arrived. That Billy Hamilton?'

Beck said nothing.

'It is, isn't it? So that's the bugger?'

'How is your mother, Mikey?'

Mikey's eyes narrowed, stared at Beck. 'Do you care? No mate, I don't think so either. Billy Hamilton, eh? You think it's him maybe?'

Beck shifted, again said nothing.

'Can't you tell me any bleedin' thing? For Christ's sake.'

'I asked how your mother is. You're wrong, I would like to know.'

'And that's a stupid bloody question, mate. How'd ya think she is? There you go then. That's your answer. And where's my niece? Where's Róisín? That little baby is out there somewhere?'

'Would you like to talk to someone? We have people. Victim support.'

Mikey turned, the light catching his face. He looked older now.

'No mate, I just want to know who did this.'

'Leave us to find that out. Go to your mother, Mikey. She needs you right now.'

Mikey pushed air through his nose like air brakes on a truck. When he spoke, his voice was low, without any trace of its Aussie accent now.

'Don't tell me what she needs. You cops are all the same. I know what you're like. You're the bloody reason I left this town in the first place. You never forget, see, you never let a person move on. Always on the books, see, aren't they, people like me? I went off to Australia, just about far enough away from here that I could get.'

'Okay, Mikey. I understand. You're angry.'

'Damn right I'm angry. About a lot of things.'

'You returning home at this time?' Beck said. 'I understand you haven't been in touch for years.'

Mikey stood, took a couple paces towards the door and stopped, turned around. 'So? Got to come back sometime. Mum's getting on now. Never know what'll happen. But I never expected this.'

'No one expected this,' Beck said.

'If it wasn't for family, I'd never have come back to a crummy town like this. It never leaves you, see, it's always right on your back.'

Beck said nothing, and Mikey crossed the final few feet to the door, where he paused, and without looking back, his Australian accent fully restored, added, 'You and I will talk again, mate. Catch ya later.' And walked out of the station.

CHAPTER FORTY-SIX

Hamilton lounged back in his chair in interview room number two. It was obvious he was high, the pupils of his eyes dilated like saucers. But Beck acted like he hadn't noticed. As too must have the custody sergeant. Otherwise the interview would have had to be postponed to the following morning, allowing Hamilton time to sober up. No one wanted that.

Hamilton's arms were draped across his chest, hands joined together, thumbs twiddling. Like he was patiently waiting for a movie to begin, or his flight to be announced. His head hung back resting on the top of the chair, staring at the ceiling.

Tough guy.

'How about straightening up there, horse?' Beck said. 'There's a good man.'

'Horse!' Hamilton said, laughing, pressing his head further back into the chair. 'That's a good one. Me auld lad used to say that.'

'What about it?' Beck said. 'Horse.'

Hamilton giggled, staring at the ceiling.

'Horse. That's a good one. Naa, don't feel like it, bro. I likes it just the way it is. Here, can't you tell I'm shitfaced? Some cops ye are. I ain't supposed to be no interviewed while I'm trippin', man.' Hamilton giggled again. 'Show me to my cell, James. Here. Horse. That's a good one that is.'

Beck turned to Claire. Billy was too spaced to be of any use for anything. Then Beck got an idea.

'Would you get me a glass of water? Please, Claire. Here, Billy, you want some water?'

'Billy! Everyone's so friendly. *Billy, you want some water?* No, I don't want no friggin water.'

When Claire was gone, Beck stood and moved around the table. Hamilton was still looking at the ceiling and didn't notice. He walked behind him and placed two fingers into his nose and pulled back his head, clamping the palm of his free hand across his open mouth. Billy could not move his upper body, if he did, he'd tear his nose clean off his face. And nor could he breath. He trashed his legs about, hitting them on the legs of the metal table that was bolted to the floor.

Ouch!

Billy stopped, had to, sat motionless, his wide eyes staring up at Beck.

'Did that get your attention, Billy?' Beck relaxed the hand covering Hamilton's mouth, felt the air through his fingers as Billy sucked in. 'Sorry horse, but that seems the only way to do it. Now, horse, concentrate, okay.' He gave a sharp tug on Billy's nose, reapplied the pressure onto Billy's mouth. Billy's eyes widened, fear in them now. 'Sobering up there a little, are you Billy? Never fails to do the trick.'

Billy blinked.

Tap tap…

Beck released his grip. A sound like a groaning hippopotamus as Hamilton sucked air into his lungs.

Tap tap…

'Beck, can you open the ruddy door, please?'

'Be right there.'

Hamilton was no longer slouching back into his seat. He sat up and leaned forward onto the table. Beck could see a premature bald spot on the crown of his head. He couldn't help but smile.

'What happened here?' Claire asked, putting the water down onto the table, looking at Hamilton.

'Asthma attack, looks like,' Beck said, taking up one of the plastic cups and sipping. 'I didn't know he had a medical condition.'

Billy coughed. 'I don't...' pointing at Beck, then falling silent. He looked like a kid who'd tried to pick a fight but was now left on his own in the playground.

Claire eyed Beck, said nothing.

'Right, let's get on with it,' Beck said, returning to his chair and sitting down. 'Interview with Billy Hamilton, arrested for section three assault, namely the use of a box cutter.' Beck glanced at the clock on the wall. 'Interview commencing now, 17.05 hours.' He pressed record.

'Have you anything to say to that, Billy?' Beck asked.

'No comment.'

'No comment, really?'

'Billy, did you think that Edward Roche might have had something to do with the abduction of your daughter?' it was Claire.

Hamilton looked at her. The craziness in his eyes had gone. His expression was almost tender.

'Abduction,' he repeated. 'No one ever used that word before.'

'The search is being called off, Billy,' Claire said. 'We believe someone took her. It's the only explanation. She hasn't been found.'

Hamilton stared, and his eyes glistened. He rubbed his hands quickly across them and took a deep breath.

'I just wanted to find my girl,' he said. 'That's all. I just wanted to find her.'

'And you thought Edward Roche might have had something to do with it?' Claire asked.

'Maybe.' He looked at them. 'It's just as well you came when you did. I was out of it. I could have killed him.'

'You would have, Billy,' Beck said. 'Now, where were you between four and six on Tuesday evening last?'

Hamilton lowered his head. He stayed like that for a moment then raised it again. He was crying.

'I didn't kill Samantha. I was a bastard to her. I admit it. But I didn't kill her.' He gave a long, anguished cry. 'If only I could go back, make it better between us. But I can't.' He looked at Beck, then to Claire. 'Please, find my baby. Promise me. You won't stop looking.'

Is this the real Hamilton, Beck wondered? He decided it probably was. And stripped of the paraphernalia, there wasn't much to Billy Hamilton, he was just a frightened kid with not much going in his life. His tough guy image gave him an identity, his only identity, but an identity nonetheless.

'Tuesday evening, Billy, between four and six,' Beck asked again. 'Where were you?'

Billy was thinking.

'I don't know,' he said. 'I fucking can't remember.'

Normal service resumed.

'Okay,' Beck said. 'I have another question for you.'

'Do you now,' an edge creeping back into his voice.

'Earlier today the body of Inspector Gerald O'Reilly was found in his home. Dead. Throat slit. Just like Sam's was.' Beck paused.

Hamilton ran his tongue across his dry lips, staring at him.

'You like knives,' Beck said. 'Don't you Billy?'

'You can fuck off with that for a start. I didn't kill anyone. You're not pinning that on me so you're not.'

'We don't know when exactly he was killed,' Beck added. 'Not yet anyway. But it was probably in the last twenty-four hours, something like that. You can account for your movements during that time, can't you, Billy? I mean, you'd hardly forget twenty-four hours, would you?'

Hamilton stabbed a finger through the air towards Beck.

'I want a solicitor. Okay, horse.'

CHAPTER FORTY-SEVEN

Superintendent Wilde adjusted his tie and placed his cap neatly onto his head, then stepped through the door out of the station. The waiting press converged on him, smart phones and dictaphones held so close to his mouth that he was forced to brush them away. The glare of TV camera lights dazzled him, showing up every crevice on his face and the dark rings beneath his eyes.

An explosion of voices, an indecipherable mumbo jumbo, reporters shouting all at the one time, all saying something different: *'Do you have a message for the person who abducted baby Róisín, Superintendent?* ... *'Can you tell us anything about the body found today? Has it been identified yet?* ... *'Has the murder weapon that killed Samantha Power been located, Superintendent?* ... *'Do you think baby Róisín is dead, sir?* ... *'Has the result of the technical examination of the baby's T-shirt come back? Does it belong to baby Róisín, sir?* ... *'Are there any suspects? It's been almost two days now?'*

'Please,' Superintendent Wilde said, raising his hands. 'One at a time. Please. One at a time.'

The TV was turned to mute. Vicky lifted the floor tile and carried it to the fireplace, stood it on its side on the ground, leaning it against the stove. She looked across the room at the wall-mounted TV in the kitchen area. 'At this stage there is no indication the baby is dead. We must assume she is still alive,' Superintendent Wilde said, looking out from it, his expression grave.

The timing was perfect, Vicky thought. Sad, yes, of course, that was true, but perfect. She looked around the crumbling old house. A bit like this place, she considered, what she had in mind, full of potential. But she had to be quick, had to strike while the iron was still hot, while this dreadful business was fresh in people's minds. And if she did, if she did this thing right, secured the funding from Frankfurt, went straight into production, had everything – fingers crossed – wrapped up by Christmas, in time for the International Independent TV Production Fair in Oslo for the end of February... Well, if she could do all that, then Cobana Productions might have a TV hit on its hands, the equivalent to the publishing success of *Angela's Ashes*.

Vicky undid an extra button on her blouse and checked the time. He'd be here soon, and he was usually never late.

CHAPTER FORTY-EIGHT

Maurice Crabby drove slowly, oblivious to the traffic that was building up behind him. Once or twice when a driver overtook they honked their horn and held up a prominently displayed middle finger. But Maurice didn't notice, he didn't notice anything, and he didn't care. He continued, the big SUV hogging the road, crossing the border into County Clare. By the time he arrived, it was after five o'clock. It was a long time since he had been here, years in fact, but once he passed under the stone arch and started along the driveway to the main building, it all came back to him. The building was different now. The bars on the windows long removed. The gravel driveway had been replaced by tarmac, and parking spaces were neatly marked in white paint. The old wooden doors with their metal hinges were gone too. Now the doors were of glass, and even in the evening sunlight, he could see the bright lights inside the building. Warm, welcoming. *Hello.*

The final change he noted outside was the sign, set in the grass margin by the door. In a corner of this was the health service logo, and beneath it the words 'Psychiatric Services', and beneath this again, 'St Bridget's Open Facility'.

The old wooden sign it had replaced, in austere gothic script, had said: 'St Bridget's Hospital for the Mentally Deviant'.

All had changed. And yet all had remained the same. But Maurice found his breathing was a lot easier now.

CHAPTER FORTY-NINE

Jacinta O'Reilly lived in a house that reminded Beck somewhat of a steam locomotive: flat roofed at one end with a chimney stack rising from its centre, while at the other it was raised with a sloping slate roof. The front predominately was of glass, with huge windows and, uniquely, corners of dimpled glass bricks, two bricks thick. The house was painted a gleaming white and the window surrounds black. The door in the centre of the building was also black. It was set in from the road behind a neat lawn. There was no garden wall, no trees, no embellishments, not even flowers. It was quite striking.

'The flat roof is covered in solar panels,' Claire said, pulling up behind a green convertible VW Beetle parked at the side. 'Designed this herself.'

'Impressive,' Beck said. 'And expensive. You know her?'

'A little. It's a small town. She's her own woman, as they say. Originally, she trained as a nurse, then became a homoeopathist. It's a booming sector, alternative medicine. Chalk and cheese really. The pair of them.'

'Children? Two I heard?'

'Two boys. One's in New York, an artist, but O'Reilly called him a bum. The other, the one he was proud of, training as a solicitor in London.'

She was waiting for them when they rounded the side of the house, standing at the front door. Inspector O'Reilly's ex-wife was a small petite woman, attractive but not pretty, with a round face, small eyes and thin lips. She was dressed in a short red dress, a belt that had a large gold buckle secured around a slim waist. Her breasts were prominent, her legs perfect. She oozed sensuality, but also practicality, all at the same time. O'Reilly would have picked up on that.

'I was just about to go out when I heard,' the voice cracking. 'I can't believe it.'

They reached the door. Jacinta stared at Claire, turned to take in Beck.

'How did you know?' Claire asked gently.

'Someone rang. A newspaper or other. It doesn't matter. I know, Claire.' She turned. 'Come on. Come in.'

The hallway was tiled. It was like daylight inside. Beck considered it the only property he'd ever felt the need to wear sunglasses inside. She led them into a room, like a picture from a soft furnishings brochure, colours vibrant and coordinated, everything clinically clean and tidy. Beck saw a mural on the wall, an abstract. He worked out it was of a woman reclining into a chair, nothing but a scarf around her neck. He thought of the picture on the wall of the room where Inspector O'Reilly's body had been found. Maybe not so chalk and cheese after all.

She noticed him looking.

'Gerry liked it,' she explained. 'Picked it up at an auction somewhere. It kind of grew on me. Can I get you anything? Tea, coffee?'

'No,' Claire said.

'I'm fine, thanks,' Beck said.

'Look,' Claire said. 'Don't you worry about us, please, Jacinta. We came to…'

Claire suddenly looked uncomfortable.

Jacinta O'Reilly sat down, crossing her legs, her short dress sliding up her thigh. She cupped her hands around one knee, indicated a sofa with a nod of her head.

'Take a seat, please.'

They sat down on a button-back red leather settee.

'I'm still processing the information,' Jacinta O'Reilly said. 'I don't think I want to know the details. Is it true though? That he was, actually... murdered?'

'It appears that way, yes,' Beck said.

'Did he suffer?'

Beck balled a fist and rubbed it against the palm of his other hand.

'Unlikely,' he said, not sounding very convinced.

Jacinta Reilly picked up on it.

'Is it true, his... throat?'

You said you didn't want to know the details.

Beck nodded. 'I'm afraid so.'

She blinked rapidly, then her small eyes widened and were still.

'My, God,' she said. 'You know, we'll be seven years separated next month. And yet, in some ways, it was like we had never separated at all.'

Grief can sometimes be like a wave, Beck knew. It begins as a current, one of many currents that flow and ebb, joining other currents that hide beneath the surface, unseen and deep, so, so, deep. The grief is carried with these, the momentum building, slowly rising from the deep, breaking through the surface, rising up, curling into a white top, building and building, the white top becoming a boiling foam crust, bubbling and hissing, all the time heading to shore...

Beck knew, knew that if they needed to get questions answered, they needed to do it now, before it was too late.

'Mrs O'Reilly,' Beck said. 'If I may ask. How was Gerry lately, his demeanour?'

The question distracted her, forced her to focus on practicalities. The wave settled somewhat, fading back into the dark sea.

'The boys are grown now.' Suddenly, she looked startled. 'My God. I need to tell them. Maybe I should do that now? I mean, I wouldn't...'

'This won't take long,' Beck said. 'It's important.'

She paused, took a deep breath, settling herself.

'Gerry was not himself lately,' she said. 'No. Definitely not. We always tried to keep on good terms, you understand. And we did. For the boys' sake. But he wasn't himself. He was withdrawn, quiet… didn't you notice? Down at the station?'

Beck hadn't. He hoped Claire might answer, but she remained silent. O'Reilly wore a mask, but no surprises there, so did everyone else.

She continued, 'He said it was all futile. A waste. Said that he knew that now.'

Beck and Claire exchanged discreet glances.

'What was a waste?' Beck asked.

Jacinta O'Reilly sighed, looked down at the long red fingernails of each hand.

'Gerry had an addiction. That's what I'd call it. An addiction to sex. There, I said it. I've never said it before, not to anyone else in the whole world. But I've said it now, and you know what? I feel better for having done it. He was never happy with what he had. Including me. It was very difficult. I think it stemmed from his childhood. His mother died when he was very young, when he was only five. He had issues with commitment, that I won't go into, because I don't really understand it myself. But I had to deal with the aftermath, that's all I know.'

A light was briefly being cast into the dark corners of Inspector O'Reilly's life. For the first time, Beck felt an empathy for the man. As so often happens when someone dies, he wished he'd made more of an effort to overlook the guff and instead get to know the man.

'It was painful,' she added. 'I sometimes…' She looked away, then slowly back again, '… went along with it. Look, can I tell you something?' They remained silent. 'I've never said this before either. I enjoyed those sex parties. But unlike him, I got attached, to people…'

Beck stopped rubbing his fist against his palm. Instead he sat motionless.

'And he didn't like it. That was the reason we broke up. He accused *me* of having affairs. Unbelievable. To him, sex didn't count. It just didn't. It was a purely physical act. It was like an itch, he said, the worst itch you could get, an itch that absolutely had to be scratched. But it was the so-called affairs I was having that were the problem. Not his itch. But to me, I couldn't have one without the other. To me it was more than a bloody itch. Am I making you both uncomfortable?'

'So, he wasn't himself lately,' Beck said, ignoring the question.

'No, like I said. And he'd started coming round here, begging me to take him back. He said he had realised the futility of one-dimensional relationships. That he was tired of it all. He wanted what we once had. He was very upset. I told him he needed to see a doctor. I was worried for him.'

'In what way,' Beck asked, 'were you worried for him?'

'He rang yesterday morning and sounded particularly upset. He said a girl had been killed. I couldn't understand why he was so upset about it. He didn't know her, I don't think he did anyway. It seemed to have affected him in some way. I'd never seen him like that before. I was concerned, that's it. I don't know why, I just was.' She dropped her voice. 'But I told him it was too late for any of that. I told him I loved my new life. And I had him to thank for it, because in a way, he had liberated me, from myself that is. If you see what I mean?'

She fell silent.

'Do you know who may have done this?' Claire asked.

And then it happened. While they weren't paying attention, the wave had crept up and now smashed to shore, curling onto the sand, the white spray exploding into a white mist that stretched to the sky. Her face was lost in her hands, as she slumped back onto the couch, and a cry of anguish came up from the very depths of her soul as she cried:

'Ah Gerry. God in heaven. Ah Gerry.'

CHAPTER FIFTY

Maurice Crabby stood in the doorway, looking up at the camera on the wall, and pressed the buzzer. The automatic door slid open and he entered. It was a different world inside too from what he remembered. Unrecognisable. The wood-panelled walls and floors, the high ceilings where voices carried and echoed, the screams from hidden rooms and wards that swirled about the place, never ending, all gone. Inside the door were potted plants and armchairs spread about the vast foyer. Like a hotel. But no matter, here would always be a place of misery and fear for him, where the ghosts of inmates – not patients – flittered about the corridors and dark places, shuffling in white gowns, always shuffling, a slow procession of madness. This was the place the big detective had taken his mother to on that night, back in 1954.

He thought again of her sitting at the table, in her brightly coloured coat and that hat that tilted to the side. As if she was going out somewhere for the day. But it was here she was going to. And it was here that she had been ever since. But no one cared. She was of the Clachán. An outcast. As they all were. Who remembered them or cared less? No one, that was the answer.

A smiling figure in a blue skirt and jacket appeared before him. Her name was prominent on a badge fixed to the lapel of the jacket: *Lucinda*.

'Are you a nurse?' he asked. 'Your badge doesn't say.'

'Yes. Our name tags are generic. We do not refer to ourselves by title. It seems to help the residents. Lucinda Nally. Resident house nurse.'

Maurice detected a trace of a Scottish accent.

'I didn't tell Kathleen you were coming. The last time you never showed, you know. She was upset.'

He noted her use of the term residents, not patients, or inmates. *Residents*. Like a hotel.

'The last time. I wanted to come. Really. I just… *couldn't.*'

She gave a faint smile, but didn't comment any further.

'The first time I came here was with my father,' Crabby said softly. 'He had returned from England.' Crabby pointed vaguely behind him, towards the windows. 'There used to be a gate out there, covered in wire mesh, and a small gate house set into the wall. For a man. In a uniform. A security man.'

The nurse looked at him strangely.

'My father banged on the door,' Crabby said. 'We waited ages before someone came and opened it. It was a nun. She reminded me of a great big bat with its wings folded standing before us with her cowl wrapped about her. She didn't apologise for having kept us waiting. She said we could stay only a short while and to wipe our feet on the way in. I remember she had a big bunch of keys. She brought us to my mother's room. It was at the end of a long, dank corridor up two flights of stone stairs. I'll never forget the sound of the key in the lock. It clanged and echoed. And there she was sitting on the edge of the bed, the white of its sheet folded back over the coarse-haired blanket. Her bare feet were on the stone floor, her hands crossed on her lap.'

Crabby's voice faltered as he fought back tears.

'It's getting late now,' the nurse said, laying a hand gently on his arm. 'I'd ask you not to stay long. Routine is very important.'

But it was the bat's voice that echoed in his head, *'You will take care not to mention any talk of taking her away from St. Bridget's. Do not be putting notions into her head now.'*

'… Mr Crabby?'

Maurice focused his eyes.

'What? Oh, I'm sorry.'

'You looked…'

'Please, can I see her now?'

She looked at him, as if deciding.

'Yes, of course,' she said.

He followed her along a corridor, the walls covered in brightly coloured murals, of beaches and twinkling blue seas, glorious sunrises. A world of make-believe. A visual tranquilizer. At the end of the corridor they stopped at a door, number 43 on it.

'Wait here a moment please, thank you.'

She tapped on the door gently, then opened it a little and squeezed in, taking care that Maurice couldn't be seen from the inside. The door closed again with a soft clumping sound.

Alone in the corridor, Maurice was struck by the utter silence. It was so silent it almost hurt his ears.

And then the door opened, and Lucinda Nally stood to one side, smiling.

He entered. She was sitting by a window that no longer had bars across it. The curtains were open, a garden of cut grass, flowerbeds and shrubs framed behind the glass. Everything pretty, bright colours, anything that was dark forbidden. He stared at the little old lady seated next to the window, looking at him now. Her face was small, the features sharp, her white hair gathered behind her head in a bun. She wore a pretty dress printed with a butterfly design.

'Mother,' he said, the word catching in his throat, tears coming to his eyes now.

CHAPTER FIFTY-ONE

They had been concerned about leaving Jacinta O'Reilly alone. They offered to wait until someone came round, but she insisted they go, that she needed time alone. So they did.

Beck's phone rang as they reached the car, the screen showing Private Number. It seemed the only certainty about the uncertainty of Natalia ringing was that the timing would be all wrong. He ignored it, pressed the red termination button, finished the cigarette he'd lit as soon as he'd left the house and got into the car.

'You were never married, were you?' Claire asked, opening the window and starting the engine. She drove along to the end of the driveway, pausing before moving onto the road.

Beck still hadn't answered.

'Well, were you?'

'What?'

'Married. Were you ever married? Just curious.'

'No. I told you that before. Never married.'

'Hhmmm,' changing gear, the question unresolved.

'Don't you ever want to get married?'

What is this?

'Can we talk about it another time, Claire?'

'Of course. I was just wondering, that's all, about people, who don't get married. I was thinking, is it because they don't need someone in their lives? Is that it? A part of me wishes I could be like that.'

'Just curious in return,' Beck said. 'Where did you meet Lucy Grimes?'

'Well,' she said, becoming silent for a moment, thinking. 'It was Dublin. I was new to the city. A country girl, a redneck, wet behind the ears, call it what you will. I wanted to experiment. To splash whatever colours I chose onto a blank canvas... Make sense?'

'Makes sense,' Beck said.

'I wanted to understand who I was. Dublin was more than a freedom for me, it was a liberation. You see, I thought I liked boys, but it was such an effort. So I didn't bother trying any more. I didn't want to hide is what I'm saying, so I just went for it. I could be myself. I didn't have to bully...'

'Bully?

'Yes,' Claire said. 'Makes me squirm when I think about it. In school, with the others, just to belong. I was part of a gang. Nothing heavy, just name calling. Just... Jesus. That's bad enough. Usually we picked on the pretty ones, the nice, sweet sensitive girls, the girls we perceived a threat to our collective fragile ego. 'Hey dyke bitch,' stuff like that. I was such a stereotype. I was really talking about myself. Looking back, I hated myself. Because those girls were definitely not lesbians. I was. But I couldn't deal with it. I was in the closet, hiding from nobody but myself. I owe a lot of people apologies from back then, if I ever meet them again that is.' Claire sighed. 'Anyway. In Dublin. Freedom. Total. Complete. Beautiful freedom. I didn't just put my foot into the water, I jumped in, and to where it was deepest and wildest, and was swept along, allowing it to take me wherever it willed. The lipstick-femmes liked me – that's girly lesbians, Beck. Hey, am I making you feel uncomfortable?'

'No,' Beck said. 'It's quite a story. Continue.'

'And I liked them,' Claire continued. 'I got quite the reputation, and I gloried in it. They liked me even more because of it. But Lucy Grimes was the one. Gregarious, spontaneous, funny and gorgeous – a perfect woman. I met her at a crime scene, Beck, to

finally answer your question. She was freelancing for a daily newspaper. I was on sentry duty. We got chatting. The rest is history.'

They stopped at a junction and turned right for Cross Beg. The
sun was low in the sky now, suspended by the top of the cathedral
steeple that looked down on the black slated roofs of the town. The
road dipped and curved on its approach, following the contours
of the land instead of any direct route, laid down for donkeys and
pony traps rather than cars and trucks.

'Hhmm,' Beck said. 'You're lucky, to have found someone you
love, and who loves you in return. That's the perfect hand, better
than any pair of aces. It's what we're all hot-wired to do, isn't it?
To find someone we want to be with. Yes, we all want that. But
then, of course, being human, we usually go and mess it all up.'

'Speak for yourself, Beck?'

He thought of Natalia. And knew again, that it was a fallacy,
an illusion, that he was fooling himself. Because he didn't want
someone he could be with. He wanted someone he *couldn't* be
with. He wanted to be with Natalia, yes, but he didn't want to be
with her either. He didn't want to *be* with her, he didn't want to
be with anyone. He couldn't even *be* with himself.

He looked out the window as they passed the roadside sign
that announced 'Welcome to Cross Beg'. A little further on the
road became Main Street. Beck noticed two TV satellite trucks
parked against the kerb, a film crew on the street, cameraman
and reporter. He watched the reporter approach a woman who
stopped to talk to them.

'One more day,' Beck said. 'That's what they'll give us, before
they turn their attention on us, before we become the story, and
they'll be down on us like the proverbial ton of bricks.'

Claire turned into the car park of the station and parked next
to the custody door, where prisoners were brought in and out.
She cut the engine.

In the Ops Room he went with her to her desk, glancing over at Sergeant Connor who had just come in from the public office. He stopped by the window and looked out. The weather had dropped a couple of degrees today. The sky was edged by soft grey clouds. He could see through the gaps in the buildings outside a window to the mountains in the distance, partially obscured behind a grey mist.

'The rain is coming,' he said.

CHAPTER FIFTY-TWO

She smelled of soap and antiseptic when Crabby embraced her. She did not get up, so he had to bend down. He could feel her slender back beneath his hands, her ribcage brittle like dried wood. She reached up and touched his shoulders briefly, before she took her hands away again and held them once more in her lap.

She did not tell him to take a seat. She did not say anything. He could see it in her eyes. Hurt. And a brooding anger.

'Did they tell you I was no longer for this world or something? Well, I'm healthy as an auld trout you'll be sad to know.'

The remark rubbed against his conscience like rough sandpaper. He stood there, his hands by his side, like a little boy again.

After a moment she cleared her throat, dropped her head and turned her eyes up to look at him. Like a sly observation. Then, deciding that he had been suitably chastised, she parted her lips into a weak smile.

'At least you didn't forget me completely *a grá*. Thank you for the hampers. Will you put an extra box of biscuits in next time? I share them out with the others.'

He went to the bed. It had a foam headboard and two pillows, a beige-coloured duvet. He thought of the coarse wool blanket of before. Maurice sat down on the bed uninvited.

'You look well,' she said. 'In fact, I'd say you haven't changed a bit, but then that'd be a lie. You have changed. It's been a year after all. Did you have to go so long without seeing me? Ashamed are you? Of your own mother? *A grá* it breaks my heart.'

And in that little question was piled the rubbish, the detritus, the broken bits of… himself.

Yes! I am ashamed.

But he didn't say that.

'There's been another one,' he said.

She was reaching to the top of the dresser beside her bed, searching for something, her eyes narrowing in concentration.

'What did you say?'

'There's been another one. You probably heard.'

She found it, a radio bingo book.

'I heard nothing. I don't listen to the news. I don't read a newspaper. The world outside these walls does not exist to me. What do I care about news? They've got what?'

'I didn't say they got. I said there's been another one. A baby. Disappeared.'

She was holding the bingo book between two slender fingers, lifting it from the dresser. She dropped it now, withdrew her hand onto her lap.

Her voice was a whisper. 'Whose baby? Where?'

'Her name is Samantha Power. She had the baby in the car with her. The baby is gone.'

'What car? Where, I asked you?'

'By our village. By Kelly's Forge. The car was found. The mother was in it, but the baby wasn't.'

'When was this?'

'Tuesday.'

'The poor craytur. No sign of the child at all at all?'

'No, just disappeared.'

Her face crumpled, her eyes looking down into the tunnel of years that had passed, stepping into it now, going back in time. He could tell she was reliving it. Her eyes widened, snapping back into the present, throwing away the bloody cloak of memories that attempted to shroud her.

'Where is the mother?'

'She's dead.'

She looked at him.

'How so?'

'She was murdered.'

The old woman took an intake of breath and brought her hands to her face.

'Why have you come here?' the sound muffled behind her fingers.

'It was I who found the body.'

She took her hands away from her face again, looked at him with that same strange look.

'Why have you come here?' she asked once more, the voice insistent.

'Because I am afraid.'

'What are you afraid of?'

'That they will…'

She laughed aloud.

'That you will end up in here. In the room down the hall from me. Wouldn't that be nice? Serve you right. So, you didn't come here out of concern for me. You came here out of concern for yourself.'

He couldn't say anything to that. Because it was true.

'They'll do more than that to you my boy, you can be certain of it. *You* found the body, is it?'

'Yes.'

'And you worry you'll end up in the Big House. The Loony Bin. What about the prison, did you ever think of that?'

'What do you mean?'

She looked tired all of a sudden, very tired. She sucked in her cheeks and her eyes became her face, oversized, staring at him, the flesh around them like burnt, dry clay.

'You look more and more like your father, do you know that?' she said. 'He left me to rot in here as well. They all did. Kathleen's in the Big House and her name is never to be mentioned. Did he ever contact you again? No, he didn't, did he? I can tell by the look in your eyes. You're like your father. Selfish. Made a clean break of it so he did. After that one time when he came to see me, bringing you with him.'

'He did stay in contact,' Maurice whispered. 'But he and uncle Paddy never got on.'

'Ha, my brother Paddy was the one who took you in. Not your father.'

It suited them, he wanted to say, they had no children of their own. I worked every hour under God's sun for that pair. I was just another animal along with the donkey and the plough horse, just another beast of burden.

'They say I killed a baby,' she said, narrowing her eyes. 'Do you think that's true?'

'I saw Mícheál Peoples take her into the forest.'

'You saw it?'

'Yes. Did you think I didn't? Is that why you never mentioned it all these years?'

'It was cursed that place. Better off that it rotted into the ground. We were all cursed living there. Even you. It was not just I who took the baby into the forest. There were others. Your sister was sick, Patrick.' For the first time she had used his name. His proper Christian name. Patrick. 'Weak children didn't live long in Kelly's Forge. The winters culled them. She'd had pneumonia. Her lungs were weak. She was coughing and coughing. In such pain. She was never going to get better, not back then. Slowly she was dying before our very eyes. It was a release for her, her passing. On that night she was coughing up blood. It never stopped. I was covered in it. She was so, so pale. Mícheál Peoples decided. He was the village elder. We trusted him, and he decided that he would take her into the forest. Make her better, or let the forest take her. I followed them though. It was over in minutes. They offered her to the forest. And it was not the first time a sacrifice had been made. Later they said she was freed from suffering. Micheál Peoples promised the village would be freed from sickness. From calamity. For a while at least. Until the next time…

Crabby felt the energy evaporating from his body, leaving it like a hollow shell. He felt as if he could collapse onto the floor and disintegrate into a million different pieces. His mouth was dry, as if coated in sand.

'What? She died in the wood? She was offered? A sacrifice? What are you talking about?'

'She was coughing blood. But it wasn't the same. They needed a sacrifice. A blood sacrifice. They cut her throat.'

Crabby got to his feet, but he felt his legs could not carry his weight, so he sat on the bed again.

'Are you completely and utterly crazy? You really are, aren't you. You're crazy.'

'Bernadette,' she said. 'Your baby sister. That's what happened to her. The big policeman was right all along. I was half-deranged with the grief. They thought it was me. Of course. But it wasn't. It was the others. It was the way of the village. Outsiders knew nothing of our ways, there were rumours of course, and gossip, mutterings as we passed by on the street, but no one knew, and what's more, no one cared.'

'No. I don't believe it. You crazy bitch.'

'Now. You tell this crazy bitch. Did you kill that girl? It's in you, I have no doubt.'

The way she asked. Direct. Cold. In your face.

His own mother.

Maurice leaned forward, twisting his hands together. He dropped his head, kept it there.

She waited for an answer. He slowly got to his feet again, walked tentatively to the door, turned, stared at her.

'Maybe I did kill her. Maybe I ripped her throat open. All that fresh, hot blood. Would you be proud of me, mother? Another sacrifice too, in a way.'

His mother showed no emotion, her eyes still, unblinking. But then she slowly contorted her lips into a twisted smile.

Crabby opened the door and stepped out of the room, closed it gently, and walked away.

CHAPTER FIFTY-THREE

Danny tugged on the peak of his baseball cap.

'It's not so bad,' he said, looking round. 'But you don't have plans, do you?'

Vicky laughed.

'Yes, I do, Danny. They're in my head, that's all'

He removed the baseball cap and scratched his head, put it back on again. Both doors and all the windows in the old single storey house were open, a cool evening breeze blowing through. He pointed to the ceiling.

'What's going to happen with that? It's just rotted plyboard.'

She moved to the table in the centre of the room. It was covered in papers and home improvement magazines. She leaned over it. 'Come here. See this.' She fished out a sheet of paper and pushed it across the table towards him.

Danny didn't look at it. He was looking down her shirt.

Vicky smiled, waited a moment, then straightened.

'This is going to be one big room, pre-production facilities over there,' she pointed. 'And over there…'

'Whoa, whoa, whoa,' Danny said. 'Pre-production what? I thought you said this was a house renovation. That I can do, but…'

Vicky placed her hands on her wide hips, stuck her chest out.

'You know I do TV work, Danny, I freelance for production companies all the time.'

Danny shrugged. He didn't know the ins and outs of it.

'Anyway, Danny, this girl has plans of her own. Pre-production is just a fancy name for fixtures and fitting. The real work takes place in Dublin, at a facility there. Look at my drawings, please.'

Danny looked down now, his eyes running slowly over the neatly drawn plans.

'OK, seems straightforward enough, seems doable' he said after a while. He looked around again. 'The walls have to come out.' And looking up. 'And that ceiling too, and the new one will need to be raised. I'll need help with this, the roof especially.'

Vicky smiled again.

'Danny,' she said sweetly. 'Speaking of help. There's something else that you can help me with.'

His eyes fell away from the roof and settled on her. He suddenly looked like a little boy.

'Is there,' he said. 'And what's that?'

'You've heard of *Angela's Ashes*, Danny, haven't you?' Vicky said, clearing away papers from the table top and placing a mug of coffee down in front of him.

He picked it up and took a sip, cradled it in his hands.

'No, I haven't,' he said.

'Well, suffice to say, it's an epic of woe, in the tradition of Irish suffering, if I can put it like that.'

A vacant look crossed Danny's face.

'I'm going to do something similar, Danny,' she said. 'But centred on Cross Beg, on recent developments, and old ones too…'

'Can I be honest, Vicky,' Danny said. 'But you've lost me.'

'I'm going to make a documentary about what happened in 1954, Danny. Remember, a baby disappeared. And I'm going to tie it in with what's happening now, with Samantha Power's baby, and how she was murdered. I'm going to build a chronicle between the past and present, a crossover if you will, between the *History Channel* and *True Detective*. Something like that.'

Danny took a sip of coffee.

'Still lost,' he said. 'Anyway, that was a long time ago. There's no connection between the two, what happened then and now, is there? No one even remembers it.'

'No matter. Can't you see? It'll make for great TV. I'm going to use the current investigation as a backdrop. And I'm going to do some digging of my own.'

'Ah,' Danny said, 'like your one in *Murder She Wrote*. That the kind of thing you mean?'

'Yes, Danny, exactly… something like that anyway. And I need your help?'

His eyes widened. 'Me? How?'

Vicky paused, then continued, her voice low, conspiratorial.

'Samantha Power was in Crabby's supermarket before she was killed, I heard about it. I heard the cops were in there for ages looking at the CCTV. I want that footage, Danny.'

He frowned.

'I dunno, that's best left to the cops, Vicky… anyway, how am I supposed to help you get that?'

Vicky gave a vague smile. 'Because you do all the maintenance work right, don't you?'

Danny pursed his lips.

'I wouldn't call it maintenance work,' he said. 'More like bits and bobs. But it's regular. A couple of times a week. I'm due in there day after tomorrow in fact. Here, I don't want to upset Crabby now.'

Vicky gave Danny her best smile yet, moved around the table, closer to him.

'No one needs to know. I just want to get that CCTV. It's straightforward. You give me a ring when you're there, I go in and can have it all on a memory stick in seconds.' She ran an index finger over the back of his hand.

Danny looked down, but still, he shook his head.

'I don't like the sound of this,' he said. 'This sounds like trouble.'

'It's called investigative journalism,' Vicky said. 'And I'll win an award for it one day. Especially if the cops can't solve it, because you know what? I think I can.'

Danny angled his head to the side as he looked at her.

'What?' he said.

'I think I know who killed Samantha Power,' she said.

His eyes narrowed.

'You serious?'

She nodded.

'You've got to go to the gardai. You can't keep that to yourself. Who is it?'

'I can't say.'

'And what about the baby?... Ah no, Vicky, you've got to go to the cops.'

She shook her head.

'No I don't. I've got nothing, no real evidence anyway. But the way this is going, I'll have it solved before they do.'

Danny shook his head, as if none of this was making sense.

'What about the baby? The poor baby?'

'That's a conundrum I can't explain. Not right now.'

'This is too crazy. I don't think...'

She reached out and held his hand gently, squeezed it, took a step closer. Her face was inches from his. She was wearing a belted skirt, the buckle touching the buckle of his jeans, a dull, soft metallic chiming sound.

'No it's not, Danny, trust me, okay?'

Danny smiled. 'OK, I trust you.'

Vicky laughed, took a step back.

'I knew you would,' she said.

CHAPTER FIFTY-FOUR

Beck carried Claire's suitcase into the house and up the stairs to the spare bedroom.

'Thank you. And thank you for insisting.'

'That's okay,' he said.

She was referring on his insistence on leaving the station, of leaving work behind. Delegation, he had said; the belief that others can carry out and execute a task. There was a night shift coming on duty. That is why the job was split into shifts, a seamless transfer of duties and functions.

'Are you ambitious?' he asked her now as an afterthought.

She looked about the bedroom. It was simple; wardrobe, bed, bedside table.

'I wasn't. Well, I was. But then I wasn't, that's what I mean to say. But I think I will be again. To get purpose, you know, back into my life. Can I tell you something?'

He was hoping now she wouldn't, he wanted to make a meeting.

'Of course,' but without enthusiasm.

'I know this isn't the right time. But I just need to get it off my chest. We were trying for a child. For three years actually. Since before we got married. Don't look at me like that.'

'Like what?'

'Like that. Like you think it wasn't a very good idea.'

'I'm not thinking that. You are. I'm thinking that I'd like to make a meeting, that's all. An AA meeting.'

The news brought no reaction. Had he already told her he was going to AA? He couldn't remember.

'We went to Spain,' ignoring it. 'To a clinic. We could have done it here. But it's less expensive there. They cover more options too. They organised everything. A donor. Blood tests. It was all very straightforward. Until it didn't work. So we tried again. And again. Or should I say, Lucy actually tried again. We thought that was better. She's five years younger than me.'

Claire swallowed a number of times in quick succession, her voice wavering.

'Claire. You don't have to tell me any of this, you know.'

A flash of anger.

'Why, don't you like hearing it? Or is it that you just couldn't be bothered?'

'Not at all,' Beck said.

The truth was, it was a bit of both. He hoped she wouldn't start crying. The last time had used up all his reserves of emotional empathy. *You're so up your own arsehole, Beck, do you know that?*

'I need to tell it,' she said. 'For myself. I need to make sense of it. So you're going to have to listen. Not a very appreciative guest, am I?'

Beck determined that he would listen. He crossed the room to the window, looked out.

'You have a view,' he said. 'You'd never believe it, but there was supposed to be a public garden out there. All weeds now. From here it doesn't look so bad.' He turned. 'Go on.'

Yes, he would listen, for no other reason than to be there for someone who was prepared to open the valve and not, like himself for instance, have it explode in his face.

'It all changed after that,' she went on. She remained standing at the door. Rigid. Formal. To sit would add a cosiness to this that didn't belong. 'I wanted to forget about it. Move on. We still had each other, right? That's how I was looking at it. But Lucy wanted to try again. *Again!* And since it hadn't worked for her, she wanted me to be the one to carry the baby. But I couldn't go through with it. I just couldn't.'

She allowed herself to lean against the door now and bit her lower lip.

'We're constantly rowing' Claire said. 'It's just constant. We say we'll stop arguing. But we never do. We just start all over again. We can't help ourselves. One word. That's all it takes. And we're at it. She's said some things… things I can't forgive. I can't take it any more. I really can't. I want it to stop. And… she scares me a bit sometimes. If I wasn't sure about carrying a baby, I'm *really* not sure about bringing it into a house where every word is said in anger. So we need a break. From each other. To give us time.'

Beck thought of Natalia. The illicit rendezvous. Her guilt afterwards. *'We have to stop,'* she'd say. *'This is the last time'.* But it never did stop. Because that was the buzz for both of them. The fact it was illicit. The fact they shouldn't be doing it. The fact they shouldn't be together. It was just another way for him to escape. Maybe if he could turn the handle, open the valve, just like Claire was doing here, run a little steam off. The meetings at the top of the rickety stairs in Ozanam House weren't doing that for him. He doubted they ever would. But he'd give it one more try anyway.

CHAPTER FIFTY-FIVE

Beck noted the looks when he went into the room. He closed the door gently, looking about for a chair. He spotted one, against the far wall. He walked towards it, the room falling silent as he crossed. The floor creaked with each step he took. Beck could feel a collective contempt for him that far outweighed the mere act of being late and disturbing the meeting. Since he'd started coming here, he'd never once been on time. He reached the chair and sat down. Another glance from someone, and a voice sounded, warning the room that tardiness was a symptom of carelessness that led to relapse. Satisfied, the meeting continued.

At the top table, behind a row of AA slogans – *Keep Coming Back, A Day At A Time, Keep It Simple* – sat Vicky, telling her story. She glanced at Beck and nodded. Beck could see Joe in the front row, half turning, before stopping, seemingly resisting the urge to look back.

'… I was on that misery-go-round that we all know about, just one never-ending misery fest. It's usually the man who's the alcoholic in the relationship, right? There are women, but it's usually the man? Right? But in my marriage it was me. My ex-husband was a good man, but he didn't know what he'd gotten himself into, God love him. He walked up the aisle with this cutie – if I say so myself – and woke up with Godzilla.'

The room laughed. Laughter in the face of misery. The more miserable, the greater the laugh. Which made Beck wonder if there didn't exist an attraction for rolling in the gutter again for these people? *These people?* That included him. If nothing else, it would always make for a good story at a later meeting.

'And when I drank it was lights out. Literally. I'd never remember anything. I got into all sorts of situations. Did things I'm not proud of. And my husband stuck by me. Even having my kids didn't stop me. Nothing did. And he stayed by my side through it all, through thick and thin. He was always there for me. The strange thing is, when I finally got sober, you know what I did? I left him. That's what I did. Funny old world, isn't it.'

The room broke into laughter again, but more energetic this time, like the comedian had told a cracker. Beck had to admit, the punch line had gone above his head.

She spoke for another quarter hour. A verbal collage of black-outs, bar-room fights, infidelities, car crashes, arrests, lost opportunities, each paling into the other. When she'd finished, the meeting was opened to the floor. And so it continued, stories from the misery-go-round, each more miserable and fantastic than the one gone before. He was asked to share, but Beck declined. The contempt was back again briefly, but was then swept along by the next story.

'Anyone else?' Vicky asked the room when it eventually fell silent. 'We have a couple of minutes left if there's anyone who would like to share.'

'G'evening. My name's Mikey. And I'm an alcoholic.'

Beck turned. Mikey was seated at the far end of the room against the wall.

'I've been in Australia ten years now. But I'm originally from Cross Beg. Australia's been good to me. It's given me back my self respect. I'm home on holiday. It's my first time back. Ever. But something terrible's happened. My sister, Samantha, she's the one was found dead the other day.' A murmur went through the room. 'Aye, the girl never had it easy. Always made wrong choices see. Just like me. But at least I got a second chance, to learn how to choose to make the right ones. She never did, I guess. That's what AA taught me. I don't remember my last drink, but I'll never forget it. It was here, in Cross Beg. I woke up in a police cell. They'd beaten me, the coppers. They did that back then.' He shot a look at Beck, meeting him square in the eyes, held them, before looking away. 'But I gotta thank them too. If it weren't for the coppers, I'd never have left this town. I'd still be here, hangin' round, drawing the dole, fucked up and miserable. Aye. But I got out. I got out. It's good to be here, thanks for listening.'

When Beck looked back to the top table, Vicky was watching him, and their eyes met, briefly, before she looked away. Again, he wasn't certain. But he thought he caught it, he wasn't sure what.

But *something*.

Mikey was smoking a cigarette on the street outside when Beck came through the front door of Ozanam House.

'I thought you might be in this club,' he said. 'Coppers have a lot to feel guilty about. Guess that's why they drink, eh?'

Beck smiled. 'Don't you ever give it a rest? That's a great bloody rock on your shoulder. Not a chip.' Mikey clamped his cigarette between his lips and flipped open the pack he was holding, held it out to Beck. Beck took a cigarette and looked at it. 'If I was in your shoes,' he said, 'I'd be the same way too. This menthol?'

'Yey, mate, it is.'

Mikey offered him his lighter. Beck took it, lit the cigarette and handed it back.

'Thanks.' He took a long draw. 'We're doing everything we can, Mikey,' he said, blowing out a thick stream of smoke. 'I'd like you to understand that.'

'Yey. But it's fucking raw, y'know?'

Beck nodded.

Mikey flicked the stub of his cigarette away. He smiled.

'You're not too bad for a bloody copper. Mum's out of the hospital. I'll give her your regards.'

Mikey zipped his padded jacket and turned up the collar.

'They call this a heatwave, mate,' he said. 'More like bloody autumn, if you ask me.'

Beck watched as he walked away, and checked the time. Gumbell would be waiting.

CHAPTER FIFTY-SIX

The tinkling chimes of a piano filled the lounge in the Brown Water Inn. The music was subtle but commanding, filling the entire space with a soothing audio glow. The carpet was luscious, and the lounge was filled with what looked like antique settees and armchairs. Floor lamps were placed strategically throughout, just enough to offer an aura of yellow light, a sort of aurora borealis. The bar was a horse-shoe shape against the wall at one end, without stools to discourage lingering. Shapes sat on the settees and armchairs, and others in white shirts and red waistcoats flittered about, carrying trays and putting down drinks, but it was difficult to discern anything, the place was like a hall of mirrors.

'Give me a double cognac and a bottle of chilled lager. Make sure it's chilled now.'

'Of course, sir.'

'Beck, what do you want?'

'A ginger-ale.'

Gumbell guffawed.

'No. A real drink, Beck. You've seen the alternative. Alcohol fundamentalism. You don't want to end up like that, do you? An insufferable dry drunk.'

As opposed to an insufferable wet drunk?

'A. Gin. Ger. Ale. Thank you.'

'You really are serious, aren't you?'

'Yes.'

When the drinks arrived, Gumbell took a long swallow of cognac. It was in a balloon glass, but it could have been in an old shoe.

After a while, Gumbell spoke, voice much calmer now.

'I'll be conducting an autopsy on the body tomorrow. Of Inspector O'Reilly. I deem it necessary. I want to make sure he wasn't made to drink weed killer, or something like that. That would be a double whammy. A bit of, ahem, overkill. Not trying to be funny, old boy.'

Beck could tell the alcohol had already shorn away the sharpest edges from Gumbell.

'I see,' he said.

'But I doubt it,' Gumbell said. 'Never struck me as the particularly thorough type.'

Beck swirled the ice cubes in his glass before taking a sip. Without the alcohol, the ginger ale tasted insipid, cowering on his tongue. It had no reason for existence on God's green earth without a brandy in it. The only other purpose was to give the impression a person had a real drink in their hands. Like now.

'How long have you been going to those bloody meetings anyway?' Gumbell asked.

'You said not to mention it.'

'Just answer the bloody question.'

'Couple of weeks.'

'Do they actually make you feel any better?'

'Actually...'

'Bad bender was it?' Gumbell interrupted before he could finish. 'Your knee hit anything else while you jerked it up?'

Beck put his glass down on the little oval-shaped holder attached to his chair. It slid in and out of the armrest. Original, he considered.

'Is it the same person, do you think?' Beck asked.

'This throat-slitting you mean?'

'No, the bloody Zodiac Killer. Who'd you think I mean?'

'Steady on there, Beck. You're very tetchy. Get yourself a drink and settle yourself down. Good man.'

Beck got to his feet.

The State Pathologist gave a rare smile. 'Just call a waiter, they'll do it for you.'

'I'm not getting a drink. I'm bloody leaving.'

'Be like that then.'

'Shouldn't have bothered coming here in the first place.'

'Toodle-oo, you're a miserable bastard tonight anyway. No company for a refined gentleman such as myself.'

'And my question. As to whether it's the same person?'

'I don't know. Not yet. But when I do… Now leave me alone to enjoy my drink.'

As Beck walked away, Gumbell's words trailed after him: 'Self-righteous fecker.'

Beck ordered a taxi at reception and went outside to wait for it. He lit a cigarette and held it next to his mouth, taking short, frequent puffs.

'Penny for them.'

He turned. And did a double take. Coming through the door: Vicky.

'Didn't expect to see you here,' she said.

'Nor I you.'

'AA open meeting coming up soon. Needed to finalise some details.'

She didn't ask why he was there.

'I was meeting a friend,' he offered anyway.

'A female friend?' with a coy smile.

He realised he'd smoked his cigarette down to the filter. He stubbed it out in the ashtray on the wall.

'No. Very much the opposite.'

She smiled again, not coy this time, brushing a hand through her hair.

'You didn't make it to Frazzali's.'

He nodded towards the hotel.

'I know,' she said, 'your friend. Look. I'd better be on my way. See you at the next meeting, hopefully.'

He felt disappointment. That something he'd thought he'd felt wasn't a *something* after all.

She moved past him, was about to step from the pavement onto the hotel car park. She stopped.

'Are you waiting for somebody?' she asked.

'I'm waiting on a taxi.'

Again, the smile. A return to coy. He could get lost in it.

'Ridiculous. I'll give you a lift. Come on.'

She drove a two-year-old Mercedes. Her perfume filled the car. And there was something else. He felt it immediately. Like a static charge. The car seemed to fizzle with it, radiating from her. He noted the curve of her hand around the steering wheel, the glow from the dash on the lower portion of her face, the lipstick on the folds of her lips glistening in the faint light, like rain on a night-time street.

She drove fast. Beck watched the lights outside flash by. Up ahead, the street lamps of Cross Beg came into view in the near distance, a chain of orange glows on either side of the road, meandering into the town. The pitch of the engine changed, the car slowing down.

'The town of secrets,' she said, adding, with a soft laugh, 'my secrets.' She looked at him. 'Are you good at keeping secrets?'

'Not very good,' he answered. 'Secrets I mean. Are they?'

'But necessary,' she said, softly, as if to herself, then, her voice solemn. 'Any developments in the investigation, if you don't mind my asking?'

'I don't mind you asking. It's progressing, is what I'll say.'

'Not giving anything away then, are you?' she said.

'No,' Beck replied, an edge to his voice now, a hardness that hadn't been there before. 'I'm not.'

Silence.

After a moment, Vicky turned the steering wheel, moving from the road.

Beck strained and made out the sheen of grey light ahead. As they drew closer he realised the sheen was water. It was a lake. She turned from the road onto a rutted track and then there was the crunch as the tyres moved over pebbles. The car stopped by a water's edge. Vicky turned off the engine.

'You never once asked where I was taking you?'

'I didn't care.'

She laughed, tugging with both hands at the front of her shirt. The stud buttons popped apart. He was looking at a black lace bra with two brimming breasts. The static in the car changed, morphing into an energy. Charging through their bodies.

An energy. Called lust.

Later, he asked Vicky to drop him off at the top of Main Street. He wanted to walk home he explained. But he didn't need to explain. Vicky didn't ask. Because Vicky didn't really care.

'You'll be at the next meeting,' she said, but it wasn't a question.

What it really said was, *See you around.*

Beck watched the car disappear along the brightly lit street.

The air was warm. A rare epoch in a cold, rain-soaked land. Cross Beg looked pretty during the summer months. Even the empty buildings and the upper façades of all of those along Main Street, normally grubby and faded, with cracked windows and mottled curtains stuck to glass panes, looked fresh behind that explosion of colour from their hanging flower baskets. Beck noted that the buildings seemed naturally brighter during the warm summers, the yellow and purple streaks left by the winter storms fading like the colour of an old bruise. Passing the Hibernian Hotel two men in baseball hats and bandanas, one wearing a sweatshirt with 'I'm a 1%'er' across the front, were smoking cigars. They spoke in that loud confident way of Americans.

As Beck passed, one of them said in a slurred around the edges voice, 'Hi there, buddy.'

'Good night,' Beck said, and walked on.

He thought of Inspector O'Reilly. He thought of Samantha Power. He thought of baby Róisín. And he thought that somewhere out there on this night was the person responsible. He wondered what that person was doing right now? At this very moment? Were they sleeping, free of guilt, incapable of feeling remorse for what they had done? Or were they awake, tortured by the memories.

It was late. He needed sleep. He walked on, along the deserted street.

CHAPTER FIFTY-SEVEN

Maurice Crabby did not go home. Where was home anyway? Kelly's Forge? Cross Beg? St. Bridget's?

He drove north west, towards the ocean, and along the coast road, passing through darkened sleeping villages, the white of the breakers visible on his left even in the darkness. Near Ballyvaughan he turned onto a track that ended in the dunes of a beach. He turned off the engine, and he could hear the clinking noises of it as it cooled. He opened the window and could hear the sea, a rhythmic breathing of water on sand.

It was as dark as that night, that night when it had all started. And when, in a sense, it had all finished too. He watched through the windscreen the gentle curls of white over the tops of the dunes that were the waves breaking on the shore.

His own mother. The thought would not leave him. His own mother.

He began, again, to cry.

He squeezed the steering wheel, tighter and tighter, until he could feel his nails biting into the flesh on the underside of it. He opened the door and got out, looking at the sky. There was nothing in that blackness. Not a star. Nothing.

And then he looked to the sea again, to the faint flashes of the white wave tops. And began to walk towards it. Through the dunes, losing sight of the ocean momentarily, and then re-emerging, there it was, a little way ahead, across the beach. The tide was in, the dark ocean, mysterious, unquantifiable. He closed his eyes and listened to its breathing, and, as if in a trance, slowly began walking ahead. He did not open his eyes again until the sound of the waves were loud and seemed to surround him. And when he did, finally, the water was lapping at his feet. Before it he felt his insignificance. Another step, into the water. It would be easy. So easy. To just walk into it, become lost. Forever.

Crabby took another step.

CHAPTER FIFTY-EIGHT

Beck turned the key, pushing open the door, stepped into the hallway. He was tired, suddenly so very tired. He climbed the stairs in the darkness and made his way to his bedroom, pulling the curtains and unbuttoning his shirt at the same time. He piled his clothes onto the floor by the bed, and climbed in. It wrapped itself around him and carried him away. Within seconds, the room was filled with the sounds of his stuttered snoring.

I have returned. Did you think I would just walk away? Forget all about you? Leave you in peace? I will never forget you. I will never leave you. Certainly not in peace. You ridiculous fool. You gobshite. You moron. You cretin. Now, take my hand you idiot, come with me.

Beck tossed his head from side to side on the pillow, his legs kicking beneath the duvet, trying to break free. He opened his mouth, a low croaking sound coming from it. But it was too late. The Scarecrow had him in his grasp. Who led the way quickly, dragging Beck behind, with that unmistakable smell of his wafting behind, of leather and soap. The ground held no difficulty for either of them, they seemed to float above the gorse and ditches. Beck recognised this place. He pulled on the hand that gripped him, his hand so small, like a child's, but the grip of the Scarecrow was too strong. They did not linger at Kelly's Forge, but continued on, over the ditches and on, disturbing the sleeping cows who opened their eyes but could see nothing, merely felt their presence passing them by. They stopped eventually at an ivy mountain, it seemed to rise forever, a wall that reached to the sky. He had seen this before, a glimpse, the other day, when he came to the wood. But now it didn't look like a wall, it looked like a living creature, its green, dark coat shimmering in the breeze.

A flash of lightning lit up the night sky, with it a sound, low and sharp. Yet it was not thunder. The lightning struck again, and so too with it came that sound. Higher now, more piercing. Beck felt the grip of the Scarecrow weaken. The lightning flashed once more and with it the sound came again. The grip almost non-existent now. Then gone.

Beck opened his eyes. He looked about the room, breathing rapidly. The light of the street lamps through the fabric of the curtains was a blue hue.

He turned his eyes and stared at the ceiling.

No, don't think.

He threw back the duvet and got up. He dressed and left the room, went down the hall and knocked on Claire's door. When she opened it he spoke.

'Don't ask any questions. Get dressed? We're going out.'

'Going out...' still not a question. Her eyes were alert, there were no cobwebs of recent sleep. Her eyes searched his, then she said, 'Give me a minute,' and the door began to close.

CHAPTER FIFTY-NINE

The trees are of birch, poplar, Norway spruce and in the centre a mighty ash almost 300 years old. It is cool here, and even on the hottest day it is shaded, the tree tops catching the sun like a web. This forgotten corner is hidden behind the remaining section of high stone wall that once formed part of the Kendrel estate boundary. The wall itself is almost hidden by wild bramble and bushes now. This spot is beautiful, peaceful. But so too is it eerie. The locals say it is more than eerie. They say it is haunted. They say the banshee prowls through the trees when darkness falls. Many have heard her, or so they claim, when her soft wailing sound wakes them from their sleep. Yet it is not a fearful sound. It is alluring. It is a sound that many want to follow. Some do, and they never return. They call this place, this piece of ground, the Banshee's Garden. It is the forgotten place. No one comes here. Ever. Not even teenagers for dares at Halloween. No, no one comes here.

It is silent, so deathly silent.

A fog had settled on the abandoned village, and as they crossed the ditch and walked along the overgrown track, the bushes and trees on either side crowded round like silent, ghostly, witnesses. The light from their torches cut hollows into the swirling air, and the crackling of the undergrowth beneath their feet was carried off into the darkness, the sound appearing much louder than during daylight. They continued through the remains of Kelly's Forge until they reached the end. It was surprising how quickly nature had reclaimed this place. Although the cottages had been constructed of dry stone, without mortar or cement, such dwellings can stand for centuries. But not here. Here, they had been skewered by the trunks of trees and weakened by their roots, leaving behind nothing but indistinct accumulations of stones and, though gable walls still stood, these were lost to ivy and foliage. Soon, there would be no trace left of the place called Kelly's Forge.

The ditch rose before them.

'We're going over that,' Beck said. 'Okay?'

Claire turned her torch to either side of it, illuminating the ghostly witnesses, the freakish trees, pointing at them with their spindly arms.

Beck used his free hand to grip a fuchsia branch. The grass was wet with dew and his feet slid as he grappled his way up. At the top, he leaned down and offered his hand to Claire. She ignored him, used the same branch to pull herself up.

They shone their torches into the field beyond, the eyes of the cows lying between the rushes, dots of yellow, reflecting back the light like laser beams between the rectangular glow of their ear tags.

Behind them, where the land sloped, the fog had cleared, and in the distance, scattered through the darkness, particles of light from houses and hamlets.

Beck turned left, the sound of his and Claire's feet as they walked through the grass a low swishing noise in the open air. They walked to another ditch, the sides sloping down to the bed of a dried stream bed. Was this the same stream he had encountered the other day? Beck wasn't certain. He calculated he could jump it. When he tried he landed short and slid to the bottom. The light of his torch revealed the dry bed veering right ahead of him.

'Can you get down here?'

For the first time, Claire's uncertainty began to change into resistance. She stood motionless.

'I'm getting second thoughts about this whole thing. Look at us. What are we doing here?'

'We're here now. Can you just come down?'

'No. You need to tell me.'

'Jesus Christ, Claire.'

'Tell me.'

Beck stepped forward, the sharp edges of the stones squeezing into the soles of his sneakers. He cursed for not having worn boots. He began walking away.

'Beck. Where the fuck are you going? Beck…'

Beck ignored her, continued on.

After a moment he heard the scraping sound as she clambered down the sides after him. He slowed, waiting for her to catch up.

They walked on in silence. The stream bank levelled out into a low impression strewn with mossy rocks and stones. Beyond it the land fell away, joining the sweeping curve of the surrounding hills. Beck moved left, the land soft and pitted, a labyrinth of gorges between peaty, gorse-covered mounds. They stepped carefully from mound to mound, Beck missing his mark at one and his leg disappearing up to his knee in the crevice between.

The world began to brighten, any lingering mist dissolving along with the darkness, the new day slowly stretching to fill the spaces between the horizons.

The soft rough ground gradually gave way to firmer, stonier territory, hard, sun-baked soil with thin grass sprouting from it in clusters. And just beyond, a high wall of ivy, bushes and bramble, curling into a mane at the top, giving it the appearance of a vibrant green tsunami.

Beck froze, staring at it. Claire was silent. Then Beck began quickly walking ahead. Up close, glimpses of grey stone through the ivy. Beck pulled some of the growth away, revealing a portion of the wall. He looked along it in both directions.

'A secret place,' he muttered.

'What's that?'

'A secret place,' he said, and louder, 'Looks like.'

Beck turned and walked ahead to where the wall ended in a pile of rubble. Claire followed. Only those rocks on top were visible through the weeds and nettles that wrestled for possession. It was a corner section. The other section lay ahead, intact, stretching off into the trees.

They stepped over the rubble, to where the air was flavoured by wild orchids and lilies. Ahead, gnarled and knotted trees, towering above them, ancient and ragged. Beck saw a mighty ash, brooding, as if sensing his presence. Beck felt he was not wanted here, in this place of feral trees. And with it came the unmistakable sense that he was being watched.

He walked slowly along the edge of trees inside the wall. There was a soft murmuring sound as the mighty branches moved. The air was cold, but the morning sun sent shafts of light down between the branches, creating pools of lights on the ground about them.

He came upon a dip, a cut in the ground, like a fold on a giant's chin. His eyes were drawn to what looked like wild cotton on top, disappearing down the sides into it. He led the way and when they reached it he could see that the wild cotton was, in fact, wool. Beck turned his head slowly and looked into the dip. It took a moment to distinguish them, the bones had darkened and merged with the colours of the earth. They were small skeletons. Three of them. Animals. Perfectly intact; legs, ribs, tailbone, head. The jaws open, a row of white teeth top and bottom, the gape so wide Beck knew their deaths had not been peaceful.

'What is it?' Claire, her voice low.

Beck was thinking about it.

'This is where it feeds. A fox. Probably. It's quiet here, and safe, close to its den.'

They went down the sides.

'They've been picked clean,' Beck said. 'Completely. Look like lambs to me.'

He peered ahead, studying the ground, its contours. It appeared unnaturally uneven, not following the smooth contours of the incline behind them. Ahead, the moss and lichen had a bubbled effect. He walked ahead slowly, stopped and pressed his foot down onto one, felt the grit beneath. More bones, but now covered by the forest floor, like a mat. Looking ahead again he saw another, slightly larger than those about it, against a tree, as if pushed into it, the moss and lichen creeping up the trunk. Beck walked to it, knelt down and pulled back the covering, exposing the tips of bones resting against the wood. He pulled carefully on one, and it slid out, nothing to hold it back. But it was old, coarse with age and deeply pitted, bronze in colour. The bone was small, semi-circular in shape. But unmistakable. Especially with the six little teeth set into it like pine nuts. It was the lower portion of a human jaw bone. More specifically, a baby's jaw bone.

CHAPTER SIXTY

Dr Gumbell was dressed in a beige linen summer suit and stood, staring down at the selection of bones he had spread about on the ground. He had taken the precaution of wearing wellington boots. Beck wondered where he had gotten these at this hour. They looked brand new. For a long time, he stood motionless, stroking his chin between two fingers, the smell of stale alcohol wafting from him like a bad cologne. Finally he spoke.

'This case is throwing up the rarest of scenarios, and all at the same time. Quite compelling. Quite amazing actually. From a professional point of view. Everything is here, from what I can see,' he said. 'Mail order skeleton. We have a calcaneus – that's the heel bone, Beck, in case you didn't know – a fibula, tibia, a femur, and a pelvis. I didn't arrange them all.' He pointed vaguely towards the ground. 'Have here a vertebrae, a couple of ribs, and a scapula. Then things get a little messy.' He pointed towards the tree. 'The cervical vertebrae, the neck, and that jumble of bones there, the skull. See what I mean? Like the end of a butcher's bucket, all piled there.'

He picked up his medical bag from where he had left it by his feet, opened it and took out a large magnifying glass and pencil torch. He closed the bag and put it down again, then stood it on its end and sat on top of it, stretching his legs, placing one on either side of the bones. The pencil light illuminated the remains as he leaned forward, bending his long back, peering through the magnifying glass. After some time he sat back and sighed, held up the magnifying glass.

'Beck. My back is killing me. Take this. And the light. Inspect those other bones behind me, there. Tell me what you can see.'

Beck took the glass and light, studied the other remains through the magnifying glass.

'The bones are ribbed,' he said. 'Or gnawed, whichever you'd prefer. Why didn't it eat the bones as well?'

'Why would it?' Gumbell said. 'There's nothing to gain from eating a bone but a lot of ultimately wasted hard work. And probably a painful stomach. But then again, I'm no vet. The human bones are gnawed too. So, what does that make it? If an animal eats a child, maybe it kills it too? An every day occurrence in some parts of the world. The question is, is this a crime scene?'

Beck didn't know the answer to that question. Not yet.

'I mean,' Gumbell added. 'I've never seen a wild animal standing in a dock myself. Have you?'

'We don't know how it died,' he said.

'True,' Gumbell replied. 'We'll have to wrap these up and take them to the lab in HQ. Have an anthropologist look at them. No need to stand on any ceremony, anything of forensic value has long since disappeared. Except the bones themselves, that is.' He seemed distracted, and leaned forward. He pulled the covering back further about the tree, a handful of bones tumbling out. He picked one up and dusted it off, held it up for inspection.

'Inspector,' a voice from behind Beck.

Beck turned. The uniform was walking purposefully towards him.

'The station's been trying to contact you. The call came through on the radio. There's no mobile cov…'

'What is it?' tetchy.

'Edward Roche, boss. He's dead. He died during the night. Cardiac arrest. He'd lost too much blood. They couldn't stop it.'

Beck was surprised. He thought of the wide set, tattooed Roche, and nodded. At least that might get finance out of Superintendent Wilde's hair. For a while at least.

'I've another one,' Gumbell said then.

Beck turned back to the State Pathologist.

'Well,' he said. 'That's no surprise. There's plenty of them here after all?'

'I mean a different one. A different bone.'

'Yes, I know,' Beck said, still not getting it.

'I mean from a different skeleton. There's more than one. Wake up, Beck.'

'More than one?'

'Afraid so, old boy.'

Gumbell held up a piece of bone.

'A section of pelvis. A male this time. A male baby.'

Beck exhaled a long stream of air between puckered lips, making a sound like a strong wind.

He shook his head, lost for words.

CHAPTER SIXTY-ONE

Detective Garda Somers sat at her desk in the deserted Ops Room. The sun was high now, shining through the window above her desk. She bought down the blind and a cool breeze blew around it onto the side of her face. Her mobile phone was on the desk in front of her, turned to mute. It was turned to mute because Lucy had already rung nine times. But Claire had not answered, and Lucy had not left a message.

Claire sat back in her chair and ran a hand absentmindedly through her hair. She thought of Lucy. God, she missed her. Her desk phone rang, the number displayed on screen. She recognised the first three digits; Garda HQ in the Phoenix Park, Dublin. She picked up.

'About time,' the voice on the other end. 'I've been trying to contact Inspector Beck. There's no reply from his mobile.'

Claire didn't recognise the voice.

'And you are?'

'It's the lab at Forensic Science Ireland, Garda HQ, I'm Derek. I was told to ring Inspector Beck directly.'

'Inspector Beck is still at a... possible crime scene. There's no coverage there. What is it?'

'You can tell him the DNA sample we extracted from the item of clothing, namely a baby's T-shirt, fou...'

'I know where it was found.'

'Okay. It's confirmed. The DNA sample matched that extracted from the murder victim, Samantha Power.'

Claire felt no surprise, just sadness.

'Elementary now,' Claire said, more to herself.

'Elementary? What you mean?'

'Nothing. Anything else?'

'Yes. Tyre marks. Specialist tyre analysts identified these as a particular type fitted by the manufacturer Tata Motors, owners of Jaguar Landrover, to the Landrover Discovery and Range Rover models, specifically the V6 petrol models. The tyres had little wear. It states the vehicle was new or the tyres had recently been changed. That's unlikely. I'll forward these results on anyw…'

'Why?' Claire interrupted.

'Why?'

'Why do you say that's unlikely? About the tyres having been changed.'

'Because tyre shops don't normally stock that particular tyre. Maybe in cities they do. But not anywhere else. No demand. They have to be ordered in.'

'And you know all this?'

'Yes, I know all this.'

'Anything else?' with a sigh.

'I thought that was plenty.'

'It is,' Claire said.

'What's your name?'

'Detective Garda Claire Somers.'

'Don't think I ever spoke with you before,' the voice softening like warming molasses. 'My name's Derek.'

'You already told me that. Thank you, Derek. Bye bye.'

Claire hung up, but immediately her mobile phone started to flash.

Lucy.

Claire turned it upside down so she wouldn't have to look.

CHAPTER SIXTY-TWO

Sergeant Connor rang from the video room in the station as Beck headed back. Beck was sitting in the passenger seat of a marked patrol car, staring at, but not seeing, the world passing by outside. He was thinking of bones, his mind swirling, trying to catch a clog of understanding that might stop it, but finding none.

'I've gone over everything,' the sergeant said. 'Again. And again. And again. Nothing. Someone has to have gotten into that vehicle somewhere outside Cross Beg. She stopped for that person and picked them up. Someone she likely knew. There are no other CCTV cameras. I got a couple of truck dash cams. Nothing. CCTV's not going to solve this, if you ask me.'

'Hhmm,' Beck said, thinking, forcing himself to concentrate. 'Maybe.'

'There's nothing more I can do. Perhaps I should move onto something else?'

Beck cleared his throat, but said nothing.

It could finish right here. CCTV. Move on. Dig somewhere else in the garden.

Those bones.

Instead.

'Listen,' a clog catching, an idea formulating in his mind, 'can you put everything onto a memory stick for me? From Crabby's. From everywhere. Traffic cameras. The lot. Everything you have.'

'Why?'

Why? What does that mean? Why? So I can choose a colour, count the number of blue cars, the number of green cars, play a game with myself and see if I win. Why?

'I want to have a look at it, that's why,' keeping his voice calm.

'Oh, of course,' like the idea had just occurred to him. 'I'll get it ready for you and have it by the time you get back… There's something else.'

Slipped in as an afterthought, but Beck had a feeling it wasn't. 'Yes?'

'Maurice Crabby. As Samantha Power drives away from the supermarket, he comes out almost right behind her, in the shop van, stays like that until they pass the last camera and I lose them.'

Beck was right, definitely not an afterthought. His mind drifted. *Those bones.*

CHAPTER SIXTY-THREE

It was ringing again. Her mobile phone. Lucy. She ignored it, her mind instead focusing on V6 Landrover Discoverys and Range Rovers. Two screens were open on her computer: one on Pulse, the other Google. A montage of V6 Landrover Discoverys and Range Rovers filled the Google page, a list of owners of Landrover Discoverys and Range Rovers in the county of Galway filled Pulse. The photographs portrayed the Discovery as predominately a work horse. There it was, sloshing along a muddy track, climbing rocky hills. The Range Rover, however, was displayed on leafy streets, in a royal enclosure, and another had a movie star arriving at a premier. A Range Rover was not common on the roads around Cross Beg and district.

On Pulse, she narrowed down the returns by completing the engine size search field, inputting a displacement range between 2,900cc and 3,100cc. Much of the screen disappeared. She was left with just twelve V6 Discoverys and Range Rovers in the whole of Co. Galway.

As she clicked on owner details, she saw Beck enter the Ops Room. He came and stood next to her. She told him about the call from the lab in HQ.

'Just about to check owner details for these vehicles.' She right clicked the mouse. 'According to Pulse. There is a Landrover Discovery V6 and a Range Rover owned locally. The Discovery first.' *Click.* 'Owner is one Colin Hegarty... that name rings a bell. Has form.' *Click.* 'Assault. Shop Street Galway. July 2005.

Injured party was a young female student. One punch. Knocked her out cold in the street. Alcohol consumed. She lost a couple of teeth. Victim was not known to him, and he fled the scene. Arrested a short time later. The incident appears to have been a one off. There's nothing on him before or since... that we know of, of course.'

'Where's he live?'

'A place called Cus-na-Tol.'

He gave her a blank look.

'It's a parish out by Lough Sheebeen, five miles towards Ballinasloe.'

'And the other vehicle. The Range Rover.'

Click.

'Well well. I know him. So do you.'

'Who?'

'Maurice Crabby.'

CHAPTER SIXTY-FOUR

She pushed the roller along the wall by the corner of the window, applying an even coat of paint. Vicky liked painting. It always took her mind off things. The trick was to keep the pressure nice and even. That way you ended up without blotches or run offs, you didn't have to start all over again. Yes, she liked painting, took her mind off things. And right now she wanted her mind taken off things. Because she needed to be patient. She needed to stop thinking about Frankfurt, about the International Independent TV Production Fair in Oslo, of missing babies and whether or not Danny Black would hold his nerve and actually help her obtain that CCTV. But most of all, she needed to stop thinking about that person, the person she thought was a killer. She wanted to take her mind off all this, but it was damn hard. She thought of Finnegan Beck. The man was so blasé. He hadn't seemed in any way bothered getting out of the car the night before. He hadn't even asked for her phone number. She was usually the one who behaved like that. She didn't want to think of him either.

She thought of her plans for this place. Once the work started, when everything was in place, she didn't have to be here, well, not for everything. Danny could look after all that himself. So maybe she should tell Joe to work it out some way, to get away for a night, before everything started – one night, surely he could do that? He could tell his wife whatever he wanted, she didn't care… she thought again about Beck. At least Joe was crazy for her.

She bent now to apply more paint to the roller. And waited while the excess dripped off. Then she straightened again. She could hear Danny in the kitchen, the loud drone of a drill sounding intermittently. Since arriving this morning he had been in there, ripping out the old fittings and taking up the floor covering. Apart from a brief greeting, they hadn't really spoken. He didn't seem to want to talk about what they had discussed the previous evening. Maybe I need to push him, just a little? she thought. Vicky pressed the roller against the wall and applied the paint briskly. When she'd finished, she put the brush down onto its tray.

'Danny,' she called, rubbing her hands on the old shirt she wore. 'Time for a cuppa. Put the kettle on please.'

The drill sounded again, but when it finished she could hear the gentle thud as he placed it on the mantelpiece, then his footsteps across the floor. She heard the sound of a tap running, and water being poured into the kettle. When she went into the kitchen she crossed to the worktop by the sink. There was a packet of chocolate biscuits turned upside down on it, to keep them fresh. She turned it right side up and pulled the wrapper apart, held it out. Danny took a biscuit. She reached for a couple of mugs from the wooden holder next to her.

'The answer,' Danny said, reaching for the teabags. 'To what we spoke about yesterday.'

'Oh, yes,' Vicky said.

'I've slept on it. I'd like to help you. It's a story that needs to be told. So, I'll do it.'

Vicky smiled. 'Good. As soon as possible, okay? This waiting is getting to me. You're at Crabby's tomorrow, right?'

'Yes, in the evening,' he looked about the room. 'But I wouldn't do any more painting anyway, if I was you. Most of these walls are coming down.'

'I know,' Vicky said. She took a sip from her tea. 'I did the gable wall in the living room; that's staying.'

She had a feeling about this story. It was going to be big.

Vicky smiled.

Yes, she thought. Very big.

CHAPTER SIXTY-FIVE

'Sergeant Connor.'

He was standing in the public office, talking to Garda Ryan. *Best friends.*

'Yes, boss.' He held up something. Small and black. 'Memory stick. It's all here.'

He walked across and handed it to Beck.

'Thanks,' Beck said, putting it into his pocket. 'You know a place called Cus-na-Tol?'

The sergeant shook his head.

'You need to. And how to get there? Take Garda Ryan with you.' Beck then explained why.

'Crabby's not at work today,' Claire told him when he got back to the Ops Room. 'I just checked.'

'Isn't he? Where's he gone to?'

'Don't know. The staff say he took off around lunch-time yesterday, didn't tell anyone where he was going.'

'What about his wife?'

'She doesn't know either. I'm not so sure about her, thought she sounded a little odd to me on the phone.'

'Odd?'

'Odd. Yes. As in, well, *odd.*'

'Okay,' Beck said, checking the time. 'Why don't we go and talk to her?'

*

The Focus climbed the narrow mountain road to Crabby's house, the fields about them yellow and anaemic. Even so, some contained cattle, mooching around sniffing for grass or staring over the hedges as they passed. The blue sky held light brush strokes of white. The sacred mountain of Croagh Patrick was just about visible, way off in the distance, rising sharply to one side like a celestial spear.

She had been watching them approach for some time. From her bedroom window Julie Crabby had a view all the way into Cross Beg. If she had known they were coming, she could have followed their progress from the moment they had driven out of the town. Apart from some trees and the occasional farm building, she had a clear view of all the traffic on the mismatch of roads to the west of Cross Beg.

But it was only when the blue Focus had turned from the road at the bottom of the mountain and started up did she realise it was coming to her. Because this wasn't the type of car to meander about a mountain without purpose. Not like the little vans of the elderly farmers who came to check their plots of bog or to simply pass the time of day. She knew it was a garda car. She'd been expecting it.

The policeman was tall, with piercing brown eyes in a handsome face, his hair receding on a high forehead. His female companion was smaller, stocky build, tight haircut. There was a masculine energy about her, she considered. She stood in the doorway, observing them, folding her arms across her chest.

'My name is Detective Inspector Finnegan Beck. This is my colleague, Detective Garda Claire Somers. And you are Mrs Crabby?'

She pursed her lips. 'Yes. I am.'

'Could we come in for a moment? This shouldn't take long.'

She said nothing, debating whether to tell them to come back when *he* was here. Why should she have to deal with *his* business? But she just knew the tall policeman would have none of that.

'Yes. Yes. Come in,' she said, turning.

*

Beck considered that she was appraising him when the door opened, sussing him out as it were. This was something he was used to when he knocked on the doors of criminals, but he had not expected it here. He put it down to the natural inclination of one who liked to be boss, who called the shots. She wanted to see if she could call the shots with him.

She led them down a hall to the living room, deep pile carpet, matching settee and armchairs, piano in one corner next to a bay window, grandfather clock in the other, an entire wall taken up by rows of books. Beck noted some of the titles: *Ancient Rome, King Richard I, Greece and Modernity,* but these far too pristine to convince him they were for anything other than appearances.

'Surely it's my husband you need to speak to,' she said, sitting down, her tone that of a school mistress.

'Yes. But he seems to have disappeared,' Beck said.

'I'd hardly call it disappearing. He's probably gone to see a supplier, something like that.'

'Perhaps you could help us?' Claire said.

Mrs Crabby's eyes narrowed. 'How so?'

'Mrs Crabby,' Beck said. 'I won't beat about the bush. Tyre marks found at the scene of the brutal murder of Samantha Power near Kelly's Forge are consistent with those fitted to the type of vehicle your husband drives.'

Beck spotted a change immediately. Subtle. Like a shadow passing across her eyes.

'What does that mean?'

'They are from a Range Rover. That's what I mean. It's not difficult.'

'I don't like your tone. Nor that sergeant's yesterday. I demand to be treated with respect.'

Beck raised his eyebrows, held them there. *And your point?*

'He's not the only one to drive a Range Rover you know,' she said.

'Why? You mean you drive it too?'

'No. No. I mean yes. Well… I mean… Of course I drive it… What are you getting at?'

'Mrs Crabby. Why are you so nervous?'

She ran her hands over her face, held them there, then slowly dropped them onto her knees.

'Has someone been speaking with you?' Her body folded and she sat back into her chair.

Like a hawk can spot a mouse lurking in high grass from a distance of a mile, so too could Beck spot a gouger, a criminal. And his instinct told him now this woman was no criminal. All he had to do was push. Just a little. He pushed.

'Yes,' he lied.

She sat forward again, her head hanging low between her shoulders.

'I was there,' her tone without her customary arrogance, meek even. 'But. But… it was before. I thought, oh, I thought… He didn't take the Range Rover. I know now he was making deliveries. I thought he was meeting someone. I went there. Thought I'd surprise them. He wasn't there. I didn't catch them…'

'Them,' Claire said. 'Who's them?'

Mrs Crabby dropped her head again. Claire could see the grey roots through the parting along the centre.

'I don't know. Them. One or the other.'

'Mrs Crabby,' Claire said. 'Did you catch him with *them* before? Ever?'

Mrs Crabby opened her hands, stretching out her fingers. She looked down, her answer lay in her silence.

'So you were there,' Beck said. 'What time was this?'

'Afternoon, around two o'clock…'

'The same day,' Beck said, 'as Samantha Power was killed. You were there. The same day as your husband was seen driving out of

Cross Beg. Which was just after the victim was observed driving the exact same route. It's the last sighting of Samantha Power's vehicle on CCTV the day she was killed that we have. We have no evidence he was there. But you were. You just admitted it. Are you trying to tell me this is coincidence?'

Mrs Crabby couldn't hide it; this was the look Beck found usually came when incriminating facts were presented. As they had been now. It was Fear.

'He came home with blood on him,' she said after a long pause. 'He didn't think I saw him, but I did.'

Beck felt a sensation like an elbow nudge him in his belly, at the same time his breath caught at the back of his throat and he coughed.

'When you heard what happened,' Claire said. 'Did you think that strange?'

'Of course,' the voice rising, then dropping to an inaudible whisper as she added, 'But he's still my husband, despite everything.'

'Did you ask him?' Claire again. 'Maybe he cut himself.'

'Well,' the pitch elevating once more, 'How else would he have blood on him?'

'What did he say?' Beck asked.

'Can't you wait? Stop asking questions. Just for a moment. There's something else I want to add.'

Again, that elbow into his stomach.

'He was there too…' she began.

Silence.

Claire opened her mouth, was about to speak.

'… He was at Kelly's Forge after me. When I got there, it was deserted. There was no one there, so I only stayed a minute, then went home. But he was there later.' Mrs Crabby said.

And the nudge into Beck's stomach became a punch now.

'I know,' she added, 'because I checked the sat nav on the Range Rover. He took the car out after I got back, and I know he was there. After I'd been there. And maybe that was when Samantha Power was killed.'

Beck shook his head in amazement. 'Both of you,' he said incredulous, 'both of you were there, you're telling me?'

She nodded. Beck imagined a hawk, but instead of soaring high, it was flying low, and yet still unable to spot not one, but two mice scurrying about in the high grass below. Beck had missed this one completely.

CHAPTER SIXTY-SIX

Sergeant Connor drove the marked patrol car, his elbow resting out the open window. The sun had turned his skin a golden bronze.

Next to him in the passenger seat was Garda Ryan, brooding. She had been hoping to finish work early today. But that wasn't going to happen now. Although she was physically sitting next to Connor, the important bit, her *presence,* was missing. Subconsciously she was far off somewhere else. In her mind she was compiling a shopping list, checking off items against the contents of what she remembered to be in her fridge-freezer. Her husband had already rung twice. Like she was a family information centre. Where was the potato peeler? the first question. Where was the grill setting knob on the oven? the second. She had tolerated the first, but the second, the straw that broke the camel's back, drew the response, 'Work it out for your bloody self,' before she hung up.

Garda Ryan was sorry about the way she had reacted now. Her husband could be so domestically helpless at times. *Still.* She was beginning to sweat inside her hi-vis jacket, but it was too awkward to take it off in the car. Connor's constant smiling was starting to irk her too. What the hell had he to be so happy about?

She yawned, and rubbed her tired eyes, trying to remember when she'd last had a full night's sleep. She couldn't, so gave up.

They asked directions at a shop and post office standing in the middle of nowhere at the side of the road. It was an old two-storey building with living quarters above. There was a bus stop outside, the emblem of the national bus company, a galloping Irish Setter, across the top. A sign over the door said Cool-na-Tol Convenience Store and Post Office.

A middle-aged woman in a grey dress was sat reading a newspaper behind the counter in the supermarket section. The post-office area consisted of a single empty booth with a long counter next to it fixed to the wall. Official forms and brochures were displayed on the wall, along with a sign: 'Be Smart. Open A Post Office Savings Account Today'. The woman stood when they entered, looking nervous. Sergeant Connor could see the headline on the open page of the newspaper: *Raiders Disguised as Gardai Rob Dublin Post Office*.

'It's okay,' he said. 'We *are* Gardai.' He tapped his shoulder number, 'Look.'

'I'm here on my own. Out here, we're isolated… we've never been robbed thank God. Yet.'

'You know a Colin Hegarty?' Garda Ryan said. 'We need to know where he lives.'

'*Him.*'

'Why do you say it like that?' Connor asked.

'Because. No reason. Just because. You know how it is, some people…'

'So, you know where he lives?' Connor again.

She gave precise directions: straight ahead, second left, then first right, left again and down that *boreen*, Colin Hegarty's place. 'It's easy to miss that second left, keep an eye, and the house is hidden behind bushes, you mightn't see it from the road. Oh, and there's a rusty gate, keep an eye out for it. Be careful. He can be a little paranoid.'

It was exactly as she described. The rusty gate gave it away. Ahead, the small rough road, or *boreen*, meandered on, grass spouting from its centre. It was 18.14. Garda Ryan was thinking she wasn't going to get any shopping done now. But for Connor, nothing could shake his eternal optimism of working in the light of day.

As they pulled up, Colin Hegarty was watching them, hidden from view, running a finger along the trigger guard of his double-barrelled shotgun, angry at the whole world.

CHAPTER SIXTY-SEVEN

Sergeant Connor led the way to the rusty gate. The bushes on either side pressed in. They had parked on the roadway, there was nowhere else that they could see. At the gate he viewed the house. It was unpainted, bare plaster, a narrow window on either side of a plain wooden door, a sloping tiled roof. There was a garden of rutted grass and cowpats where animals had recently grazed. He could see a cluttered farmyard beside the house, old oil drums, discarded tyres and machinery, a car resting on cylinder blocks, a tractor and a small white van.

Connor placed a hand onto the gate. As he did so a symphony: high pitched, also a baritone, and a base line, of throaty growls, then a chorus of yelps. A pack of dogs. A long white face, a black patch around one eye appeared inches in front of his, two rows of gnashing white canines, the neck straining against a metal chain. Connor jumped back, instinctively raising his hands to protect his face, but knocking his hat off in the process. Garda Ryan, on the other hand, remained calm. Connor cursed under his breath. He felt, as the senior ranking officer, he had let himself down. A loud deep voice rumbled through the air: 'Go back! Now! I'm tellin' ye! Go back! Go on! Now!'

Connor retreated a couple of steps. But Garda Ryan, standing behind him, did not move. He bumped into her.

'Not you,' the voice rumbled again. 'I'm talking to the feckin' dogs.'

'Stop the messing and put the dogs away,' Garda Ryan shouted. 'There's a good man.'

'When you tell me what this is about. Then I'll decide.'

'It's not for you to decide,' Garda Ryan announced. 'Let us in or we'll have an armed response unit around here in double quick order. They won't be so polite. Now put the dogs away and let us in.'

Hegarty looked down at the shotgun in his hands. He was hidden behind the bushes at the side of the farmyard. He didn't have a licence for the firearm. He used to have one. But it was taken off him, after the, what he called, incident. They took his shotgun away. The one he was holding now was stolen from a dead neighbour. After he had found the old man slumped in his chair when he went to visit, and so took the opportunity when it presented itself. And because he didn't want to bring suspicion on himself, he hadn't called an ambulance. It was two more days before the body was eventually found.

'Give me a minute,' he said.

He clicked his tongue and called the dogs. The sounds of their yelps and barks receded, becoming muffled as he locked them into a shed. He went into an outhouse, and hid the shotgun under bags of calf meal.

Connor stretched himself to full height when he heard Hegarty's footsteps approach, attempting to open the gate. It was only then he noticed that it was locked. Hegarty appeared from around the side of the house, but walked by in front of them, along the path against the wall of the property.

'Come in this way,' he said, pointing.

He disappeared behind bushes at the side of the garden.

'Down here,' he called from the other side.

They followed his voice and found him standing on the other side of a farm gate. It was completely concealed by the bushes.

'I had a gate across the top of the road there,' pointing back the way they had come. 'But the Council made me take it down. They said it's a public road, that I had no right to put it there.

There's nobody lives down this road. Nobody but me.' His face contorted. 'Bastards.'

Hegarty was tall and gangly, hollow-cheeked, the skin on his face draped over his bones like filo pastry. His hair was white and his face had a couple of days' stubble. He was dressed in a blue-and-white check flannel shirt and dirty jeans, metal-tipped boots. They knew the boots were metal-tipped because the top of one had worn away, revealing the shiny metal plate beneath. White chest hair curled out of the open neck of his shirt.

'You have problems with intruders?' Garda Ryan asked.

The face contorted again.

'If they'd half the chance I would. I had a fella here the other day askin' me had I anything for sellin'. He was casin' the place to come back and rob me later. I set the dogs on him. He didn't come back.'

'You can't…' Connor began, but then changed his mind. 'We'd like a word.'

'About what,' suspicion in the eyes.

'We need to check something, that's all,' Connor said. 'You have a Landrover Discovery. One is registered to your name.'

Colin Hegarty turned his head, pursed his lips and went 'pwut' as he spat onto the ground.

'I never had you people around here till I had that incident. Now you come here whenever something's wrong. In case I had something to do with it, whatever it is. Always something. I'm on the list now, amn't I? I'm one of your customers, an auld reliable.'

'What list?' Connor said. 'I've never even been here before.'

'Aye, but you're here now. You know what I'm talking about.'

'Landrover Discovery,' Garda Ryan prompted.

A scraping sound as the gate bolt was slid across, then Hegarty pulled on it and the gate swung open.

'This way,' turning and walking ahead of them.

He led them into the yard. A bale of animal feed was torn open, the handle of a pitchfork sticking out of it, with it the sickly-sweet smell of silage.

'In this weather there's no grass. I'm feeding my livestock from winter supplies. No one's talkin' 'bout that, are they?'

They stopped in the centre of the yard.

Connor looked around. But there were no animals that he could see. He noticed a stone outhouse with an open doorway. Hegarty watched him looking at it. At one end of the farmyard was a wooden fence, the fence posts crooked and the barbed wire between sagging.

Connor looked to the outhouse again, then turned to Hegarty. Their eyes met. Connor took a step, about to go over, see what was in there. He felt a tug on the sleeve of his jacket.

'Over there,' it was Garda Ryan.

He turned, saw what she was pointing at off to the side of the yard. There, against a low wall, parked on grass, was a vehicle. A green vehicle. A jeep. A Landrover. Specifically an old Landrover Discovery.

Connor forgot about the outhouse, started walking towards the Discovery instead. When he reached it, he squatted down onto his knees, inspecting the tyres. They were clean and in good condition.

A breeze blew across the farmyard and a flock of starlings suddenly took flight, rising up from behind a shed, performing a cartwheel and flying away.

All that remained was silence.

'Why you so interested in it anyway?' Hegarty asked.

'You heard about the girl?' Garda Ryan said. 'Who was killed. And whose kid is missing…' She let him think about that. Then: 'That's why.'

Hegarty did not reply. Not immediately.

'One minute,' he said then, walking away.

'Where you going?' Connor called after him.

'One minute.'

They watched him head towards the outhouse. He reached it and disappeared through the open doorway.

'What the hell?' Connor wondered aloud, setting off after him.

CHAPTER SIXTY-EIGHT

Dr Gumbell was in what he called the post-coital *tristesse* stage of his hangover.

The philosopher Baruch Spinoza had said the mind became so caught up in the sensual pleasure of lovemaking that afterwards the greatest sadness, one that confuses and dulls the mind, followed. Gumbell had spent the entire evening before drinking brandy and Crested Ten at the Brown Water Inn, trying to decide which he favoured most. Charged to room service, of course, even though he still had to work out how to get his expenses to cover it. His drinking gave him, while not the same pleasure or euphoria, but the same intense distraction as lovemaking. And for much longer. He couldn't remember when he'd last done the naughty. When he tried, all he remembered were messy sheets and looking for a taxi afterwards.

He pushed the protruding tongue aside and peered into Inspector O'Reilly's mouth. As he did so a chuckle forced its way from his own. He hadn't expected it, but it had accompanied a joke he'd just remembered: *Man asks another man, what's the definition of eternity, mate? Other man says, I don't know, what is the definition of eternity? The first man says: The time you finish making love and your taxi arrives. Boom! Boom!*

The chuckle disappeared just as quickly as it had come, lost to the sterile, antiseptic and formaldehyde-laced air.

It was because of his post-coital *tristesse* hangover that he had missed it. His senses, normally sharp, now sodden and slow. It was as he placed Inspector O'Reilly's hand back again by his side onto the morgue table that he noticed something glint. It was a glint different to that which he had been experiencing all day. The glint caused by disruption to the electrical impulses of his hungover brain, causing him to see bright particles like little shooting stars across his vision. He was used to those.

But this was different, part of a cluster, centred on the palm of the hand. He reached for tweezers and leaned in, picked one up and placed it into a vial. He crossed to the microscope, tipped it out, blinked, then looked into the lens. Next, he went to a shelf and took down the box of exhibit samples. He found what he was looking for and went back to the microscope. He compared a fragment taken from the knife handle with what he had just taken from the hand. Then he stood back and took a deep breath. He went to the sink and washed his hands, then crossed to a chair on which he'd hung his jacket. He fished out his mobile from a pocket and rang Beck.

CHAPTER SIXTY-NINE

Hegarty emerged from the shed just as Connor reached it, brushing past him, striding back the way he had come.

'Stop, Hegarty,' Connor commanded.

Hegarty had something in his right hand: a piece of metal, short, stubby, grey.

Connor was wary now.

'What's that? In your hand.'

'Relax,' Hegarty said, slowing down but now stopping, looking back over his shoulder as he went. 'It's a jimmy bar. Not a bloody shotgun.'

He laughed. It was his private joke. But neither guard laughed.

Connor, relieved, followed him.

'What you need it for?' it was Garda Ryan.

'I'll show you.'

The three of them walked towards the Discovery.

'Where were you on Tuesday last?' Connor asked when they reached it. 'Early evening say, from 'bout four o'clock on.'

'No foreplay, eh? Straight to the point.'

'Watch your bloody mouth.' Garda Ryan hated smutty talk. 'A careless word can bring an indecency charge. If that's what you want, keep it up.'

'I'm like someone with a bad bloody credit rating, aren't I?' Hegarty sounded sorry for himself. 'It'll never be forgotten, will it? That night. The incident. It wasn't all the way it was presented to be in court you know.'

'Really,' Garda Ryan, her voice rising. 'Wasn't it now? You pleaded not guilty if my memory serves me correct. The jury decided. Were you wronged then? Miscarriage of justice, was it?'

'I'm not getting into it again. Not now. It's over with.'

'Then why the fuck are you bringing it up?' Garda Ryan's face was turning red. 'You don't want to *get into it* because there's nothing to get into. And you know it. Isn't that right now, sunshine?'

Hegarty's hand tightened around the jimmy bar. He smirked, walked to the front of the Discovery, pushed it between the grill and bonnet, pressed down sharply, and the bonnet opened with a clunking sound. He ran his fingers under the rim, released the catch, and pulled the bonnet up. He held it while he clipped the supporting arm into place. Then stepped back, outstretching his arms in a theatrical gesture.

'You'll not see a Discovery like it for miles around,' he said.

They stepped up and looked into the engine bay.

'There's nothing there,' it was Connor. 'It doesn't have an engine.'

'Exactly,' said Hegarty with a smug smile. 'And hasn't for at least a year.' He pointed. 'It's over there.'

They looked. It sat on a wooden pallet, rusting, covered in bird droppings.

'I'm planning on putting a diesel in,' Hegarty said. 'That V6 would drink Lough Erne dry so it would.'

From above, the low rumbling sound of jet engines as an aeroplane crossed the sky.

'Now,' Connor said. 'I want to see what's in that outhouse of yours.'

The smug smile disappeared from Hegarty's face.

CHAPTER SEVENTY

Pulse Alert. Cross Beg Gardai seeking Maurice Crabby of Mountain Top View, Doirelog, Cross Beg, driving vehicle reg 172G for Golf Zero Zero Four Three Niner black Range Rover. STOP AND DETAIN. Wanted in connection with the murder of Samantha Power Pulse incident number 647564539 refers. Approach with CAUTION. Investigating officer Inspector Finnegan Beck, Cross Beg.

STOP AND DETAIN.
STOP AND DETAIN.
STOP AND DETAIN.

CHAPTER SEVENTY-ONE

'*To what do I owe…*'

'Shut up, Beck, and listen,' Gumbell said. 'I've spent all afternoon in the company of Inspector O'Reilly. In twenty-six years of doing this job I can safety say I've never seen anything quite like it…'

Gumbell lapsed into silence.

'Like what?'

'Can you get over here? Someone should come and talk to me. Instead of me having to ring around like some kind of telephone sales person.'

'Where are you?'

'I'm just about to go up on deck for some pre-dinner cocktails. Where the hell do you think I am? The morgue, Beck. The morgue.'

An image of Gumbell massaging his head with his hand, two bloodshot eyes peering out from a pale face, and a temper – obviously – foul. Beck allowed himself a self-righteous smile.

'I'll be right there.'

Before he had finished speaking, Gumbell had already hung up.

The State Pathologist looked up abruptly as Beck entered the room. It was obvious he had nodded off. His breath and every pore of his body were throwing off enough fumes that even in the morgue it was sufficient to add a coarse sweetness to the air.

For a moment he stared at Beck, confused. Beck was tempted to ask if this was further proof of what can happen when brain cells go AWOL. But he did not. He considered too, that, with a little colouring here and there, there would be little difference between the body lying on the mortuary table and the body sitting on the stool next to it.

Dr Gumbell took a deep breath, standing up slowly. For a moment he appeared unsteady on his feet, reached out, grabbing the mortuary table.

'You alright?' Beck enquired.

'Don't ask silly bloody questions,' Gumbell snapped. 'Of course I'm not alright. Jesus, you. Of all people.'

Gumbell released the table, stood silently. Slowly he pushed himself away, walked round and stood on the other side, opposite Beck. He reached down and grasped the hand of the corpse. Beck noted he was not wearing gloves. He raised the hand and turned it at such an angle that, if he were alive, Inspector O'Reilly would be screaming in pain.

'By the way. The bones. I counted three sets. Two girls. One boy.'

He allowed the statement to settle in.

'Old as Methuselah,' he added. 'A conundrum.'

'Yes.' Beck said. 'But I can't think of that right now. To the matter at hand.'

'See this?' Gumbell said. 'Lean in for God's sake, man. You won't see anything the way you are.'

Beck craned his neck. That smell again, stale alcohol, mixed now with that of a carcass left out of the freezer too long.

Beck could not 'see this'. He could not see anything other than the hand of a dead person. Gumbell looked like he was about to speak again. Instead, he twisted the hand ever further, almost a full circle, catching the harsh florescent lighting overhead. It was then Beck noticed the tiny particles reflected in the palm of O'Reilly's hand.

'What is that?'

Gumbell gave a triumphant smile.

'About time. Bloody Nora. Metallic residue from the handle of the very same blade that was extracted from the neck of the late Inspector O'Reilly, that's what. Here. On his own hand.'

Beck was silent, considering. Gumbell threw him a look: *And?*

'Really,' Beck said after a moment, but not coming up with any conclusion. 'I suppose he'd have to have gripped it very tightly, wouldn't he, for that to happen? Like, *very* tightly.'

Again, another triumphant smile from Gumbell.

'And two plus two equals…?'

'What? Two plus two equals… four. So?'

'Plus two again?'

'Six. Where's…'

'… This going? It's the logic of the equation. Simple equation, Beck. Kid's stuff. No fingerprints found at the scene. Some old ones, but nothing new, nothing fresh. No markers for DNA either. Nothing. Not even a dirty mug. Forensically, the scene was as clean as a sterile wipe. Yet not wiped. That's key. Not wiped. Residue intact; dust, minute food particles, hair follicles. All embedded. Undisturbed. Not wiped. All there for a while. Since *before* the discovery of the body. You saw the amount of dust in the place yourself. So, two plus two equals four, and a further two is six, and on infinitum. It's the sequence. The inevitable outcome. And so is this. *Mors voluntaria*, Beck.'

The term made Beck wince. Not because of its meaning, but because the language invariably brought with it an image of him, the Scarecrow, who pointed a crooked finger at him now: *'Come on you imbecile. Did you learn nothing from me? Nothing but a talent for harbouring a grudge, you ungrateful bastard.'*

'You mean?' Beck began. 'You can't be serious? *Mors voluntaria*. Death by one's own hand. He did it himself? Slit his own throat? Suicide? Steady on…'

'It's not a case of steadying on anything, Beck. Look. Read. Interpret. Everything is in those three words. It's basic to anyone in my profession. *Look. Read. Interpret.* And I've looked. I've read. I've interpreted. And it is as plain as the nose on your face. Or the knife in his bloomin' neck. Like the equation, it's whichever way you want to look at it. Either way, it's the same result. It will always be the same result.' He fell silent, then: 'It's not as odd as you'd think. It's Western sensibilities that struggle to comprehend it. Take the Japanese for example. They've been doing it for centuries. It's considered an act of honour. Of bravery. But it does appear gruesome, I'll grant you. To our sensibilities, what he did. But the neck is a much more efficient way of speeding things along. A hell of a lot more efficient. The Inspector would have died practically instantaneously. How many suicide options can give you that certainty? Think about it. Throw yourself under a train? Terrible odds. Doesn't cut it. If you excuse the pun. Let me tell you a little story. I treated a fellow one time. Back when I was a junior doctor, just starting out. Had lain down nice and cosy in front of the evening train to Westport. Next stop the Pearly Gates… or so he thought. And there to meet him St. Peter. It turned out his next stop was the Mater Hospital, and there to meet him was not St. Peter but yours truly. I never saw anyone more disappointed. His legs were later thrown out with the rest of the offal from the surgery department. No, Inspector O'Reilly chose an effective way to end it all. His grip on the handle, i.e. his determination to see the job through, was such that it left the residue you see here now.'

Beck shook his head.

'You serious? He did it to himself?'

'Jesus, you're a slow learner, Beck. Yes. Yes. Yes. He did it to himself. And no, it's not a joke. Even I have my standards you know.'

Beck rubbed an index finger along the top of his ear.

'Okay, I'll let you explain this one to Superintendent Wilde.'

CHAPTER SEVENTY-TWO

Crabby had not walked into the water after all. The cold ocean had jarred him back to his senses enough to make him realise that he did not actually want to die. Not just yet anyway. No. Not just yet.

Since first light he had been driving. His shoes and socks were sodden so he had taken these off. He drove in his bare feet. After an hour on the dual carriageway, just past Ennis, he spotted the big road sign that said, 'Limerick 40 kilometres'. He realised he'd been heading in the wrong direction, south, when he should have been heading north.

He turned at the next junction and started back the way he had come. He drove for another ten minutes then turned off the dual carriageway, following the sign for Loughrea. He didn't know where the dual carriageway would ultimately have taken him, once past Limerick, but he knew that Loughrea was on his way home.

After another ten minutes or so he came to a village, spindly houses on either side of a road that widened as it passed through. His attention was drawn to an old set of fuel pumps at the side of the road, painted green, in front of a white building, its windows boarded up but cleverly painted over to make it look like the place was still active: a 'face' peering out behind it, another window containing stacks of Bovril and Cadbury's Cocoa. An illusion. When he looked back to the road he saw the patrol car parked across it, flashing roof lights and a sign: Garda Checkpoint.

Crabby slowed. Thinking. Telling himself that this was a mere formality. They weren't looking for him... or were they? It was possible, he knew. He thought of the sergeant. The one who'd viewed the CCTV in his office. Even if they weren't, they soon would be. But were these guards looking for him? Probably not.

Probably not.

He thought of his mother. He thought of St Bridget's, no bars across its windows now. But there might as well be. But most of all, he thought of his sister, Bernadette.

A yellow-jacketed officer was standing in each lane, the furthest one leaning into the open window of a battered-looking estate car. Ahead of Crabby was a small Nissan. The guard waved the Nissan through without stopping it. Crabby eased the Range Rover forward. The guard had his hands on his hips, glancing at Crabby's registration number and the tax and insurance discs in the windscreen.

So far so good.

The guard indicated with his hand for Crabby to stop, and Crabby eased his foot onto the brake pedal, pressing the window remote at the same time and lowering the window.

The guard approached, rummaging through a mental filing cabinet, under the heading of R for Range Rover.

'Good morning, sir.'

No smile. Poker face. The tone almost bored. Nonchalant. Just procedure, sir.

Nothing to worry about.

Crabby relaxed, pushing his bare feet further into the footwell where they wouldn't be seen.

'This your vehicle, sir?'

'Yes, guard, it is.'

'Got your licence with you?'

'Of course. Right here,' leaning across, opening the glove compartment, fumbling about, finally finding it, extracting it now, handing the driving licence to the guard.

'Always carry it with me,' Crabby said, his tone friendly: *let's get this over with and I'll be on my way.*

The officer took the licence, looking at it, then back to Crabby, then back to the licence. Then Crabby saw it. A change, understanding setting in. Reaching out now, his hand coming through the window. Crabby looked at that hand: *where's it going?* Then realised, when he saw the fingers begin to curl around the ignition key.

And then everything happened too fast to comprehend; the V6 growled, then roared, the wheels spun, Crabby jerked the steering wheel in the opposite direction to the guard, who was running alongside him now, shouting, the words indecipherable, suddenly falling away, tumbling, his hat knocked from his head, rolling across the ground. Crabby spun the steering wheel back, the carburettor filled with fuel, igniting, a surge of power, maximum revs, the big machine tearing away. He looked in his wing mirror, saw the guard getting to his feet, running towards the patrol car, gesturing to his colleague, the estate car that he had stopped taking off with a puff of black smoke. And then the flashing blue lights were in his rear-view mirror, as he pressed on the accelerator pedal, all the way, until it could go no further. The speedometer needle climbed higher and higher. But always, when he glanced in the rear-view mirror, it was there, an apparition stuck to his bumper, blue lights flashing, occasionally receding, but never disappearing completely.

CHAPTER SEVENTY-THREE

The image of Inspector O'Reilly's dead body had settled beneath the surface of Beck's consciousness. Like most news of its nature, it had first seemed distant, removed, even alien. But now, after the immediacy of the time spent with Gumbell, he could consider it objectively. The man he had known, and yes, it was true, disliked, had pushed the point of a knife into the side of his neck, and kept on pushing until it had gone deep enough to slice through sinew and veins, and then, changing direction, he had pulled that knife across his neck, on and on, the distance short but relatively as wide as Siberia. And his life, all forty or fifty odd years of it, all its trials and tribulations, its happiness and joy, everything that comes with a life, finished. Gone. In a matter of seconds. It was all over. And he had done it to himself.

'I bought you a coffee. It's probably cold now.' Claire handed him the takeaway cup. He sipped. It was cold, but he didn't care. 'What happened in there?' she asked. 'You haven't said a word since you came out.'

She was munching on a chocolate bar.

'The two cases aren't connected after all. Inspector O'Reilly. He killed himself. He slit his own throat. That's what happened in there.'

She coughed, covering her mouth to catch the spittle from flying everywhere. She swallowed, and coughed again.

'Whoa,' she said. 'Whoa. Whoa. Whoa.'

'And the bones. Found in the wood. There were sets. Two girls and a boy.'

'Whoa,' Claire said again, and looked out the window.

When they got back to the station, Beck put his head around the door of the public office.

'Connor and Ryan,' he asked the two guards there. 'They back yet?'

They shook their heads.

'No boss,' one of them said.

They should have been back by now, Beck thought. He considered going to the comms room and calling them on the radio. Instead, he looked at his watch. He'd give it another twenty minutes.

CHAPTER SEVENTY-FOUR

The road became narrower, twisting with sudden, sharp bends, slowing the big Range Rover down, lurching it about like a crazed Clydesdale horse. More than once Crabby thought he had pushed it too far, felt the big machine sliding from beneath him, crouching low onto its springs on one side, rising so high on the other it defied the laws of physics by not toppling over. For the first time in his life his thoughts were a mere sensory perception. There was a freedom to that. A dangerous, perhaps fatal, freedom.

He had been rejected by the two women in his life who he thought had mattered the most: his mother and his wife. His children? Yes, them too. Because he had spent his life working, in this supermarket, trying to prove something to someone whom he could never impress: his wife. So he had given up. Had instead created his own world, a world where his wife and his children were not a part. And the boys, his two sons, had grown up quickly. And then they were gone. First chance they got. Who could blame them?

Still, this was easier. The accelerator a metaphor for his life. Always running. The road demanded his attention. He eased back. Just a little. Because all it required was an extra nudge, a tight bend, a spin of the steering wheel, and he would lose control.

A stretch of straight road suddenly opened up ahead of him and he snapped the reins, and the big Clydesdale started to gallop. But still the blue lights were in his rear-view mirror, impossible to shake.

It was then he felt it. The energy required to propel two tonnes of metal into forward motion at this speed, that of three hundred and eighty horses, literally fading away. And something else was missing. A sound. As he listened, he could hear the grinding of fat, wide-rim tyres on tarmac. What was missing was the sound of an engine. His eyes were drawn to something glowing on the instrument panel. He looked at it. It was the fuel pump icon. Flashing. The power was not fading. It was gone.

Crabby threw his head back and laughed.

He couldn't even get this right.

CHAPTER SEVENTY-FIVE

They brought Crabby directly to Cross Beg station. Running on sirens and blues, the journey had taken less than thirty minutes.

Crabby listened to the water dripping into the bowl of the cell toilet. He lay on the thin plastic mattress on the concrete bed that had been built into the wall underneath the cell window. He could hear other sounds from outside the cell door, these drifted along the corridor, rising and ebbing; shouts, laughter, crying, the banging of doors.

He was numb now, a coldness in his body, feeling the hopelessness of it all. It was destiny. For this to happen. Again. And now it was his turn. To be locked up, just as they had locked up his mother. It had happened before. And it would happen again. It was happening now. To him.

He turned and faced the wall, closed his eyes.

And was back again. To that night. That terrible night.

Now it was his turn.

CHAPTER SEVENTY-SIX

Superintendent Wilde was subdued; he seemed to have lapsed into a daydream. He jerked forward in his chair now, his eyes focusing on Beck, shook his head once.

'I know,' Beck said. 'It's a lot to take in.'

'It is. Gerry was alright you know… underneath it all. Christ, I had no idea. What he was going through. You ever work with someone who killed themselves?'

The question struck Beck as odd. Cops all knew of colleagues who had tied ropes around their necks, or shot their brains out, usually with service firearms. Statistically, police suicide rates were six times the national average.

'I know of five,' Beck said. 'Over the years.'

Wilde's eyes widened.

'Really. Five. That many.'

'That many. And you?'

'This is my second. But I have to go all the way back to training college for the first. Andy Carroll was his name. He went down to the Cliffs of Moher one weekend and threw himself off. I never spotted it in him either. Did you ever spot it? In anybody? Did you ever say, "Ya, he's the one, he's going to do it?"'

Beck inhaled hard. 'The thing is,' he said. 'It's never the ones you think. It's always the ones you don't.'

'Doesn't make it any easier.' The window blind rustled in a breeze. 'Billy Hamilton's been transferred to Galway.' Wilde added.

'We need to get him before a judge, otherwise he's out, pending file. I think he could do himself in.'

'I don't.'

'That's a fifty-fifty chance so. One of us has to be right. For sure.' A flicker of a grin, gone as quickly. 'The DPP recommends manslaughter for the death of Edward Roche. A murder charge won't stick.'

'If he does get out, and kicks off again…'

'That's a chance we have to take. Anyway, I think he's done all his kicking off for now. Maybe forever. Something like this can change a person. Still doesn't solve the counterfeit currency issue.'

Beck didn't really care about the counterfeit currency issue. Not at this moment.

'Maybe it was just Edward Roche. Maybe he was a one-man operation.'

'Maybe,' Wilde said, looking past Beck, beginning to daydream again. 'If his death takes it out of my in-tray for a while, I'll take it. Or better still, permanently. We can always live in hope.'

Out of sight, out of mind.

'You interviewing Maurice Crabby soon?'

Beck nodded. 'Yes. Just waiting for him to be booked in. And his wife was there at Kelly's Forge too. The day Samantha Power was killed.'

'You're kidding me.' Wilde fell back into his chair as if he'd been punched. 'I won't be taking part in any interviews. I know them, so there's a conflict of interest. You taking her in?'

'Not just yet. I'll see how it goes with him first.'

'We don't have much, do we?'

'We have enough. If the fingerprints on the handle of the passenger door and the roof match. We should have the results soon.'

'Hhmm. And of course, considering he ran from that checkpoint. So if I was a betting man…'

Beck got to his feet.

'Odds on favourite then?' Beck said.

Wilde shook his head, a smile breaking through. 'His wife. Now there's a dark horse.'

'Neck and neck maybe?'

'That's enough, Beck. Run along.'

CHAPTER SEVENTY-SEVEN

They carried mugs of instant coffee in with them to the interview room, placed them onto the table top and sat down.

'Would you like something?' Beck asked. 'I can get you a tea or a coffee.'

Crabby stared into space, not replying. Beck repeated the question, louder this time.

'Tea? Coffee, Mr Crabby?'

Crabby turned his eyes to Beck and focused. He shook his head now, and spoke in a soft voice, so soft Beck could not hear him.

'I can't hear you.' Beck said. 'Can you speak up?'

'I don't want anything. Thank you. No. Wait. Water. A glass of water. Thank you.'

He sipped from the water when Claire brought it in. She sat down.

Beck explained he was to be interviewed in connection with the murder of Samantha Power, that he was not being charged for this crime, and was not under arrest in connection with it. His admissions were to be made voluntarily. If he agreed to it, that is.

'Unless, Mr Crabby,' Beck said. 'You force me to charge you with her murder, I can do that. I can charge you and work backwards. But I think it would be better if you agree to talk to us. Do you agree?'

Crabby was motionless for a long time, then slowly nodded. Beck was about to turn the recorder on when there was a knock to the door. It opened and Garda Dempsey put his head in.

'A word, please.'

Beck exchanged glances with Claire, then got up and stepped out into the hallway, closing the door behind him.

'Yes?'

'SOC,' Dempsey said. 'The fingerprint comparisons with those found on the passenger door of Samantha Power's car...'

An elbow, once again, into Beck's stomach. 'Yes...?' when Dempsey didn't answer right away, forcing himself to keep his voice down a notch.

Beck stepped back into the interview room and resumed his seat. He looked at Crabby, but Crabby would not look him in the eye.

'Listen to me,' Beck said. 'Listen carefully. Are you listening now?'

CHAPTER SEVENTY-EIGHT

Beck's tone caused Crabby to lose that vacant stare of his, an alertness creeping in now. He nodded slowly.

'Yes. I'm listening.'

'When I turn on this recorder,' Beck said. 'I want you to answer my questions. Again, you are not under arrest for the murder of Samantha Power. Will you answer my questions, or will you waste my time? Tell me now.'

Crabby spoke, loud enough for them to clearly hear.

'I'll answer your questions.'

'Right then, let's get on with this.' Beck switched on the recorder. 'Interview with Mr Maurice Crabby commencing,' glancing at his watch, 'at 17.03 hours. Present, Detective Inspector Finnegan Beck and Detective Garda Claire Somers.' Beck paused briefly, then: 'Mr Crabby, did you murder Samantha Power?'

Crabby squinted his eyes, almost closing them.

'I... don't know. I don't know anything any more.'

Beck and Claire exchanged glances.

'Were you at the scene? Kelly's Forge. Last Tuesday. Were you there? Specifically, between four and six o'clock?'

Crabby looked down, placed a hand under the calf of each leg. Beck had seen it a thousand times before. Crabby was thinking.

'I was there,' no embellishments, just matter-of-fact.

'You were there?' Beck repeated.

'Yes. I was.'

'When exactly?' it was Claire. 'What time?'

Crabby folded his arms, sat back.

'I don't know the time. Not exactly. But it was that day. Tuesday.'
Beck leaned forward.

'You know, Mr Crabby, Samantha Power was killed that day.
She had been in your shop beforehand. You were observed on
CCTV, driving out from the supermarket shortly after she had
left, travelling the same road in the same direction as Samantha
Power's Citroen Picasso. So, when you tell us you were actually
there too, at Kelly's Forge, where her body was found... Think
about it, Maurice. If you were me, what questions would you be
asking right now? What would you be thinking?'

'That I killed her. That's what I'd be thinking.' Crabby sighed,
lowered his head and cradled it in both hands, sighed again. 'Can
I tell you something?'

'Go ahead,' Beck said.

Crabby folded his arms now, and lowered his head, staring at
the table.

'They took my mother away, you know. They said she killed
her baby. That was my sister. The baby's name was Bernadette.
They locked my mother up and I never saw her again. Not really.
So forgive me if I have a sense of déjà vu about this whole thing.'

'What you're saying,' it was Claire, 'is that *if* you didn't kill...'

'I didn't kill her,' Crabby interrupted. 'I didn't kill anyone.'

'You just said you weren't sure,' Beck said. 'Which is it?'

'... if you didn't kill her,' Claire went on, 'that you can be still
locked away. Is that what you're saying? Without any evidence?
You believe you could be locked up? Just like that?'

Now that it was voiced aloud, his fear, his torment, became
like a balloon released, flittering about the room, the air escaping,
landing now, flat and lifeless. Yes, he really had believed that.

'Oh, God,' as he began to cry.

'Mr Crabby,' Beck said. 'Why were you at Kelly's Forge the day
of the murder? And why didn't you tell us you had been there?'

Crabby wiped his eyes with the back of his hands.

'My mother was never the same again,' Crabby said, still with his head bowed, staring at the table. 'I lost my sister that night. But I also lost my mother.' Crabby's head jerked up suddenly. He stared at Beck. 'The big policeman took her.'

'When exactly did this happen?' it was Beck.

'The Marian Year,' Crabby replied. '1954. October. The whole country was on its knees. To Our Lady. 30,000 people marched through Dublin in May that year in a Marian procession. I prayed to her, I prayed and prayed. Night and day. That she would return my mother to me. But my prayers weren't answered. My mother never came home again.'

'Where was your father?' Claire asked.

Crabby sat back in his chair. He closed his eyes, as if he was no longer able to tolerate the memories.

'He was in England. They said he left my mother for another woman. But I don't know. No one ever told me. My mother was only twenty-two at the time. *Twenty-Two.* He was older, in his thirties. He came back. Once. He brought me to see her in, in that place, but he went away again, left me with my mother's brother, uncle Paddy, and his wife. I heard from him down through the years, from my father, on and off. He married again too. And then he forgot all about me, and all about Kelly's Forge. A cursed place. And still is. Looking back, I can understand why he did what he did.'

'Who is this big policeman you mentioned?' Beck asked.

Crabby lowered his voice again, like he was afraid to mention the name, and his eyes opened.

'Inspector Padráic Flaherty. He came over from Galway. I remember him in the cottage, his head almost touching the roof. I went in beside my grandmother in the hag, I was so frightened of him.'

Crabby fell silent, wrapping his arms about himself.

'And then,' Claire asked. 'What happened?'

'He told my mother he didn't believe in monsters or any of that nonsense. He wasn't very nice to her. He got the village to look for the child. But they didn't look for long. His mind was made up. In the early morning he took my mother away with him in his car. Just the two of them. She never came back.'

'Where is your mother now?' Claire asked.

Crabby's eyes widened.

'Haven't you heard what I said? I told you. She's locked up. She's still locked up. They mightn't actually lock the doors there any more, but she's legally detained. In Saint Bridget's. Ever heard of it?'

'In County Clare?'

Crabby nodded.

And both detectives now understood. Beck had thought his reference to losing his mother was metaphysical. But it wasn't, it was literal. Beck understood the trauma that would cause a child, a trauma that would not have been understood back then. A trauma that might keep a part of Crabby forever five years old, endlessly reliving that night, over and over, a perpetual loop of torment. Yes, Beck knew all about that too.

'You still haven't told us why you were there,' Beck said, although he was beginning to think that he might.

'I went there that day, Tuesday, because it was my sister Bernadette's birthday. I often think of her, of her lying there, alone, in the cold earth of that place.' Crabby's eyes began to well up. 'And the next morning, I went there too. I can't get the place out of my head sometimes, see. I try, but I can't. I went there on my bike, for the same reason as anyone who goes to a grave does. To remember. To remember my sister. Yes, and my mother too. Sometimes I close my eyes and imagine that my sister has not died, but has lived, that my mother and father have stayed together, that we were all one happy family living together in a house in the woods. Crazy, isn't it, and also that the place that gives me the greatest torment also can give me the greatest peace. And that's why I go there, and that's why I went there that morning when I… I found the body. It makes no sense to anyone but myself. Because, after all, I am the one living this torment, every waking day of my life. 1954 does not exist, it is long gone. But not for me.'

He paused. 'But I did not follow her. That evening she was killed, Tuesday. I remember she was in front of me for a time, when I left the supermarket to make deliveries, but I was in the van, and I turned off for the village of Kiliter. There's sat nav in the van, so you can check. It was earlier that day I went in the Range Rover, I left a single rose. I remember thinking how small and inconsequential it was, how…'

Crabby fought back the tears.

'Why were you making deliveries?' Beck asked.

'Because my staff can't get things right, that's why,' his voice stiffening. 'It was a mix-up. And it was left to me to sort out. As usual.'

Which would explain Crabby's apparent agitation when Samantha Power passed him on her way out of the shop.

'I know it was earlier,' he added. 'When I went to Kelly's Forge. Because I remember it was before I made those deliveries. That's how I'm so certain.'

'What time?'

'I don't know. But I know it was before I made the deliveries. I went there in the Range Rover.'

'And how did you get blood on your clothes?'

Crabby's eyes narrowed. There was only one way Beck could have known about that. They had been speaking with his wife.

'She was there too, you know,' he said. 'My damned wife.'

'We know,' Claire said. 'She told us. She told us she wanted to… catch you.'

'That again,' Crabby said. 'Catch me… I cut myself on the damn shutter. Later, that evening, when I was closing up. It got stuck and I had to push it down and the edge caught me, tore my shirt. There you have it. As simple as that.'

He became quiet.

'We found fingerprints,' Beck said. 'On the passenger door of Samantha Power's car.'

Crabby's eyes narrowed further still. 'And?'

CHAPTER SEVENTY-NINE

'They're not yours, Mr Crabby,' Beck said. 'The fingerprints on the door are someone else's. Of the person who killed Samantha Power. That's what I think.'

Crabby considered those words, from the man before him, the man who had come into his supermarket that night, staggering and speaking gibberish. The man, now sombre and sober and with the full power of the State behind him. Back then he had given the policeman a bottle of tequila and Beck had left happy. The juxtaposition of the two Becks led him to a conclusion now. The detective did not have to mention anything of fingerprints. He could have left him wondering. But he didn't. This man had a *croí*, a heart.

'But we found skeletons,' Beck said. 'Of children. Babies. In a place near Kelly's Forge.'

Crabby's head snapped up to look at him.

'What? More than one?'

'Sounds like you already know about one,' Beck said. 'Do you?'

Beck watched Crabby, who slowly nodded.

'Yes,' he said. 'I do. There was a monster... but it wasn't an animal.'

'Monster,' Beck said. 'What monster?'

'My mother.'

CHAPTER EIGHTY

'I went to visit her,' Crabby said, lowering his head, resting it on his chest. 'My mother. Yesterday evening. She told me what happened, to my sister, Bernadette. She told me of how Micheál Peoples took her into the forest, where my sister was killed and offered up to the spirits of the forest, a… a sacrifice.' Crabby began to cry now. 'My poor, dear sister.'

Beck tried to make sense of it all, and did not have the patience to allow time for Crabby's grief.

'What happened,' he said. 'Tell me.'

Crabby was quiet for a moment, then he looked at Beck, and he began to tell him, exactly what his mother had said, in a voice that was strong and unwavering, as if expounding the demons from within himself.

After he'd finished, the two detectives were quiet for a time.

'That's quite a story,' Beck said.

'What will happen now?' Crabby asked.

Beck thought about that. His instinct, that innate thing that had served him well throughout his career, all his life, spoke to him, telling him that Crabby was speaking the truth. But then again, the hawk had missed the mice in the long grass, so he could not be certain.

'My priority is the current investigation. The unit for historical crimes against children will be notified immediately.'

'I'm sorry,' Crabby said. 'What she said, what she told me, was such a shock. Please, you must understand that. So that when you asked, about that poor girl, Samantha Power, I just… I just, I don't know. I doubted myself. I mean. I doubted my sanity. Because, well, anything seems possible now, doesn't it?'

'Yes,' Beck said, 'I suppose it does. One piece of good news though, Mr Crabby,'

Crabby raised his eyebrows. 'Yes?'

'We have no reason to hold you any further. You're free to go.'

'But my mother,' Crabby said. 'She's not a murderer. She did not kill my sister. She was a child herself don't you understand, the events of that night pushed her over the edge, made her temporarily insane. Whatever happened was not her fault. I can see that now. She was a victim too. Inspector, what will become of her, my mother?'

Whatever happened that night, Beck considered.

'Maybe we'll never know what happened that night,' he answered, voicing his thoughts aloud.

But there was one way that might help him to find out.

CHAPTER EIGHTY-ONE

Claire led the way down the stairs into the dank basement. She reached up and pulled a cord, turning on the light. Their footsteps echoed as they walked along the narrow hallway. They went through an open door into a room. Light seeped in through air vents high on the wall, shadows slicing across them intermittently, with it the sound of footsteps: Main Street.

She flicked the light switch just inside the door. It was old-fashioned, circular, stubby and black. In the room was a table, stacked with papers and old files, the floor along the walls similar.

Eventually she found it. It wasn't a file. It was two sheets of yellowed paper held together by a treasury tag, the tag's metal tips thick with rust. She placed it onto a stack on the table. They both stood over it, staring down at the spindly handwriting. Then Beck picked it up, brought it closer, turned it so that they both could read:

Following conversation with Dr Hillary Nugent of Mount Saint Carmel it was agreed that Kathleen Waldron would be presented for psychiatric evaluation at the first possible opportunity. Dr Nugent was of the opinion new research into the area of filicide – this is the killing of a child by one or more parents – would lend itself to what he said was an interesting case study.

It should be noted that Kathleen Waldron was covered in blood on the arrival of uniformed members. Inspector Flaherty observed same on his arrival.

Kathleen Waldron has been detained in Mill Street bar-
racks in Galway. She is twenty-two years old and appears
quiet and withdrawn and generally uncommunicative,
apart from occasional utterances about 'the monster'. This is
what she has insisted throughout came into her home and
took her baby, named Bernadette. All the inhabitants of the
place, Kelly's Forge, a mere twenty-five souls, are steeped in
superstition and folklore. They talk of banshees and faeries
and such general nonsense. In this case, I believe such beliefs
have nurtured a madness in the girl culminating now in her
killing her baby and disposing of its body, where we do not
know, as the body has still to be found. I consider the girl to be
wily and clever and so do not hold out much hope of finding
the child's remains. In this instance, extensive searches have
been conducted in the area but without result.

There was a break in the handwriting, with one line left blank.
When it continued, the hand was heavier, greater spaces between
the words, some not resting on the line but rising from it, others
dipping beneath. It was also harder to decipher.

In the last number of hours I believe I have advanced the case
to a conclusion. It will avoid the requirement for a trial and
the attendant publicity this would lend the State – including,
I have no doubt, most unwelcome international press cover-
age. The husband of the girl, Seamus Waldron, has agreed to
sign a document to the effect that his wife is wholly deranged
and with the urgent necessity to be confined within a secure
institution forthwith. My recommendation is St Bridget's
Hospital for the Mentally Deviant at Trabawn, County
Clare. The girl has one other child, a boy, named Patrick.
He will be passed into the care of his uncle, Paddy Crabby,
and his wife, who, to all accounts, are respected citizens and

good Catholics. The boy will adopt his uncle's surname and will be known by his middle Christian name, Maurice. This, it is deemed, will be in his best interests.

As agreed with the Chief Superintendent of Galway District, and in his discussions with the relevant parties, including the Bishop of the diocese and the public representative, Mr Galligan, member of Galway County Council, it will be noted officially that the child died of pneumonia and was buried with her grandfather at Ballinasloe. This summary report will be destroyed and there the matter will rest.

Signed, Inspector Padráic Mary Flaherty, Mill Street Garda Barracks, Galway, October 26, 1954...

'It was his father,' Beck whispered, putting the report down. 'He had his wife committed. Maurice Crabby's mother.'

'But,' Claire said, 'if they thought she'd killed her child, wouldn't that be a wise move to make?'

'He couldn't have known that though,' Beck said. 'He just wanted her out of the way, and this was a very convenient way of doing it.'

The only sound in the room was that of the dull thuds of feet passing on the pavement outside.

'But they couldn't do that,' Claire said, 'even back then... could they?'

'They could. And did. It was common. This little country of ours had one of the highest rates for committal to mental institutions in the entire world at the time. I know of a case where a man had his wife committed because he was having an affair. He needed her out of the way. That's how he did it. She spent thirty years in the place. The poor woman was as sane as you or I.'

Claire pointed to the report. 'Didn't Maurice Crabby know about this?'

'No. How could he? This was bureaucracy. A collusion between church and state. No one knew about this except the people directly involved. How times have changed. Thankfully.'

'So, what do we do with it?'

Beck considered.

'We defer to rank on this one. Superintendent Wilde. That's my verdict. Let him deal with it.

'Tell me,' she said then. 'How did you know we'd find those remains? Isn't it all a bit strange?'

Beck shrugged. 'Yes. Stranger than fiction. I dreamt it, in a round about way that is.'

He laid the old yellowed sheets of paper down carefully.

'Bit of advice, Beck,' Claire said. 'Don't tell too many people about dreaming up the answers to cases, okay? Because if you do, they'll think you're a complete and utter stoner. Got it?'

'Got it,' he said, but he'd got that already.

Went without saying, actually.

CHAPTER EIGHTY-TWO

Sergeant Connor was seated at a desk in the Ops Room when Beck returned from the basement, typing furiously onto a computer keyboard. He didn't notice Beck come in, or walk across the room, or stop and stand right next to him. His hands were fisted, except for two index fingers protruding like barrels of revolvers. The two fingers circled the air, over the keyboard, hunting for letters, before swooping and crashing onto the pad.

'We were getting worried about you,' Beck said. 'And where's Garda Ryan?'

Connor looked up with a start, smiled. 'Like you said. Everything goes under the case number. Writing up my report right now… Jane, she had to go home, family emergency or something.' Connor glanced back to his computer screen.

'What kept you?' Beck asked.

'Got a damn puncture on the way back. A six-inch nail in the front right. Hegarty put it there. Can't prove it, of course, but I just know he did. A slow puncture. We were halfway back before I noticed it.'

Connor leaned into his computer screen.

'Covered it all there, I think. You like the way I finished it? Sums up the place, *filthy*.'

Beck didn't answer that question. Pulse was not a platform for creative expression. It was for strategic information, bullet points preferably. If Connor wanted to tell a story he should join a writers' group. Which made him think that after all this was over, maybe

Cross Beg could benefit from a class on best practice in the use of the Garda Pulse computer system.

'The fingerprints on the door of Samantha Power's car,' Beck said. 'We just heard. Not a match to Hegarty, or anybody else.' And nodding towards the computer. 'I think we can wipe his name from the board now.'

Connor looked disappointed. His readership audience had just virtually disappeared.

CHAPTER EIGHTY-THREE

She was standing at the counter in the hardware shop, waiting for the young sales assistant to finally finish with the man whom she'd been standing behind for over five minutes now. The man with a paint colour board spread out on the counter, ruminating and indicating with the end of a pen the particular colours he was interested in, oblivious to her presence. There was another cash register, unattended. As usual, Vicky could never remember a time, not once, when that register was ever used.

Eventually, the colour board was folded away, but the man continued talking, waving the end of his pen through the air. *Chit chat.* She heard something about a football match, the young sales assistant giving polite nods of his head. But she could see it in the assistant's expression: *go away now please.* To which the man was oblivious, waving the end of the pen about, 'He spent a fortune on a team of misfits. They didn't win one game towards the end of the season. Not one…' he said.

Finally, the young sales assistant stopped nodding his head, glancing back to her, then to the man again, unsmiling: *It's time to go now. Seriously.*

The man looked over his shoulder. 'Didn't realise you were there, love.' And back to the young assistant. 'Well, I'd better be on my way then. Let me think about that, will you? I'll get back to you, young man. Thank you and good day.'

Vicky picked up one of the two cans of deck varnish she had placed on the floor.

'Hello, Vicky,' the sales assistant said, his eyes brightening. 'Twenty minutes. And still he didn't buy anything. All he's ever bought in here is a pair of fifty cent ear plugs. Two cans of varnish is it?'

'Yes, honey, two.'

'So you're finally starting?' scanning the first can in.

'I'm putting the cart before the horse with this. But so what. Can't do the decking for ages yet. But it makes me feel like I'm getting something done.'

'Uh huh,' he said. 'But it'll be worth it when it's finished. A TV production studio you said, last time when you were in. That right?'

Vicky smiled. She noticed the assistant was blushing. He seemed to do that a lot. She waited until he looked up again and she held his eyes, watching the deepening shade of red on his cheeks. How old was he anyway?

'Yes,' she said, a playful giggle. 'Watch this space as they say. I plan to do contract work for U.S. media companies, plus my own productions too of course... I just can't wait, I'm simply bursting with ideas.'

Oh go on, she thought, and ran her tongue over her lips. The lad looked away, took the money she handed him, placed it into the till, his head bowed, then mumbled something about another customer and walked away.

CHAPTER EIGHTY-FOUR

Beck opened his eyes, his body giving an involuntary jerk. He was so tired, he'd momentarily drifted off. He yawned, leaned forward, supporting his head with the palm of both hands on his desk. The Ops Room was quiet. He was sitting in a corner, behind the door. Claire was seated at her desk on the opposite side of the room, beneath the window. Sergeant Connor and a uniform were the only others present.

He had played it over twice. From the time Samantha Power had entered the car park of Crabby's supermarket until she had left again. He had followed her along the road out of town, losing sight of her when she drove past the last camera.

What happened next?

Had she stopped somewhere and picked up somebody? Somebody who was known to her? Or had somebody, instead, stopped her?

Beck sat back, cupped his hands behind his head now. His stomach rumbled. He hadn't eaten anything all day except for two sausage rolls. There comes a point when you don't feel hunger any more. When coffee dulls your appetite and makes you feel sick. It comes at the point of an investigation when nothing is clear, where you thought you were making progress, were getting close to something, only to find instead that you'd travelled in a complete circle, arriving back where you had started from in the first place. And Beck was back to where he had started, where it all had all started. He had watched Samantha Power walk out into the early evening sunshine, going to her death. Taking her six-month-old daughter with her. How did it happen?

How?

'You need to eat,' it was Claire.

He hadn't noticed her standing there.

'You going out?'

'Uh huh,'

'Get me something, will you?'

'Of course.'

'It doesn't matter what, just so long as it's not poisonous.'

Beck used his finger to reset the video progress bar, and for the third time, began to watch the CCTV footage all over again, slowing it right down this time.

It was a chicken roll, with ham and cheese, the bread hard, the cheese like wood-shavings, the ham the texture of wet paper. The chicken itself was chopped into thick slices, coated in breadcrumbs and barbecue sauce, a firewall, stopping any other flavours from getting through. But bite for bite, it fly-tipped more calories into his stomach than anything else could.

Claire had pulled her chair close. She was eating from a salad box, staring at the screen. The CCTV footage continued to play, a slow-motion action replay. Beck swallowed the last of his food. He needed water. And a cigarette. He was about to press stop to take a break, when…

He'd noticed it before, he realised that now. An optical illusion, a shadow, a spectre, with it a realisation that what is searched for is sometimes right in front of your eyes all along.

A piece of roll fell from his mouth onto the computer keyboard.

'Gross,' Claire said, oblivious.

'Can't you see it?'

'See what?'

He stopped play, rolled it back, played it again.

'There,' indicating the rear of the car.

Claire leaned in, her head almost touching his.

'Um…'

He waited for her reaction, but there was none. He stopped play once more, repeated the procedure, his finger hovering over the finger pad. At the exact moment it appeared. Pressed: Stop.

Silence.

'Christ. Look. That,' Beck said, pressing a finger to the screen.

Claire, looking towards it.

'A shadow… is it?'

'Yes. A shadow. It's not divine intervention. Something had to cause it. Don't you see? Someone is getting in on the other side of the car.'

She thought about that, her tired mind processing it. *Someone is getting into the other side of the car. Someone is getting into the other side of the car.*

'Christ,' she said. 'You're right.'

CHAPTER EIGHTY-FIVE

Claire got her breath back. Trying not to, but still feeling it all the same: foolish. She had seen what Beck had seen but yet had still completely missed it. No, not just missed it, it hadn't even registered. She'd need a positive appraisal from Beck if she wanted to be considered for sergeant. This wouldn't help. And it annoyed her that at a time like this she could even think like that. But she was. She realised she had, again, underestimated the man. She looked at him now with renewed admiration.

Beck played it over again one last time. Unmistakeable. Verifiable. Real. How could she have missed that? A shadow. And a shadow, no matter what way you look at it, can only be caused by one thing, an object that blocks out the light.

'Let's assume,' Beck said, speaking slowly, thinking things over as he went. 'He gets into the car here. At this point, this moment. Let's just assume he gets in the car and she drives away with him in it. We won't worry about the ins and outs of it just yet. Why she didn't scream. Or maybe she did. But it doesn't look that way. From what we can see. Maybe he's – let's assume it's a he – is crouching, which is why we don't see him. Let's just assume that, okay?'

Claire nodded.

'Then he will not only have gotten into the car, but into the car park, first. Had to. So we need to roll back our timeline, see if we can spot anything else. I think it would help if we had a bigger screen. You look after that?'

They pulled the blinds down at the end of the Ops Room. Claire set up a PowerPoint. There were other people here now, drifting in and taking an interest without anything having been announced. By the time everything was set up, and Claire was about to begin, about to project the image onto the end wall, there were a dozen detectives and uniforms sitting down, waiting. No one asked any questions. Not yet. They knew Beck was waiting. So they were waiting too. When it appeared, whatever that was, they'd get their answers. Or not.

Beck nodded to Claire, and using her finger on the pad, she drew back the video bar, the clock in the corner of the screen automatically clicking backwards. She stopped when she'd reduced the time frame by ten minutes.

'Ready?' she asked.

Beck answered, and was surprised when the whole room answered with him, a collective 'Yes'.

She pressed play.

The sounds drifted across the room, the same sounds as before, but louder now, relayed through portable speakers; voices and engines, the sound of the breeze, a flapping noise, the occasional banging of a door. Again, that same sense of foreboding, a sadness from knowing what was about to happen, from knowing that a blue Citroen Picasso people carrier would soon, very soon, enter this car park and park in an empty space right there.

Beck knew all this.

And yet he knew so little.

But he had a feeling, a feeling deep in the pit of his stomach, growing now, getting stronger, that soon he would do. He would know. They all looked at the screen and were silent, at this picture of utter small-town ordinariness.

Beck wondered, how is it possible to see what is different when all appears the same?

CHAPTER EIGHTY-SIX

'See that vehicle? There, at the back?'

The room turned. In the doorway of the Ops Room was Garda Ryan. She'd wandered in from the public office.

'There,' she said again, pointing.

'Where?' someone asked.

'Just off the middle right. One, two, three rows back. Actually, the last row.'

Beck spoke. 'Why don't you come up here and point it out, exactly?'

Garda Ryan walked through the room, stepped up beside the power-point.

'Go on, Jane' Claire said. 'Show us.'

She extended an arm, her high-vis jacket making a squelching sound, pointing at the vehicle.

'Nothing unusual in that,' a voice. 'So?'

'Well,' Garda Ryan said, doubt creeping in now. 'I noticed this. That it had started reversing from its parking space. Then, when the victim's car came along, it stopped. And when she moved into the parking space, that vehicle, there,' she tapped the image with her finger, 'drove back into the space it had just left.'

No one spoke.

Beck hadn't noticed that. He'd been looking for a person, not a vehicle.

'Let's have a look,' he said. 'Replay it, Claire.'

It was a high vehicle, so it stretched above those around it, but not by much. There was an aerial in the centre of the blue roof, a row of four spotlights in front with an air horn behind, also a strip of sun visor vinyl across the top of the windscreen. Beck could see the roof and the top portion of the windscreen as the vehicle reversed from its space. In the middle forefront, the cobalt blue Picasso of Samantha Power appeared.

The rest was exactly as Garda Ryan had said: The blue Picasso reversed into its parking space – Beck noted this was directly opposite the other vehicle, but three rows back. The other vehicle lingered, then slowly edged forward, occupying its parking space again.

Of course, Beck knew, there could be a perfectly legitimate reason for it all. It was too early to tell.

'Claire,' he said, 'let's go forward now. Jump right ahead. By two hours this time. Let's just have a look at how things are then. See if this vehicle is still there.'

Claire pushed the video bar with her finger, watching the time line click forward now, jumping to 17.30 hours. She stopped.

It sat alone. The same vehicle. He could see it properly now for the first time. It was a blue and silver Mitsubishi pickup.

CHAPTER EIGHTY-SEVEN

Vicky left the hardware shop, walked across the car park, placed the heavy tins of deck oil on the ground by her Mercedes and fumbled in her pocket for the keys. She extracted them and opened the boot, lifted up the tins one at a time and placed them inside.

She got into the car, placed the key in the ignition. Thinking. She had already rung Frankfurt. A tentative arrangement had been made for a meeting the following week. She'd have to fly out on an overnighter. She got a crazy idea: maybe the cool policeman might come with her? She dismissed the thought, but not completely: we'll see, she thought. But she needed to act fast. Because if her theory was right about who was responsible... well then, wow! That would be enough to make prime-time TV worldwide. And a podcast. Don't forget the podcast, she thought. She smiled. A podcast, that would be a first. And Danny was due in Crabby's the following day. By lunchtime tomorrow, she thought, I might have what I need.

She was about to turn the ignition key when she saw someone come round the corner from the farm and building supplies yard at the back of the shop. A fleeting glimpse, check shirt open, billowing over a black T-shirt, wearing a baseball hat. She drove forward, looking left and right to make sure nothing was approaching. When she glanced back again, the person was gone.

She drove out of Cross Beg, swung onto River Road, driving by the big houses behind their ivy walls. The people here controlled the town, more or less. The movers and shakers. Or the hand-me-downers. Protecting their status and passing it from one generation to the next.

She thought of this as she drove. At the end of River Road, she turned left onto Atlantic Drive, heading towards the coast. When a westerly blew, the salt air blew in from the sea. Maybe she should have bought a property nearer to the sea, she wondered? That would be something. But she had limited funds, and even a tumbledown shack with sea views was fetching €75,000. Easy. And without plumbing. Or central heating. Take another €75,000 just to make it habitable. No, she was fine where she was. It might not have sea views, but she could still smell the salt on the air. Who knew, if this worked out, she could afford to renovate her exiting property *and* buy a seaside house too. Because she was talking millions here, not piddly €75,000. Bring it on!

She turned onto Atlantic Drive. The land was good around here, lush and sweet. It was horse-breeding country too. Often, when she went for walks along the beach she would see horses from the local stables being galloped across the sand, running at the waters edge, throwing up a fine mist of spray. To her left, over the grey stone walls, the land was flat, stretching to the Atlantic Ocean, and beyond, next stop, New York.

Around here, the blight of emigration had emptied the landscape of young people for generations, each one like a death, because until recently, few ever returned. The American Wake they called it.

An unusual sadness crept into her now, passing the ruins of cottages, relics of lost generations, whose descendants now called themselves British, American or Australian. These ruins, from where they had left, forgotten about now, the ghosts of long dead mothers and fathers still waiting for their return. There was a story to tell in that too. Maybe she could combine the two? Now, wouldn't that be something?

She was approaching the junction now with the coast road. Still, she thought to herself, stopping, checking both ways, it wasn't like that any longer. The thought cheered her, as she pulled out, turning right for home.

She glanced in her rear-view mirror. There was a car there. It had appeared out of nowhere, a small car, coming up fast behind, overtaking her with a roar from its big exhaust. The boy racer disappeared into the distance.

She sat back, thinking of American Wakes again. She should count her blessings more often. Okay, so she was no longer married, and granted, she didn't have children, but there were enough children in the world, right? Maybe it would happen, one day. She was still young enough. But if it didn't… She smiled. Life was good anyway. And she was going to ride this wild friggen horse for all it was worth. Ya, baby!

It was then she saw it. In the rear-view mirror. Turning onto the coast road further back. A silver and blue Mitsubishi pickup.

CHAPTER EIGHTY-EIGHT

'Now we have to wait,' Beck said.

There was a charge in the room. He could almost reach out and touch it. Everyone could. He considered that forensics and scientific wizardry do not always solve cases. Sometimes they have no influence at all. Under the hegemony of the western political system, or civilization, An Garda Síochána formed part of a sophisticated international crime-fighting apparatus headed by the FBI, and which included Interpol and Europol. They had access to the most sophisticated crime-fighting tools, including satellites.

But in this case, as in many others, none of that mattered. Right now, what it came down to was one CCTV camera high up on a pole.

They waited.

CHAPTER EIGHTY-NINE

She watched. There was something about the way it had swung onto Atlantic Drive. Too fast, wobbling before it managed to straighten up again. Something familiar about it. Approaching fast now. Maybe there was an emergency? Which would explain why it was being driven like that. Emergency. Had to be. She eased her foot from the accelerator, wanting the vehicle to catch up, to overtake. Slowing right down, the speedometer needle barely registering twenty-five miles an hour. She watched it, the pick-up growing larger and larger in her rear-view mirror, and then it was filling it completely: the silver grill, the ugly black bull bars, and above it, that face, behind the wheel, everything off kilter.

She relaxed. What was he doing here? She hadn't seen him in that truck before. He wore a check shirt and had a baseball hat on. She realised it was him she had seen outside the hardware shop too.

Should she stop?

A sudden, intense, blinding flash of white light. She closed her eyes and opened them again, her vision pockmarked by a thousand swirling stars. She focused again, on the rear-view mirror. And again, an explosion of white light, her vision disintegrating into a kaleidoscope of flashing wispy threads, all shapes, all sizes. She slowed down almost to a stop now, her vision a blizzard, impossible to see the road ahead.

And then an earthquake. The world literally shaking beneath her. With it a cacophony of sounds – thunder, a ship's klaxon, persistent and angry. She shook her head, the car just about crawling forward. She looked in the mirror, squinting her eyes, through the swirling, flashing stars, could just about make it out. As it came a second time. The blue and silver machine. Bigger. Bigger. Bigger. Filling the rear-view mirror again. And then the earth shook once more as it rammed into her a second time. Receding now, fading, then coming forward once more, the ugly black bull bars, closer and closer, finally disappearing from view as they drew level with the back of her car and…

This time there was no earthquake.

This time it was different.

CHAPTER NINETY

The CCTV gave the time as 18.47. Crabby's supermarket car park was less than a quarter full. The blue and silver pickup stood alone in an empty row of parking spaces. Fat off-road tyres, bull bars, spot lights, air horn, the vehicular equivalent of a body builder showing off his stack in a tight T-shirt. The screen was so still it appeared almost as a painting. They had been watching the CCTV for almost ninety minutes. No one had slumped into their seats yet, bored. No one had spoken. No one had even taken a comfort break.

They waited.

At 18.52 the figure approached from the rear of the vehicle, the distance lending it a fuzziness. The room sat forward in their seats. The charge had become a static, buzzing through the air, almost *tingling*. Senses razor sharp. Adrenalin pumping. Total focus. Nothing else in the whole world mattered.

Now.

He was medium build, balding, wearing a dirty white T-shirt, an unrecognisable motif across the front. Claire zoomed in. He walked quickly, looking about, nervous, moving down the side of the pickup towards the driver's door. Fumbling with the key in the lock, all the while looking around, the door opening as he then sat inside. A second later the engine started with a throaty roar. Reversing from the space, the engine revving.

'Stop,' Beck said. 'Stop it right there. And play it again. Slower this time.'

CHAPTER NINETY-ONE

The driver in front of him took her chance, the Mercedes pulling away just a fraction, but he nudged the accelerator and the big pickup was right on it again, this time the bull bar catching the right rear end of the car. The famous PIT manoeuvre, Pursuit Intervention Technique. He'd seen it plenty of times on American reality cop programmes. He'd always wanted to do it. And now he had.

'Woo hoo,' slapping his hand on the steering wheel. 'Now bitch.'

The car spun in one complete circle and one partial, slow, lazy revolution, coming to a stop at the edge of the road, tottering over the edge to a ten-foot dip. He'd chosen it for this specific purpose, knowing the crash barrier had not yet been installed over the new drainage pit.

The car was sideways across the road in front of him, facing the edge. He revved the pickup's diesel, brought the truck round to the back of the car. Quickly now, before anyone came along on the road, before she had time to react, before the shock wore off. He drove forward, connecting with the car square on. It went over the side like a pin in a bowling alley.

It happened so quickly it was almost as if it wasn't really happening at all. A rollercoaster ride. The sensation of spinning, of slowing, then from behind, an impact, her head bouncing back against the headrest. Then, moving forward, the sensation of falling, as the car slid into an abyss. Down it went. Screaming now. But just as suddenly it stopped again. This wasn't a crash. More like a thud. She was sitting, strapped into her seat, an astronaut waiting for launch. Except she was facing the wrong way.

And with it a panic.

A blind panic.

Screaming, unclipping the seatbelt, opening the door and pushing the full weight of her upper body against it. But it wasn't locked, of course, and she tumbled out onto the gravel of the freshly dug drainage pit. She thought of a grave, of being buried alive. She clambered up the side, digging her nails into the gravel, her feet grappling for grip behind her, moving upward, sliding back, then upward again. She reached the edge of the road, pulled herself over. Standing, feeling the sun on her face. There was nothing ahead of her but a clear road. She began to run. But something was stopping her. She pulled harder against this invisible force, felt the fabric of her blouse tighten about her. Confused, she looked over her shoulder.

He was right there, his hand clamped around the tail end of her blouse hanging from her jeans. A triumphant smile on that slightly deformed face. Like he'd been fishing and just got a prize catch. His back against the pickup. The bull bars, like the lips of a monster.

Her body sagged. This was impossible. She felt her legs give way beneath her. And then she was falling. His arms hooked in underneath her, stopping her fall.

She stared at her shoes as they dragged across the ground. She could not take her eyes from them. Those feet, which she'd been in control of all her life. That always did what *she* told them to do. Now, she had no control over them at all. She thought of screaming, but knew it was useless. She prayed a car would come along. Surely someone had to? But they didn't. Because, although it had seemed like an eternity, everything had happened in less than one minute.

CHAPTER NINETY-TWO

On the second replay, Beck ordered the image frozen and magnified as the man approached the pickup. He could now see that what he had thought was a motif was, in fact, a streak of dirt. The T-shirt was also torn along one sleeve and down one side. The expression on the face was one of agitation. Beck looked for something else, saw it splattered on the T-shirt: blood. It had been over two hours since Samantha Power had driven from the car park. That was when this man had arrived. Where had he been since?

Beck instructed Claire to trawl back further. It was exactly nine minutes before the arrival of Samantha Power that the pickup entered the car park. The driver got out of his vehicle and went into Crabby's supermarket, re-emerged a short time later with a bag of groceries. What happened next they already knew, the pickup reversing from its parking space, then into it again as Samantha Power drove by a couple of rows in front of him.

They waited, and some minutes later, as Samantha Power made her way back to her car from the supermarket, the driver got out of his pickup for a second time. He walked between the row of vehicles in front of his and stopped. One row now separated him from her. There he stood, staring, body stiff, arms by his side: *Predatory.* Samantha Power walked, in that bouncy way of hers, mass of curly hair rising and falling with each stride she took, the final few feet to her car.

She stood out, this beautiful exotic fish, in a small, stagnant pond.

Knowing what he knew about her now, her life had not been easy. And now it was almost over. He felt that bitter sense of sadness well up inside him again.

Run. Before it's too late.

Beck recognised that man's face. The reg check had already provided all the details. But he didn't need a reg check to tell him who this was. A name like his was easy to remember.

Beck looked back towards the man, it wasn't an invisible elbow that he felt hit him in his stomach this time. It was a kick from an invisible horse.

Because he had disappeared from the screen. The man. Whose name was Danny Black.

CHAPTER NINETY-THREE

She placed her groceries into the back of the car, and looked at baby Róisín. The baby's eyes flickered, and she turned her head from side to side a couple of times as if she was about to wake up. But her eyes did not open. Róisín settled again. Samantha went to the driver's door, opened it and got in, closing it gently. Still, baby Róisín did not wake. She turned the key and started the engine, reversed from the parking space, drove forward along the roadway, glancing in the rear-view mirror, smiling, whispered, 'You make it all worthwhile, my darling. You make my life worth living.'

But there are times when a person's mind lags behind the comprehension of the reality they face. A sudden reality, one they had not anticipated nor prepared for. Often when the mind becomes stunned, when neurotransmitters are unable to process information, confusion sets in. And it all happens in the blink of an eye, when all a person can do is stare, frozen...

Now, moving slowly along the roadway, she remembered... the passenger door opening, how she had instinctively turned, had seen a person slithering in. That's how she thought of it, slithering in. This person now rested half on the passenger seat and half in the footwell of her car. She stared, looking back to the road again, driving on as normal. As if nothing had happened. For she couldn't process what had happened, or make sense of it. All in the blink of an eye. But it'd been long enough for Black to press the chisel into her side.

'Drive. Just drive,' his voice low and hard, a verbal punch.

She knew him. That was her first thought. And: What's he doing here? That was her second.

Still, she said nothing. She just drove. Glanced in the rear-view. Róisín turning her head from side to side again. Soon, she would wake. Her mind processing again. All in the blink of an eye.

Danny Black.

Who had been a year ahead of her in secondary school. A builder now… no, no, a handyman. Called himself a builder, but he wasn't. Had a job in Dublin with one of the biggest construction companies in the country. For a time. But something happened, no one knew what. Now he was back in Cross Beg. Quiet, but weird, was the general consensus. She'd seen him in a couple of pubs around town. Or passed him by in the street. Always on his own. He always looked at her, in that way. Most men in Cross Beg looked at her in that way. She was used to it. Danny Black. What the fuck is he doing in my car?

All in the blink of an eye.

Danny Black. Pressing a knife into my side.

She glanced back at Róisín again. Thought of screaming. But it was different now. Now that she had a child. It wasn't about her. She had Róisín to think of.

She drove on.

'You at the road yet? Turn left at the road. Turn left, okay?'

She nodded. At the road. Turned left.

They were heading out of town now, along the Mylestown Road.

'Why?' She found the word escaping from her mouth. Had to open it wide and push it out.

He didn't answer.

'Why?' she asked again, louder.

She drove on, and still he didn't answer.

Mylestown was eight miles away. Ten minutes should cover it. There, she'd stop, in the middle of the road if she had to, honk the horn, one long continuous blast, wouldn't take her hand away until someone noticed, until people came and helped her. They would help her, she had no doubt. All she had to do was keep that horn pressed. Once she got to Mylestown. Just a little further on. Ten minutes should make it. The thought reassured her.

He was sitting very low in the seat now, disappearing beneath the dash whenever a car appeared ahead of them, or behind, then peeping up again, enough to see the road ahead.

Not far now, she thought, Mylestown. All she had to do was get there. People would help her. In Mylestown. Not far now…

'Turn right.'

Oh, Christ.

It was the turn off for Kelly's Forge. Nothing down there.

Nothing.

Why's he taking me there? Why? Why? Why? Her mind thought of the possibilities, kept returning to just one. No. Please. No. Not that.

She looked in the rear-view again.

Róisín was awake, smiling back at her. Samantha Power looked into those small, crystal blue, beautiful eyes, and her heart ached. Her beautiful baby girl was awake. So innocent. So placid. Such a happy child that she rarely cried.

'I have a baby. Please let me go. Pleeeease…' panic in her voice now, speaking low, didn't want Róisín to hear, didn't want her to sense that something was wrong.

And Róisín started to cry.

And she knew she had to get away, pressing her foot down hard onto the accelerator, the car speeding up. Forward. Forward. Had to get away…

'What the fuck you doing?'

Forward. Forward. Speeding up. Faster and faster. Looking in the rear-view all the time. Róisín screaming now, hysterical, waving her arms. I have to get to my baby.

At the end of the road. Nothing ahead but a low, weed-covered embankment. Kept going. Forward. Forward. Help is somewhere. Just so long as I keep moving. Don't stop. Keep moving. Help has to be there. Somewhere.

He yanked the steering wheel, and the car wobbled, then straight-
ened again. She kept her foot on the accelerator. Forward. Forward.
He yanked on the steering wheel a second time, the car wobbled again,
but this time didn't straighten. Instead it juddered, the front dipping
and rising like a boat in a swell. A mountain of green rose before her,
she could see bushes, dangly branches of trees. No, no, no. Have to
keep going. *She screamed, covering her eyes with her arms as the car*
ploughed into the mountain, then through it, dangly branches snap-
ping, bushes falling away beneath the car, but somehow, somehow,
avoiding the trees, emerging on the other side, bouncing over the rough
ground, her foot still pressed to the accelerator, the underside of the
car scraping the undergrowth, the detritus collected from the impact
forced up by the turning wheels, compacting tighter and tighter into
the wheel arches until finally the wheels stopped turning, the engine
whined, then stopped and died. Stalled. No sound. Nothing but the
screaming of the baby.

She unclipped her belt, pushed herself from her seat, fumbling over
the seat towards her baby. Oh Jesus, please spare us. I'm coming, Róisín.
I'm coming. It's all going to be alright. Mummy is coming. Mummy
is coming. *Her hand shaking, but finding the clip on the front of the*
child's chest, her palm pressing against it. Clunk. It opened, the straps
falling away. Reaching for her baby now, so close, her fingers touching
the child's hands.

Oh sweet Jesus in heaven. No. No. No. *Feeling herself being*
dragged back.

His hands upon her. She could feel them running under her skirt,
pulling at her pants, all the time being dragged back. Another hand
on her top, ripping it open. Pushed against the dash, her legs pinned
against the seat, facing him. Those small, black eyes staring, in front
of her, in that strange head, as if behind the slits of a mask. Behind
his head, her baby, no longer screaming, but looking at her strangely,
as if trying to decipher what was happening. It was a look Samantha
had never seen before, a look far beyond the baby's years.

As a rage erupted in Samantha. A rage that had never been there before. Not when Billy Hamilton had struck her all those times. Not when Edward Roche had shouted at her, had insulted her, had laughed and ridiculed her, belittled her.

But it was there now.

'You BASTAAAARD!' Launching herself at him, pushing against him, smashing her knee on the gear knob, but feeling no pain. 'You BASTAAAARD!' And Black, momentarily stunned, merely staring at her. Frozen. She was on him, and they both toppled back towards the passenger door. She reached for the lever and pulled it, the door snapped open. But Black had taken the opportunity, grabbed a handful of that thick curly hair, wound it around his hand, and pulled it back. She felt the pain now, as he squirmed out from beneath her, wrapping an arm around her as he came up, the shift in axis giving him the advantage of his superior strength and weight, pulling her backwards, off him, forcing her down onto her belly across the seats, and then he was lying on her back, half in, half out of the car. She bucked against him and he half fell sideways, but came up again, on top, heavy, immovable this time. And Róisín continued to scream. He glanced back at the baby, looked at those little blue crystals with his black pools of evils. He looked away, and pushed against Samantha's body beneath him, harder and harder. But still he could feel those small blue crystals upon him. He had wanted her body beneath him. All his life he had wanted it. He had fantasised about it. He had imagined it. He had imagined her face instead of those others in countless porn movies. In his sick mind he thought she might want him. Like in those movies. That he could abduct her and she would want him. And if she didn't want it, well then, he could just take it. But she didn't want him. She didn't want it. So he was taking it. He pushed against her, reaching down for his zipper, glancing into the rear seat. The screaming of the child tearing at his ear drums now, the small blue crystals burning into him, and realising he had nothing. He didn't even have a hard-on.

'YOU BITCH!' driving a corner of the chisel into her neck, slicing it open, all the way across.

A geyser.

Of blood.

The child screaming.

Little blue crystals following him as he fled.

CHAPTER NINETY-FOUR

Vicky was lying in the cramped footwell between the front seats and the narrow back bench of the pickup. Hogtied, legs and arms bent behind her back, roped together, duct-tape wound around her mouth, her face pushed into the back of the seat: she could see the lines in the leather, like satellite imagery of a brown and barren landscape. The stiff suspension bounced her up and down, the vehicle shaking and rattling as it moved over rough ground. Her hip hit the floor and she winced.

They travelled for what seemed a long time, but then the road became level and smooth, the drone of the engine steady and constant. She twisted her head, peering into the gorge between the two front seats. Could see his profile, one stubby hand on the wheel, dirty jeans. After some time, the pickup turning, with it a noise, like a yard brush being pulled along the sides. Slowing down, bouncing again, but not much, now turning in a wide arch, pushing her against the back of his seat.

Finally the pickup stopped, the engine died.

Silence.

A deafening silence.

She held her breath, her heart loud inside her, like the beating of a drum, filling an auditorium in her ears, a rhythmic booming: *Boom. Boom. Boom.*

The creaking of the seat as he moved, the door opening. He hesitated before getting out. Then the sound of his footsteps, walking away. She held her breath again. *Boom. Boom. Boom.*

Concentrating, trying to decipher sounds.

But there were no sounds.

There was nothing.

Boom. Boom. Boom.

Then, behind her.

'Hello sweetie.'

Sweet Jesus Christ.

'You don't look very happy, sweetie. Something wrong? I'd have thought you'd be happy to see me. I mean, although you're my second choice and everything, but still. You see, I had someone else in mind, an old friend you could say, from way back, but... how shall I put this? Why let a good plan go to waste, eh? That's what I say. Vicky. Vicky. Vicky. You love a good time, don't you? Oh yes you do. So what d'ya say. How about you and me? Having a good time.'

His voice loud, filling the car. His hands, squirming under her shoulders, dragging her out, *plop* as her legs and ass hit the ground. The sun dazzling, she squinted her eyes against it. She looked down, at the dry, chalky earth, then up, at the grass along the edges of the chalk, to the bushes and trees further on.

She shook her head... Danny Black.

Jesus.

Danny Black.

'Think you're so hot, don't cha? Think you're above everybody else, don't cha? Above me. Don't cha? *Bitch.* Teasing me... think that was enough to get me to do what you wanted? Really, you think I'm that stupid? So who did you think the killer was, Vicky? Come on, I really want to know. Tell me.'

Vicky made a whimpering sound.

'Come on,' he said. 'Tell me.'

'Crabby,' she said. 'Maurice Crabby.'

Danny threw his head back and laughed.

'That's so lame. Call yourself a what... TV producer, investigative journalist? That's the best you can come up with? Jeez, and you thought I was stupid? That's the most stupidest thing I ever heard of. It was right in front of you all along and you couldn't see it. Me.'

And his eyes, rummaging over her entire body now, aggrieved and angry, staring at those certain hidden places, smirking now. His voice dropped to an ugly whisper.

'Did you ever think? You might, you know, like it? With me? No, I don't think you ever did. No one thinks of Danny Black in that way. So then, there's only one way to do this. If ol' Danny can't have it, then ol' Danny has to just take it... I mean, it's not my fault, I got needs too you know. I ask you, what am I supposed to do? Look and not touch, is that it? I dooon't think so.'

He released her and moved off to the side. She turned her head. He was staring ahead, his back to her, as if contemplating something. Then slowly he turned again, and she could see his brown boots stomping across the dry earth towards her. He went behind her again. His hands on her wrists now, his hot breath on her neck. She felt a sharp tug, then a slackening, as he began to untie her.

He came round and stood in front of her.

'Get to your feet,' looping the rope between an elbow and the crook of a thumb and index finger.

Her legs were numb, struggling to her feet, like a new-born fawn. When she stood he threw the rope into the back of the pickup, reached out and grabbed her right wrist, began walking ahead, dragging her behind.

'Time to get serious, sweetie.'

And she heard nothing then but a long, anguished, feral scream. He did not react. Because he did not hear it. It was in her head.

CHAPTER NINETY-FIVE

Superintendent Wilde took his everyday dress uniform jacket from the coat stand in his office, hesitated, returned it to its hook, selected the tactical fleece instead, put it on, looked at Beck.

'Do you really need that?'

He was referring to the Walther 9mm parabellum in the leather holster that hung from Beck's shoulder.

'I don't know. I hope not.'

'We don't normally…'

'Bother. Maybe you should. Dublin South Central took away any illusions I had.'

'It's your choice of course. But note my objection.'

'Noted. ERU would take an hour to get here, at least. If you could note that?'

'Don't act like you know everything, Beck,' Wilde said, heading out the door. 'It's tiresome.'

In the station car park, the superintendent got into the passenger seat of an unmarked Volvo V60, two uniforms climbing into the rear. Claire and Beck went to the unmarked Focus. A marked estate with Garda Ryan, Sergeant Connor and a couple of detectives took the lead as the three cars headed out of the car park. It was 17.35. A time when Black might be home, or heading there, or thinking of heading there. After all, he had no idea they were coming.

CHAPTER NINETY-SIX

She could see the back of a house ahead, at the end of a track, a two-storey, traditional farmhouse, fading white paint, moss-crusted edges on the roof slates. Rounding a corner, a farm shed to her left, a big blue tractor inside, next to it a bank of turf. To her right, another track, leading to a long narrow building with a low red roof, beside it a green-painted grain silo. He opened a gate to the house and pulled her along a path that led to the back door. Two dirty cats slunk about by their feet, making short mewing sounds, hungry. At the door he stopped. He pulled the tape from around her mouth, some stuck to her hair, she felt the hot pinpricks as it was torn away.

'If you scream. It won't make any difference. Just so as you know.'

But now she knew what she had to do if she were to survive. Go along. Obey. Watch. Everything. For an opportunity. Any opportunity. To escape. But most of all. To stay calm.

He opened the door, up a single step, into a small kitchen, she could smell rancid cooking oil. A sink, piled with dishes rising out of dirty water. He pushed her to the left, up another step.

It was *him*!

He killed the girl. He killed the police inspector.

Him.

Jesus!

'That you, Oliver?'

The old woman appeared from a doorway. Small, scraggy, stooped, with long, white, matted hair partially covering her face, wearing a long, stiff, pinafore dress.

If she screamed now, wouldn't this woman… But something stopped her.

'I keep telling you,' he said. 'I'm not fucking Oliver. Oliver is dead. Has been for years. My father is gone to hell, mother.'

'You brought her home. At last. Hello dear, my name is Loretta. It's about time Danny met a nice girl.'

'Listen, you've got to help me,' Vicky said. 'I've been kidnapped. This man…'

He laughed.

'Say hello to mother.'

Vicky's throat was dry. She coughed.

'I thought she'd died,' the old woman said.

'She did. But she's back. Aren't you, Mary?'

He pushed her down the hall.

'Oliver. I have some news. We're going to have another baby.'

'I'm not fucking Oliver. Jesus.'

'And did you hear? He's dead. President Kennedy. It was on the wireless… Oliver, Oliver, where're you going? Come back. You're always leaving me, Oliver.'

At the end of the hall he stopped. They were by the foot of a steep stairs, steps of bare wood, worn at the centre from the weight of countless feet.

'Go back into the room mother. I'll make you a cup of tea.'

'You will?'

'I will.'

'What did you say you'll do, Oliver?'

'Go back into the fucking room. Or I'll put you into the shed. Again. Your choice, mother.'

The sound of shuffling feet, fading, as she retreated into the room, a door closing.

He pushed Vicky onto the stairs.

'Up.'

She began to climb. But she was not moving fast enough. He pushed her again, hard, and she stumbled forward. At the top she felt his hand rough on her back again, this time remaining there, shepherding her forward, then to the side, like an animal, along a short hall and in through an open door. A musty smell. He closed the door, pitch black. He turned a light on. The window was covered in stripes of black plastic. There was a double bed, linoleum-covered floor, heavy dark dresser and wardrobe. The light glowed from inside a glass floral shade hanging from the ceiling. He pushed her again, harder, across the floor. She sprawled onto the bed. He was right behind her. She felt his rough hands on her left foot, a cold hardness wrapping itself around her ankle, with it a clunking sound. She pulled back her leg, could hear a rattling noise, with it felt the pain as the clamp bit into her flesh.

He stood, looking down at her, then turned and walked across the room and out the door onto the landing, his footsteps fading along the hall. The sound of a door opening, a low squeaking noise, for a moment silence, then the squeaking sound again as the door shut. Silence. She sat up, looking down at her feet. Saw that her right foot was manacled to a leg of the bed. She stood, grabbed the base of the bed with both hands, pulling, attempting to lift it. But it was useless. It was too heavy. Just like the dresser, and the wardrobe, the bed was made from heavy, dark wood.

She heard something. Listened. A door opening, the same squeaking sound as just before. Footsteps, heavy on the wooden floor. Approaching. The booming in her ears sounded again as she realised he was coming back. She held her breath. *Boom. Boom. Boom.* The foot stomping on the drum pedal, a lone instrument in an auditorium, filling it, the only sound. Still she held her breath, until it felt like hot claws were inside scraping at her chest.

Breathing out at last, trying to control it, not wanting to make any sound. The effort made her dizzy.

The footsteps drew closer. At the back of her throat she felt bile rising, bubbling into her mouth. She gagged once, twice, three times, then threw up onto the floor.

He was standing in the doorway, looking at her as she wiped the back of her hand across her mouth. Shook his head as he stepped into the room, closing the door behind him, sliding the latch across. It made a scraping sound that echoed through her.

Oh Jesus...

She watched him, his face, stared at it, wondering...

He walked to the other side of the bed, unbuckling his belt as he went. Her breath caught in the back of her throat. He swung it a couple of times above his head. She exhaled, welcoming the sight of the swinging belt. She didn't mind if he beat her. Anything was better than... than that.

But instead, he dropped it to the floor. His small eyes observed her, in that weird head that looked like a goat's. His top lip rolled back, exposing his big teeth, saliva oozing out through the gaps. And now he was undoing the button on the waistband of his jeans. She started to gag again, a dry gag, but nothing coming up. The sound of his zipper like the buzzing of a swarm of wasps, or pieces of flesh being pulled from inside her head. It mingled with the booming sound, everything so loud she felt her head would explode.

He spoke, his voice from somewhere far off.

'Just a taster,' he said.

He leaned onto the bed on fisted hands, like a primate, moving towards her, pushing between her legs, her short skirt riding up as his elbows forced them out. He lowered himself, settling on her, lay there still. She could smell his hot, clammy breath, could smell it, like old vegetable peelings. Gradually, she felt something against her leg, through his pants, a throbbing, a dull pulse, like a mouse's heart.

Still, he lay there, an ostrich sitting on an egg.

'Oliver,' the sound so faint she wondered if she had actually heard it at all.

He dipped his head to one side.

'Oliver,' the voice a little louder, enough to convince her that it was real.

He smiled, a twisted smile, in that twisted face, looking down at her with deadpan eyes.

'Oliver. There are cars outside.'

He froze, his smile evaporating.

CHAPTER NINETY-SEVEN

The roadway to the farmhouse led into the back yard. The three garda cars pulled up and Beck got out of the Focus. He stared for a moment before approaching the house, pushing through a green painted gate and walking along a path to the door. He noticed someone standing by a window, an elderly female, her face framed within long white hair, before she was gone again, shuffling out of view. He felt something brush against his leg, glanced down, saw a cat walking alongside. When he looked back up again, the door had opened and she was standing there, skin and bones, confusion on a leathered old face, and as he drew near, he detected the pungency of stale urine filling the air about her.

'The President's dead,' Danny Black's mother said, her voice shrill. 'They said it on the wireless.'

Beck noticed the unkempt hair, the filthy pinafore, the swollen legs inside the grubby black shoes.

'We're looking for Danny Black.'

'Oh, I remember. Did he win? Did you pull his name out of the hat? Did you?'

Beck noted the distant eyes, the expression, a mixture of perpetual fear and surprise.

'We'd like to come in,' he said, already gently passing her.

He heard Garda Ryan speaking from behind.

'It's okay, my love, come with me and we'll sit you down.'

Beck, Wilde, Connor and two detectives filed down the hall. Beck opened the front door. The two uniforms were standing there.

'One of you wait there. The other come with us.'

He looked back down the hall. Claire was emerging from a room. 'This way,' he called to her.

He led the way up the stairs. Wilde and the uniform began going through the remaining downstairs rooms. Beck crossed the landing, the linoleum floor covering worn through in places to the wooden boards beneath. He selected a room, turned the door handle, and entered. There was a picture of the Sacred Heart on a wall, the red bulb beneath broken. There was a single metal bed, a jumbled collection of blankets on top, a crumpled dirty sheet, old clothes strewn everywhere, a wardrobe open, cardboard boxes piled inside, an open empty suitcase by the bed, and a table, an alarm clock on top, old style with metal cylinders like ears on top, streaked with rust. The room was cold with the smell of bodily waste. And there was something else. Beck could see it lying on the floor by the wardrobe, its wooden frame broken in one corner. A photograph, of someone he recognised: Michéal Peoples.

Claire's voice. Sudden. Loud. From further down the hall.

'Beck. Down here. Quick.'

The woman was curled up on the bed when Beck entered the room, Claire standing above her, both hands on her shoulders, gentle, reassuring. He noticed immediately the manacle securing her foot to the bed. The two detectives were standing in the doorway. The woman began to sob.

'It's okay,' Claire said. 'You're safe now. What's your name?'

'Vicky,' Beck heard her reply as he crossed to the window, partially covered in black plastic stripes, torn in the centre. *Jesus.* Vicky. He turned. The woman he knew, the cheeky, confident, sexy, sensual woman, a quivering wreck on the bed. He was about to speak, but there was no time. He went to the old sash window, one panel pulled down and flush with the other. He noted the sturdy metal drainpipe outside running down the wall next to it. This was the side of the house, invisible from the yard and from the front. He cursed, clenching his fists. The sound of an engine, in the near distance, a throaty diesel. He looked towards that sound, to the track that ran past the house. Through the bushes and trees he could see a flash of colour, silver, moving fast.

Beck was already running from the room, calculating the distance, the odds of making it in time, scrambling down the stairs, out the front door, along the path running down the centre of the overgrown garden, and finally, out through the gateless pillars.

And at that very moment, as Beck emerged onto the track, it rounded a curve maybe twenty yards away, heading towards him: a blue and silver Mitsubishi pickup. It bounced over the rough ground, riding high on its springs, bearing down.

Beck stood, legs astride, knees bent slightly, one leg back in a boxer's stance, reaching for the Walther, pulling it from its holster, extending his arms, one shoulder slightly angled forward, pistol butt held tight – but not too tight – in both hands, the way he'd been trained. Lining up the front and rear sights, both eyes looking down the barrel. Ready.

The pickup, slithering and jumping, but big enough to always remain dangling at the end of those sights.

Beck pulled the trigger, the sound a crackling thunderclap through the air, every bird for a half mile taking flight. The hole appeared in the windscreen, on the passenger side, as intended, a spider's web of broken glass spreading out around it.

I'm not messing around here, fella.

But the pickup kept coming.

Beck realised a part of him didn't care, even as he heard the grinding of gears, the high-pitched squeal of dry springs rising and falling as the pickup bounced over the rutted track.

Come on.

His body stiffened, lining up the sights again, aiming for the wide area of chest just beneath the neck of the driver. He followed that jumping, moving target, keeping both sights on it, ignoring Black's face, just that target, offering the best possibility. His finger, moist on the trigger, feeling the resistance as he began to press.

A shower of pebbles and dirt on his legs, bouncing off his trousers, a scraping sound, a hundred sticks of chalk dragged across a blackboard. The pickup, tyres grinding and tearing at the track for grip. The back end swinging round now, lurching back and forth as it came to a stop side on, the sound of the engine, a diesel tic-toc, the smell of hot oil and rubber.

Beck ran and tugged on the passenger door.

'Hands on the wheel! Hands on the wheel!'

Black ignored him, climbing out of the pickup, walking round the front end towards him. Something in his hands. Beck glanced. A chisel. The voice of Gumbell in his head, *Something like a shank, maybe.*

Beck aimed at the centre of Black's forehead.

I'm not messing round here, fella.

A smile played on Black's lips. It altered his already altered face. Gave him a look like there was no evil he was not capable of. He began walking slowly towards Beck.

As Beck's finger began to press…

'Beck! Don't.'

Black couldn't help it. He stopped, his head shifting, eyes peering from the corners of their sockets, away from Beck, back over his shoulder, to the source of that voice. Beck, in the blind spot, took the opportunity. He had not forgotten. It was like riding a bike. A church hall in Central Dublin, martial arts class, Sok Ti, the slashing elbow. Forward on the balls of his feet, at the same time twisting in the opposite direction, bending the elbow close to his side, rising now, above Black's head, and as Black looked back, slashing down, with the elbow, the power of Beck's entire upper body behind it, a sledgehammer, right into the front of Black's face... *Crack!*

The head went back as the body collapsed. Dropped like a rock. Or a sack of potatoes. Whatever. There was little blood, but Black's nose had fallen into what looked like a sink hole in his face. He roared in agony. They allowed him to roar. *Feel free.* Handcuffed him, led him to the marked squad car. He roared all the way to the station, where they were obliged to call an ambulance. They could have taken him directly to hospital, that would have saved time, but they didn't want that. No one wanted that. The sound of his roaring satisfied in each of them a belief, that in some small way, justice was already being served.

CHAPTER NINETY-EIGHT

Beck had remained at the scene. With Claire. And a couple of uniforms posted at the top of the road. Forensics and a search team would arrive eventually. But it was after the fact. That is, unless the property hid other secrets. Other surprises. If it did, they would find them.

Right now, though, Beck was waiting on a social worker to return his call. Already it was out of hours. Vulnerable elderly did not warrant the same response as vulnerable children. He was standing in the yard, from where the cats had disappeared.

As had Danny Black's mother.

'She's not in the house,' Claire said emerging from the back door of the house, 'No one thought about this. Did they?

Beck looked ahead, through the open gate of the back yard, noting a series of tiny footsteps meandering through it. Claire followed his gaze. Without a word, they both began to follow the thread of small indentations. It disappeared when they reached the middle of the yard outside, where it was dry, the ground elevated slightly. Beck knew it had been a run off, from the time the empty pens at the side of the yard had held cattle. He raised his hand. They both stopped.

There was no breeze. The day was still hot, clammy. Beck felt a drop of sweat roll into his eye, stinging him. He wiped at it with one finger. A sound, like a rustling of paper. He listened as it came again, from somewhere ahead, towards the corner of the yard. Beck cupped a hand behind his ear and motioned to Claire: Listen. They stood without making a sound, then Beck began to walk slowly ahead, towards that sound. Claire followed. It grew louder with each step they took.

Unmistakeable.

In the corner of the yard, hidden from the house, was a small stone building: sloping slate roof, door with a window on either side of it. One window was open, a lace curtain as white as a snow flake hanging out of it and motionless in the stagnant air.

The baby was no longer crying, but instead was making a series of gurgling sounds. Which was accompanied by singing, an aged and hoarse voice but one that was in perfect harmony. It was a lullaby.

Beck moved to the door. He placed his hand gently on the knob and turned it. He pushed and the door opened. The inside of what looked like a doll's house revealed itself, bright colours, little chairs, a little bed, and a plastic toy kitchen with plastic pots and pans.

Danny Black's mother had her back to him. Her filthy old clothes and body were alien in this place. And alien to what she held against her chest. Looking back over the old woman's shoulder at Beck was a baby, its beautiful blue eyes of innocence twinkling before the detective inspector's smile, a red blob on the side of her head. Baby Róisín.

The old woman, as if sensing their presence, turned.

'I always wanted a girl,' she said. 'Oliver and I are over the moon. It's only a touch of colic. She doesn't really need the doctor. I keep this place spotless. You won't find a speck of dirt in here, doctor.'

Beck stepped to her, gently but firmly gripped the child. Claire was already placing her hands on the fragile old wrists. Danny Black's mother released Róisín. Who was clean. Appeared healthy. Well cared for. Smelt as a baby should. Beck breathed in that baby smell deeply, closed his eyes and leaned his forehead gently against the child's.

'Thank you,' he whispered. 'God. Thank you.'

Róisín pulled at his ear.

The child was strong.

CHAPTER NINETY-NINE

Beck stood inside the door of the conference room in the Hibernian Hotel, hurriedly converted to hold a special sitting of Cross Beg District Court. It was six thirty in the evening and Judge Constance Canavan observed Danny Black standing handcuffed before her between two uniformed guards. The centre of his head was swathed in bandages, a smudge of blood soaking through. Twice he was asked to confirm his identity before he did so, the painkillers he'd been given responsible for the lethargy of response. He was then remanded to Castlerea prison to appear at Galway Circuit Court the following week.

'At that court,' Judge Canavan announced, her soprano voice cutting through the room, 'a preliminary psychological evaluation will be available for consideration, because it is my belief that those wilfully evil acts perpetrated by the defendant can only be understood against the backdrop of a virulent form of mental illness.'

As Beck smoked a cigarette outside afterwards, a man in a burgundy suit and fawn-coloured leather shoes approached. It was a suit Beck would expect an entertainer to wear, a compère on a cruise ship, someone like that. George Noone had fair hair, moulded into a quiff at the front, a strong square chin with a dimple in the centre. Beck had heard it said by women of his acquaintance that they would not trust a man with a dimple in his chin. Noone extended his hand and introduced himself. On his wrist was a massive, ochre-faced watch.

'I had to come. To see what he looked like. The animal.' The voice was softly spoken. 'I'm Vicky's husband, ex-husband. I just want to thank you for saving her life.'

As they shook hands, Beck decided he didn't like George Noone. No reason. Just his gimp. He was… Beck searched for a word but couldn't find it.

'How is she?'

'Under observation at the Galway Clinic. She'll pull through, thank God, but something like this…' His voice trailed off.

Beck took a long draw on his cigarette.

'I'll call to see her very soon,' Beck said.

Noone hesitated, a silence hanging between them for a moment. 'Well,' he said then. 'Thank you again,' as he turned and walked away.

Beck watched him go.

Smarmy, the word he'd been looking for. Yes, that was it. *Smarmy.*

Beck saw him then, standing at a corner of the court house, looking across at him. It was Joe, his posture that same veneer of defensiveness as displayed at meetings and afterwards at Frazzali's. But he raised a hand now and waved, and Beck waved back. Then he too turned and walked away.

Beck made it to the meeting on time for once, just about. He sat in the back row and when he was asked if he would like to speak, he even said a few words. Innocuous words, about how wonderful it was to be sober, and how he thanked God every day for helping him to stay that way. He didn't mean a word of it of course, it was just some shit he'd heard others say.

As he dried his coffee mug afterwards, Mikey Power came and stood beside him.

'Alright, mate? I want to thank you for what you did. Finding that bastard. And getting Róisín back. It means everything.'

Beck hadn't noticed him at the meeting. He thought again of the question he wanted answered.

'If I may ask. How long have you been in Australia, Mikey?'

'Ten years, mate. Why?'

'You come across as more Australian than a kangaroo, that's why.'

'I'll take that as a compliment, mate. Once I bury my poor unfortunate sister, and my little niece is settled in with my mother, that's where I'll be going straight back to.'

Beck realised he was still holding the cup. He put it down onto the draining board.

'And your mother? What about her?'

'What can I say, mate? What about her? I know what I've got to do. My mother can look after herself. Sorry. That's how it is.'

Beck nodded. 'You don't have to be sorry. Not to me. I understand. Really.'

'Thanks,' Mikey said, putting the cup down without washing it.

Beck offered his hand, but instead found himself pulled into a reluctant bear hug.

'You're emotionally stunted, mate, you know that?'

Beck did not reply, thought: I already know that.

It was a bar near the river. The 'C' in the name over the door missing, so it read AROLANS. When he walked in the few punters seated at the counter turned, watching as he walked towards them. A barmaid sat on a high stool behind it, busy filing her nails. She was young, bored, passing time, waiting, for something else, anything else, to come along. She placed the file down on a ledge behind her, beside a stack of glasses, and slid off the stool, turning to look at him.

'It's you,' she said.

Beck immediately thought this signified he had been in here previously in some drunken state or other that he couldn't remember now. But then she smiled. No, all was well.

'You were on the telly. A while back. When that crazy headcase had the town terrorised.'

'Ah ha, that's who it is,' a voice further along. 'Taut I recognised him.

'He looks different so he does,' it was someone else.

'You got the bastard,' the barmaid said. 'That's all that matters. Well done.'

Beck wasn't certain which bastard she was referring to.

'What'll it be?' She asked the question Beck was most interested in.

'Guinness. Pint. And a chaser. Whiskey. Thanks.'

He sat in a corner, draped in the shadows. He knew the hushed tones were concerned with him, could tell by the furtive glances thrown in his direction. He felt the sensation he'd missed for so long and had feared in equal measure, could feel it softening him like a warm sun on hard, frozen ground. Had they nothing better to do than gossip about him? He knew the answer to that: Probably not.

He drank until he didn't care any more, until he passed through the arrivals department and became a denizen of alcohol utopia, immune to anything other than the muddled blissful state of stupefaction, until there was nothing left but a vast, black, emptiness. From somewhere in this emptiness came a flash, of four shot glasses, being lined up on the counter, clear liquid poured into each. Along with the flash was a face, but he couldn't quite work it out, whether it was a man or a woman. An image of something else now. He concentrated, willing his skewed memory to crystallise it into something meaningful. He stared, at a worm, an eel, wrapped around a wrist, the bar busy, the sound of laughter, a band playing, a woman in an extravagant blonde wig, singing. He knew that song. Jolene. Staring at the worm, or the eel, whatever the fuck it was. And along the arm, into the face. He knew that face. A man named Darren Murphy. Member of the town's criminal class. Whom he had dealt with in the past. *He's well known to us, your honour.*

He asked himself: Am I dreaming?

'Alrite der, bud?' Murphy's face lopsided in a drunken smirk.

The lime green tracksuit top was open, a gold medallion visible beneath.

The worm, the eel, he knew what it was: a thin braided leather bracelet, loops of red thread woven through it. Where had he seen that before? A shape floated across his altered mind. A machine. Black offal. Beck groped through the hall of mirrors that was his sozzled brain. And saw something. A fleeting glimpse. He chased it, caught a corner, and pulled. The shape revealed itself.

Of course: the black Heidelberg.

Beck shouted, a word, so loud it drowned out the sound of the Dolly Parton tribute band. His last memory was of squeezing something soft in his right hand, tighter and tighter, and as he did, he heard the sound of Darren Murphy screaming louder and louder. And then everything went blank.

PULSE INCIDENT: NUMBER 74649372

Gardai responded to anonymous report of disturbance at Carolans public house, Church Street, Cross Beg. Darren Murphy, one of those interviewed claimed to have been assaulted by off-duty member. No off-duty member found on the premises. Darren Murphy searched under section 23 of the Misuse of Drugs Act, found in possession of a number of counterfeit $50 notes. Subsequent search of his home revealed large quantities of counterfeit notes to a street value of over $1 million. Darren Murphy arrested under the Criminal Justice, Thefts and Fraud Offences Act 2001, released pending file to the DPP.

CHAPTER ONE HUNDRED

Some months later...

Cross Beg is a child-friendly town. But no one without kids would ever think it. There are three large play areas, two public parks, two riverside walks, and, a little outside of town, a mature wooded area, the remnants of several large land estates now being amalgamated into a single public amenity. The proposed name of this is the Gertrude Wolfe Park.

It was mid-October and the autumn was so far unseasonably mild – by Irish standards that was. To Mikey however, he may as well have been in Antarctica. Back from Australia for several weeks, he had on a jacket of duck down, with a thick scarf wrapped around his neck, and his mop of hair lost beneath a yellow and black woolly hat that had two strings of twisted wool hanging from it over his forehead: a bumblebee woolly it was called.

Róisín thought the hat hilarious, pulling at the strings any chance she got.

Mikey stood behind her, gently pushing her on the swing. Róisín whooped each time she rose through the air. This child was his life now. He had made a vow to himself. That he would show her. That not all men were bad. And that there were more good men in the world than bad. Good men who loved. Who didn't hate. And that, more than anything, he would always be there for her. That he would never let her down.

He took off the bumblebee woolly hat and plopped it onto her head. Róisín squealed with delight.

'Come on you two. It's time for tea. It's Shannon's butcher's sausages. You could never get those in Australia. Could you, son?'

Mikey turned. His mother was sitting on the bench a few feet away.

He smiled.

'No mother, I could not.'

He scooped Róisín from the swing and held her close.

'I'll never let you down, sweetheart. Never. Not your uncle Mikey.'

EPILOGUE

Superintendent Wilde was pleased. Even if the case against Darren Murphy was eventually dropped; he denied all knowledge of counterfeit notes, and said those in his possession had been given to him in payment for a horse by an unknown individual. A preposterous story, but one impossible to prove or disprove either way. In any case, no further counterfeit notes were discovered in Cross Beg or district afterwards. Which was good enough for Superintendent Wilde. *Out of sight, out of mind.*

The funeral for Inspector O'Reilly was a lowkey affair. The suicide of a senior officer was not something that would draw sympathies to the same degree as that of, say, a serving officer killed in the line of duty.

Danny Black was not deemed insane. He was arraigned before a full jury in the Circuit Criminal Court in Galway. A forensic computer analyst from Garda HQ described how in the preceding twenty hours before the attack on Samantha Power, Danny Black had accessed porn sites on over a hundred and twenty-five occasions. Before the attack on Vicky, it had been constant, both via his home computer and his mobile phone. A psychiatrist told the court that it was his belief that Black had repressed deviant sexual urges all his life, a condition exacerbated in the recent past by a growing addiction to porn. He also said that Black displayed classic sociopathic tendencies and it was his belief, given the chance, that Black would strike again. He may even have already struck before and gotten away with it. No one knew. To find out the answer,

The National Serious Crimes Unit had begun a frantic cold case search of unsolved incidents with a similar M.O. That search was ongoing. The jury took less than an hour to reach a verdict. Black was given a life sentence with a minimum time to serve of thirty years before he could be considered eligible for parole. He would not cooperate with gardai at any point.

His mother was placed in a government-run nursing home in Galway where it was discovered that sometimes, perhaps once or twice a day, she had moments of complete lucidity. It was also discovered that she was a niece of Mícheál Peoples, although appeared to have no other connection to Kelly's Forge. During those brief moments of lucidity she would describe to nurses going to Kelly's Forge as a child to play with the children there. But then always, as the lucidity began to ebb, she would tell them of how Danny had brought home a baby to her one day. Which would explain how Róisín's T-shirt had been found where it had. When the nurses asked about this she would babble about how she always wanted another baby, that she and Oliver had always wanted a little girl. And then she would cry for the baby, and cry for Oliver, and wonder when they both would come to visit.

Beck felt sick when he considered what might have become of Róisín had Black not been apprehended.

The team from the Historical Crimes Against Children unit spent two weeks in the area where the three baby skeletons had been found. They walked to the location each day and dug with spades and shovels. But no further bones – human that is – were found. The skeletal remains were deemed to be more than a half century old. Analysis showed evidence of calcium deficiencies and general malnutrition. But no foul play. Cause of death was unde-termined. The babies were all between seven and fourteen months old. Officers interviewed Kathleen Waldron, and Maurice Crabby too, but ultimately it was recommended a criminal investigation would be futile. Who would they investigate? All adults related to the village from that time were long dead.

So, the file was quietly placed along the thousands of other files relating to resolved children's deaths in the latter half of the twentieth century in Ireland.

Sad, but true.

Maurice Crabby and his wife continued as before, still apparently living separate lives in their mountainside house on the outskirts of Cross Beg. But Maurice Crabby never cycled his bike again. There was a rumour he and his wife had been spotted enjoying a candlelit meal in a swank Galway hotel one evening. But nothing could be substantiated, of course. However, it was true, a verifiable fact, that Mrs Crabby had begun spending more time at the supermarket. That she and her husband had been spotted laughing together on more than one occasion. Never had the mere act of laughter between two people drawn so much speculation. It was agreed that generally, the artic ice of their relationship was melting as it encountered warmer waters.

Claire and Lucy got back together too. But the issue was never truly resolved. Lucy still harboured thoughts of having a child. She just didn't mention them any longer. She was content to wait the long game, until the time was right. She had Claire back, and that's all that really mattered. They were still fighting. But a little less, perhaps.

Kathleen Waldron, Crabby's mother, was offered sheltered housing in Galway City but refused. She said she was happy where she was. When it was mentioned that residential care of this nature was not suitable or cost effective, she said it would be less cost effective if she were to sue the State for the way she had been treated. There was no further mention of the matter.

Beck found a new cure for his drinking, which was running the treadmill in the sports hall in Cross Beg. He'd joined the gym after his last bender. With nerves rattled, he'd listened back to the call made from Carolans pub. He recognised the slurred and disjointed voice as none other than his own. But no one else did. He smiled when he thought about it later. Call themselves policemen.

A LETTER FROM MICHAEL

Firstly, may I start, as I did last time, by saying a huge thank you to you, the reader, for choosing to invest your time in *The Child Before*. If you did enjoy it, and want to keep up-to-date with all my latest releases, just sign up at the following link. Your email address will never be shared and you can unsubscribe at any time.

www.bookouture.com/michael-scanlon

The inspiration for this book came to me when I was out walking my dog in the woods near Kiltimagh in County Mayo, where my wife comes from. I came across the carcass of a lamb picked clean and about it mounds of wool. On subsequent visits I found further mounds of wool, (but no more carcasses). It got me to thinking about how I might tie this in with an idea I was already developing about a missing child. Near to this spot too is an abandoned village, nothing but stony ruins now. And I wondered how I might also tie this in. And so, *The Child Before* was born.

So, now that my first two books are under my belt, I can say that the process is both enjoyable and challenging. It was Lee Child who said something along the lines that he learns from each book he writes, and believes his next will be a smoother voyage. But it never is, because each book throws up its own unique challenges and difficulties. And always will.

Sometimes I feel a bit like an imposter. I say this because down through the years I've met some truly wonderful and inspirational writers who, for whatever reason, be it bad luck or circumstance, have never been published. Because of this, I feel truly privileged to finally be a published author. I just hope that you enjoy reading about Beck as much as I enjoy writing about him. Once again, therefore, two simple words, to both my readers and publisher, Bookouture: Thank you.

If you did enjoy *The Child Before* I would be very grateful if you could write a review. I'd love to hear what you think, and it makes such a difference helping new readers to discover one of my books for the first time.

I would love to hear from you too, and am on Twitter if you'd like to reach out! Also I now have a Facebook Author's page – quite a feat for a technophobe like me. Why not visit?

Thanks,
Michael

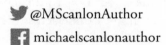

@MScanlonAuthor
michaelscanlonauthor

ACKNOWLEDGEMENTS

Firstly, I would again like to thank you, the reader, for taking the time to read this book. Equally, I would like to thank Isobel Akenhead and the Bookouture team for their hard work and dedication. Also to all the reviewers and bloggers who have supported me. To my family, my wife Eileen and daughter Sarah. Also, to Breda Jennings and Jennifer Mulderrig for reading the first draft and giving me their invaluable feedback. Also to my crazy half-Pomeranian half-something-else dog, without whom I would not have bothered going for walks on those cold winter mornings. Such walks afforded me the space to reflect on my story and see where I was going wrong if there was a problem, and where I wanted to go next if there wasn't.

Thanks to all.

CPSIA information can be obtained
at www.ICGtesting.com
Printed in the USA
LVHW092313230619
622120LV00001B/69/P